# LADYBIRDS

## R. RAETA

Afeia Books

*Ladybirds* by R. Raeta

Published by Atera Books

First paperback edition April 2022

Cover Art by R. Raeta

Paperback ISBN: 979-8-9855547-1-7

www.rraeta.com

*Dedicated to the family members who are deserving of the name. And, as always, to my readers.*

# PROLOGUE

It's not wishes that lure him so much as desperation.

The venue changes, naturally. Casinos are promising—pawn-shops even more so. All those people down on their luck, cursing their bank accounts and drowning in their debt. Simply begging for his helping hand… a snap of his fingers, gold lining their pockets.

Simple.

Too simple, of course. Money may make the world go round, but it certainly doesn't inspire most to hand over their *soul*. And, if he's being entirely honest, the ones that do are hardly his type.

Besides, over the years he's learned that the people who typically agree aren't the ones in danger of overdrawing their pitiful bank accounts. The truly desperate are the ones afraid of losing their family, their friends. *Themselves.*

He makes a point to stay far and away from making any such deals with the dying—they always turn out especially ill tempered after the deal is done and, really, time may be a commodity he has in infinite supply, but he certainly doesn't want to waste it on *that* nonsense.

Children also get a hard pass—that is one mistake he won't bear repeating (no matter how many mothers may tempt him with it).

1

Nothing good ever comes out of the deals involving little ones, and he'd rather suffer through a few more years of boredom than to tempt fate with another poor decision.

So, he follows the clientele away from the pawnshops and the dive bars and into sterilized rooms.

In his early days, hospitals were a breeding ground for illness and futile prayers. So many people calling to God and insisting they would do *anything* so long as so-and-so and what's-his-name get better. Now, with the nauseating amount of disinfectants they slather around (truly, how the staff is capable of smelling anything with constant exposure to the fumes is something he considers a small miracle) only one of those things has truly changed. More may leave the hospital alive, but there is certainly no shortage of prayers being sung in the waiting rooms and so called "chapels".

When he finds himself sick with boredom, this is where he usually haunts—listening in on those dramatic mumblings and knowing most of them don't mean it. Not really. Most are selfish enough to know better than to trade their soul for whoever is dying in the next room. But, every now and then, he finds someone desperate enough to strike a deal. He has enough practice now to know who to ask.

Unfortunately, experience has also taught him that the ones who accept are, inadvertently, the old and feeble. Which, in their own way, can be fun. They're certainly capable of providing their own particular brand of entertainment. And it really is *quite* handy that no one calls in an exorcist when dear old Gran Gran starts talking to no one.

He finds elderly women infinitely more pleasant—and far less likely to reach for a firearm— than their counterparts. The last one kept calling him by the name of her sad excuse for a grandson who lived across the country. She scolded him daily for never eating all the way up until she flat lined in this miserable little hospital in the middle of nowhere, surrounded by long stretches of highway and corn.

A sickening amount of corn.

Iowa is a place full of it and, frankly, he would rather suffer through New York's grating noise levels than be left with nothing but bloody cornfields for scenery. He is ready to abandon the ugly vegetable for a place with a more interesting landscape. It's been a while since he's been to the West Coast, or perhaps he will do some traveling overseas. After all, since Gran Gran has (quite selfishly) left him without entertainment, variety is now one of the very few spices of his wretched life.

Then he sees her.

He hadn't planned on tempting anyone that night—truly. Striking a deal in the wake of losing the last a mere hour before seems bad form even by his standards, but opportunity can be a fickle beast and he's loathe to waste it.

She's in the parking lot, sitting on the filthy cement and leaning against the bricked exterior wall outside the emergency department when he sees her. She's rather sad looking in the oversized t-shirt hanging like a shapeless bag over her willowy frame, but fashion sense aside, she's pleasant enough to look at. Strawberry-blonde hair braided over her shoulder, long limbs, and a spattering of freckles over her nose and cheeks that he finds irritatingly adorable. Best of all, she's *young*. A college student, if that ghastly logo over her chest is any indication. Young enough to be saddled with him for longer than the measly four years the last one left him with, and the eleven before that. The thought of being heard without those rubbish hearing aids alone is enough to make his palms itch in anticipation.

There are no prayers passing her pale lips, but he knows that look. The longer he studies her, the more convinced he is that she's simply too perfect to pass up. Perhaps he is willing to suffer through a few more years of this blasted, intolerably bland landscape after all. Besides, he may not recognize the logo on her chest, but where there is a college campus, there is usually *something*.

He reveals himself; plays the part of the charming gentleman and offering answers to her unsung prayers.

She accuses him of lunacy.

He shrugs it off (he's been called far, far worse) but then he says her lover's name—throws it in the air between them like bread crumbs and watches the questions, the tentative hopes, light her hazel eyes like fireflies on a summer night. Still, she is young; full of realism and free of the superstitions previous generations harbored. He's ready to write her off as a failure (she wouldn't be the first and far from the last) when she accepts.

There's sarcasm dripping from each syllable, honey thick but not half as sweet. She doesn't know that a deal set in words is as binding as if she shook his hand with those snot-backed knuckles; that her flippant dismissal is just as good as a signature drawn in blood. It's a cheap win, but it doesn't matter.

The magic takes.

Her lover is spared.

And she is *his*.

# CHAPTER ONE

FOR MOST GIRLS IN HER SMALL TOWN, THEIR EARLIEST MEMORIES ARE OF princess dresses and tea parties with dolls and invisible friends—maybe putting on their mother's lipstick and parading in front of the mirror in her stilettos.

Sara remembers doves.

The echo of a shot ringing through the hills; the burst of feathers. She remembers the warmth of their bodies when she cradled them in her palms—the weight of her father's approval when she delivered the tiny corpses to his waiting, callus-lined hands. Her mother had scowled when she saw the blood streaking her skin and staining her sleeves, but had praised her for her help all the same. Dove had always been Mama's favorite. If she really tries, Sara can almost recall the smell of the meat roasting—garlic and rosemary—in the skillet.

Mostly, Sara remembers being happy; her family whole.

Her father sober.

Her mother *there*.

After, Sara would turn her mother's flea-market reading chair, its upholstery threadbare, till it faced the living room window. For hours, she would anxiously play with the strands of her hair and watch for her mother's red sedan on the long gravel drive. So naive and hopeful, that she could almost hear the crunch of gravel under the tires and smell the dust kicked up in its wake. She never came and her father, from the bottom of his bottle, would never hesitate to tell her why.

"She ain't coming back. Bitch got herself a new family." A swig, or perhaps the twist of another cap, and he would add, "Stop wasting your time waiting for her."

Eventually, Sara did. Seasons changed, and the driveway remained empty save her father's work truck and the occasional visit from his bar buddies. Sara learned to hate the color red with a passion born from resentment. Her Oma—her mother's mother—is the only blessing Mama left her with.

Every day after school, the bus would drop her off at her grand-mother's house. Oma always had something baked—muffins, strudels, cookies—and Sara would run to the peeling, navy blue door, open it wide, and breathe deep. Beneath the scent of flour and sugar, cinnamon and vanilla, was something intangible but warm— the complete opposite to the smell of stale beer and mildew that assaulted her the moment she stepped into her father's house.

It took her a few years to figure it out, but she realized on her tenth birthday when Oma baked her a three-layered cake and her father didn't show up for dinner. Sara blew out the candles, wishing he was there. When he finally arrived, it was well past dark. She overheard Oma chewing him out in the entryway for stinking of whiskey.

Sara slept over that night, and in the morning she ate chocolate chip pancakes with fatty, thick sliced bacon and homemade sausages. When her father (finally) came to pick her up that after-noon, she didn't want to leave. Her father didn't want to hear it.

On the ride home, cans rattling beneath her feet and a fresh twelve pack sitting in the seat between them, Sara understood. Oma's house felt like *home*. Not a shell of a house with nothing but cable tv and microwaved dinners eaten alone. Oma felt close; avail-able and easy to love. Warm. Real.

Her father felt like a stranger at best.

A ghost, at worst.

Always there—a quiet, broad-shouldered figure lurking at the edges of her memory—but never there *for her*. If Oma was the ship keeping her afloat, her father was the figurehead. There for looks, but nothing else. But he tries, Sara knows he tries.

On the weekends, when it's in season, he takes her hunting. Grouse and pheasant, mostly. Never dove. She sees him then—those sober moments where he becomes more human than booze. Most of the time she even likes him, but there's always a chasm between them; an awkwardness she can never quite cross.

Even now, with the landscape unveiling its beauty in every sense—*with* every sense—she can't help but feel like she's toeing the edge of a cliff. Lean too far forward and she'll plummet; stand too far back and she'll never be close. She walks several paces behind her father's stocky frame, the weight of her camera strap on the back of her neck more comforting than the silence between them.

The sun's warm rays, spilling into the valley, reach across her favorite hill. The tall grasses, dry from the summer heat, turn to gold while the lone oak tree in the distance softens from a hard silhouette and into something three dimensional. Her father's spaniel tracks a scent, white and honey coat nearly disappearing in the high grasses. Sara stifles a laugh when the dog hops over a particularly thick patch of brush.

"You best not be laughing at my dog." Thick, graying eyebrows rise over hazel eyes—one of the few features she inherited from him. "Unless you want to take Miss Belle's place and start flushing out my birds." The hands holding his shotgun gesture to the large expanse of field still needing to be covered.

"No thanks." Sara lifts her camera pointedly in response. "I'm just the photographer, remember?"

He grunts, eyes flicking to her most prized possession before quickly flitting away. Sara tries to tamp down the disappointment souring her stomach. Three years in, and her choice in major still tips him into the realm of firm disappointment.

She hurries to change the conversation. "Belle looks good out there," she says, nodding toward the rustling grass. "She's listening a lot better than last year."

Roy adjusts his cap before returning his grip to the firearm—ready to snap up and shoot at a moment's notice. A shrill whistle passes his lips, and Belle comes bounding through the brush. Roy gives his daughter a pointed look over his shoulder. "Yeah. Amazing what happens when a certain someone isn't here to spoil her."

Sara's lips pucker in a failing attempt to withhold a smile. Belle pads over to her, tongue lolling out of her mouth, and nudges her hand. She sneaks a scratch behind her ear. "You're just sore because I'm her favorite."

"Will you knock that off?" he scolds, more exasperated than angry. "How many times do I gotta tell you not to pet her while she's working."

"I'm giving her positive reinforcement."

Faintly, she hears a mumbled, "Millennials," pass his lips as he moves a few giant steps deeper into the field. Belle bounces enthusiastically at his side, pink tongue lolling out one side of her freckled mouth.

Sara's smile falters, but she sets her irritation aside for the sake of keeping the peace. "I heard that."

He sends a disapproving look over his shoulders. "You best not have, because then I'd know you didn't put those earplugs in like I told you to."

She flushes guiltily, fingers quickly find the two orange pieces of foam in her back pocket. Rolling them between her fingers, she puts one in each ear—feeling the foam puff and fill the canal snugly until her hearing becomes noticeably muffled. "Sorry."

"No, sorry would have been you going deaf at the age of thirty," he says flippantly, though his voice carries no sharp edge. It's a lecture that's as overused as telling her not to waste water on long showers. His eyes observe the dog's movements as she weaves circled trails through the grass.

Sara shrugs her freckled shoulders, despite knowing she isn't in his line of sight. There's a witty retort ready to be fired from her lips, but she bites her tongue. She's irritated by his tone, but she knows better than to pick a fight.

Body tense in anticipation, waiting for a bird to startle, Roy offers an olive branch. "What classes are you taking this semester?"

"British Literature, Calculus, and Art Appreciation."

Her father scoffs, casting her a bemused look. "British? What the hell's wrong with American?"

"Nothing other than it being booked full." Sometimes his disapproval is so predictable it's painful, but she's mostly just glad he didn't decide to comment on her art class. When he still looks skeptical, she adds, "It counts towards General Ed, so who cares? I'm sure I'll hate it just as much."

Roy hesitates, seeming torn between offering (false) words of support and grudging acknowledgement. Sara hates English. Getting her through *Catcher in the Rye* in her junior year had been like trying to force a cat to swim—she kept her head above the water, but she came out soaked and thoroughly pissed off. Her unfortunate teacher at the time had struggled to hide her annoyance at Sara's lack of enthusiasm. The parent-teacher meetings she had called her father into were one of the only times he had stepped foot onto her campus.

"And that boy of yours?"

Sara stiffens, sucking in a bracing breath. Talking to her father about David is like walking across a minefield. She's learned from a young age to avoid the topic of love and marriage like it was the plague (probably because that's *exactly* how her father treated it). "David is starting his internship in October."

She makes a point of saying her boyfriend's name as much as her father does to avoid it.

Roy makes a sound in the back of his throat; acknowledgement but not approval. Sara has had plenty of practice deciphering the difference, and she's glad she insisted on coming up to visit with her father alone. He's hated all of her boyfriends, but the disdain he holds for David has always gone deeper. Sara blames it on the seriousness of their relationship more than anything else. She had intended to break the news to him about the apartment she and

David signed for, but the longer she visits the more excuses she finds to hold off. Sara wonders how many it takes before it qualifies as a justification.

Her father may have written off love as a fool's errand, but she's never let him convince her. In Oma's bedroom is a wedding photo framed in tarnished brass; a candid moment between the bride and groom smiling and happy with a simple buttercream cake between them. When Sara was little, she caught Oma talking to the picture and pressing her lips to the glass in a goodnight kiss. Even as a child, she could sense the ritualistic nature of it. Sara has no doubts that her grandmother wished her departed husband goodnight, and good morning, every day.

The years have taught her that Oma and Dad are a study in opposites: love found and love failed, life lived and life tolerated. One leads to a house full of warmth and memories, the other a telltale chorus of glass and tin in the recycle can. Sara knows who she would rather take after.

A retort sits, hot on her tongue, but she swallows it down—feels it settle in her stomach like coal. No amount of arguing will change his mind (or hers) and she's learned better than to waste her time.

"Sara!"

She looks over her shoulder, surprised to hear her name rolling over the soft, rustling grasses. In the distance, beside her father's black F250, is a beat up Ford pickup with rust eating through the faded blue paint; its driver side door swung open. Sara recognizes it more easily than the man yelling in front of it.

Roy's irritation is written in the heavy, controlled sigh through his nose and the flexing muscle of his jaw. "Damn it all. Gonna scare off my birds." He shoos her off, already marching deeper into the fields, away from the racket her old classmate is causing. "Go on and see what he wants, then. I'll see you back home."

Sara can't say she blames him. Austin's a hunter himself—he should know better. Still, there's an edge to his voice that makes her anxious, and she moves just a little faster. When she makes it within a yard from the parked trucks, she can easily make out his pallid face under the shadow of his baseball cap.

His brown eyes are blown wide, lip trembling and pale. Sara frowns, glancing at the cab of his truck and finding the passenger seat empty.

Her stomach drops.

Austin shouldn't be alone. He's supposed to be with David.

"The phones weren't working," he blurts, a bead of sweat running down his stubbled jaw. "I didn't know what else to do, and—"

She cuts him off, eyes still pinned to the empty passenger seat. "Austin, where's David?"

His chest heaves, anxiety pinching his face. "He's—he's at the hospital. There was an accident and—Sara, I'm so sorry. I told him it was a bad idea, I swear. You gotta believe me."

Behind her, Sara hears the shotgun go off—her father's short whoop—and envisions a hollow-boned body falling to the ground.

Sara thinks of doves.

# CHAPTER TWO

Sᴀʀᴀ ʜᴀs ɴᴇᴠᴇʀ ʟɪᴋᴇᴅ ʜᴏsᴘɪᴛᴀʟs, ʙᴜᴛ ᴛᴏᴅᴀʏ sʜᴇ ʜᴀᴛᴇs ᴛʜᴇᴍ.

The sickly green walls and the smell of bleach make the waiting feel endless. She's been there for over three hours now, alternating between sitting in the stiff chairs and pacing the length of the waiting room. David's mother sits with her, hands shaking and pale as she continues to wring them in her lap. Sara wishes her presence soothed her fear, but the truth is she only amplifies it. It's not that they dislike each other, but there has always been a quietness to Mrs. Mclintock that sets her on edge. Sara suspects it has more to do with her own anxiety than the woman herself.

"What's taking them so long?" Sara mutters, biting her thumbnail and staring at the emergency room doors. "Why haven't they come back yet?" The last update they had told them little to nothing: internal bleeding, broken ribs, pierced lung, possible spine trauma… They said nothing about the outlook, only that they were still making every effort to stabilize him. Sara hates that word almost as much as the hospital. 'Stabilize' sounds too much like his life is hanging in the balance.

Mrs. Mclintock doesn't answer right away. Her dark blue eyes dart to the clock, her hands moving in time with the second hand.

"It's ok," she says, but the tremor in her small voice betrays her. "He'll be fine."

Sara wishes she could find comfort in the older woman's fragile optimism, but it only makes her stomach twist. Nausea rises, hot and acidic, in her throat.

She needs to get out of there—she's suffocating on anxiety and bleach fumes. "I'm," she swallows thickly, trying to smooth the crack in her voice. She's not very successful. "I'm going to get some air."

Mrs. Mclintock nods, her eyes vacantly staring at the door separating the ER from the waiting room. With her pearls and perfectly coiffed hair, her *stillness*, she wouldn't look entirely out of place in a Rockwell painting. Sara's not entirely convinced she fully heard her, but she's too desperate for space to bother repeating herself.

The automatic doors slide open, the rush of hot, humid air a stark contrast to the air-conditioned room at her back.

Sara takes a deep breath. Another. Another.

Each one feels less satisfying than the last, more water than air, and she feels herself falling apart—every carefully stitched seam unraveling faster than she can patch it. She leans against the wall, brick scraping painfully against her shoulder blades as she sinks to the ground, drawing her knees up to her chest. Her fingers tangle in her hair, the heels of her hands pressing against her temples as she drags air into her lungs between smothered, hiccuped sobs.

She tries to calm her heart—tells herself there's still hope—but between every weak self assurance is another stab of doubt. She thinks of her mother's red sedan, the bitter words her father loves to utter between bottles.

*They all leave you eventually.*

But this is different—she *knows* it's different. Because David loves her and would never *want* to leave. David is made of wild smiles and romantic gestures; candies on her pillow, love notes in her fridge. Surprise camping trips in the mountains and dances in the living room. Her hand, always finding its way into his, fingers linked and the warmth of his lips pressed against the backs of her knuckles.

Her breathing slows, but the tears won't stop. They fall, one after another, the pain deepening with each and every memory because it doesn't matter. It doesn't matter if he wants to go or if he's taken against his will, because the result is the same.

"Who are they to you?"

Sara starts, head snapping up at the sound of his voice—deep and melodic, but clipped with an accent she's unfamiliar with. She had been certain she was alone, but she must have overlooked him. Or, maybe, she's just been out here longer than she realized.

He's tall; a shadow of black and charcoal finery her small town only ever sees at weddings and stage plays. Full suit, high collar—a glint of a gold chain peeking between the folds of his coat. Sara wonders how he's not sweating in the summer heat.

She sniffs, scrubbing at her eyes with the heel of her hand. "I—" Her voice is a rock slide, jarring and rough. She clears her throat. Tries again. "I'm sorry, what?"

His hands slip into his pockets, gaze unnervingly intense. "The person you're crying for. Who are they to you?"

Sara stills, pulse jumping in her throat. A quick glance proves they are the only ones around, but she consoles herself with the knowledge that she's close enough to the Emergency entrance that someone would hear her if she screamed. "How—" She shakes her head. Of course he knows; why else would she be crying in front of the ER? "My boyfriend."

"Interesting," he murmurs, more curious than empathetic. His eyes, dark in the dim light, flick to her left hand. "I would have expected more."

His reaction is off. The way he looks at her… as if he's measuring her up instead of offering sympathy, sends a warning trill up her spine. Sara stands, brick against her back and adrenaline buzzing under her skin. Something isn't right, and she doesn't plan on staying long enough to figure out what. "Look, I'm just going to go back inside."

She's already halfway to the double glass doors when he speaks, stopping her in her tracks. "I can save him."

In her chest, her heart stutters painfully—her body turning back to him numbly. "What?"

He rolls his eyes; the picture of annoyance. "Honestly, do you plan to make me repeat everything? I said I can save him."

Sara scoffs, shaking her head. "How?"

"A life for a soul. A soul for a life," he croons; invitation coated in temptation. "It's simple, really."

Right. She wants to kick herself for even asking. "You're crazy. What, did you escape the mental ward?"

He cocks his head, an amused smile curling the corners of his mouth. "Is that a no, then?"

"Yeah... think I'm going to pass." Sara looks around, the beginnings of trepidation trailing up her spine. There's no one else in sight, but she feels like there should be. "Seriously, is someone looking for you?"

He shrugs, completely unconcerned. "Very well, I'll leave dear David to his own devices, then. Ta." He turns, ready to leave. Sara doesn't let him.

"Wait!" In her chest, her heart beats so fast it feels like the screaming, violent hum of cicada wings. In his eyes, she sees a nauseating combination of amusement and *knowing*. "How did you—I never told you his name."

"Unless you fancy a man with denture cream, it was fairly easy to guess." His arms cross over his chest, finger tapping against his elbow and eyes reflecting the hospital entrance's cold, fluorescent lighting. "Terribly unfortunate—to be named David, of all things. What with the whole, getting done in by a bull." He must take her numbness as misunderstanding, because the sigh he gives is steeped in disappointment. "David and Goliath? David, the little man who beats the big bad giant? You must see the irony, surely."

It should be impossible for him to know. Unless... "What. Do you work in the back office or something? Because whatever your game is—"

"I *do*, in fact, have other places I'd like to be other than this corn themed hellhole," he drawls. "So, I would be most appreciative if you could make up your bloody mind."

God, this guy really was crazy. "Whatever. If I say yes, will you leave me alone?"

The corner of his mouth curls, crooked. "For the time being."

The sound of sirens in the distance has her glancing back towards the highway. She can just see the flicker of red cresting over the sea of white headlights. "Fine. It's a deal. Now will—"

He's gone.

Baffled, she searches, but the parking lot is empty and there's no way he could have made it to the door in the time she glanced away. He just couldn't have. It's impossible. How—

"Sara!" Mrs. Mclintock yells for her from the waiting room entrance, voice as watery as the tears streaming down her face. Sara's stomach drops, fearing the worst, but the older woman pulls her into a hug so fierce, she can feel her ribs groaning under the pressure. "He's going to be ok. The doctor said he's going to be ok."

Sara's knees go weak, and she's suddenly grateful for the strength of the other woman's hold.

THE DOCTOR DOESN'T LET ANYONE BACK TO SEE HIM FOR ANOTHER HOUR. The waiting is still torturous, but the weight on her chest has loosened—a necklace instead of a noose. When she finally enters David's room, sees the tangle of IVs and wires, she has to grip the doorframe to keep herself upright.

He's pale. So, so pale. The small mole on the ridge of his cheek stands out like an ink spot on paper, and with all the bandages and tubes, he looks almost nothing like himself. She hates that his eyes are closed—that if it weren't for the insistent beeping of the monitor, she would assume his heart wasn't beating. Suddenly, she's glad the doctor made them wait until they removed the intubation tube. At least they can see his face.

Mrs. Mclintock chokes on a sob, kneeling at the bedside and grasping his hand. "Oh, my baby boy."

Numbly, Sara moves to his other side. She brushes the bangs from his face, breath hitching as she struggles to hold back a fresh wave of tears. When she laces their fingers, his skin is too cold to feel familiar.

David stirs, groaning. His eyes flutter open, voice slurring as he focuses on his mother's face. "Mom?"

Mrs. Mclintock nods, bringing their clasped hands to her cheek. "It's me, son. It's me. You were in an accident, but I'm here, honey. Sara, too."

"Sara?" He frowns, his head turning towards her. When he looks at her, his eyes are the exact shade of blue she fell in love with, but there's something unfamiliar in his gaze. Something off. His mouth twists, but it's not a smile—it's a *sneer*. "Who the hell are you?"

# CHAPTER THREE

After shuffling between her father's and the hospital for the past two weeks, seeing Oma's house feels like coming home.

Sara lingers in the car; the radio turned low and the engine humming. The bright teal rocking chairs she helped her paint three summers ago are still on the front porch and the house's cheery yellow siding with white trim still makes Sara think of Better Homes & Garden magazines. She's planted a mix of brightly colored dahlias and foxglove in the flower beds this year—petunias in the window boxes. Sara releases a heavy sigh, feeling the tension in her neck and shoulders relax. If happy were a place, it would be her grandmother's house.

She turns off the engine and unplugs her phone from the charger. Sara doesn't bother checking for messages—the last two weeks have had her phone on loud and her nerves so raw that missing a text is next to impossible. Jen, her best friend, reaches out at least once a day just to check in and let her know she's only a drive or a phone call away. Sara responds to her faithfully, but never takes her up on her offer. It's easier to hold herself together when she doesn't have to explain her feelings out loud. Just typing out the words with her thumbs makes the tightness in her chest double and her eyes burn.

*He still doesn't remember me. They don't know if he ever will.*
*He hates me. Why does he hate me?*
*What am I going to do?*

Jen doesn't give her any answers (how could she?) but every text she sends back is thoughtfully constructed; emphatic in a way that is neither pushy or dismissive. She takes care to address her every concern, validate her every fear, before soothing her with words of comfort. She knows, instinctively, that Miles is there too—his condolences are weaved between every line Jen writes. Outside of classes, they spend so much of their time together that messaging one is as good as messaging the other. Sara sometimes wonders if it's an engaged couple thing or just them.

The morning after David's accident, Miles sent her only one message.

*'We're here.'*

Somehow, those two words offer as much relief as all of Jen's gentle assurances.

Sara didn't ask him to elaborate; she understood what it meant. Jen is her best friend, but they're more different than alike—a study in opposites. Miles and her? They're cut from the same cloth. Stubborn with their pain; hoarding their trauma to themselves as if sharing it would mean letting it run wild. Jen calls it internalizing. Miles calls it handling his business and avoiding casualties.

Sara thinks it's probably a bit of both, but she just calls it *surviving*. Right now, with the bruises under eyes and the aches in her limbs—evidence of all the sleep she's missed—she thinks her definition feels the most fitting.

The first thing she notices when she steps out of the car is the smell. Oma's windows are wide open, letting the evening breeze in and the scent of her cooking *out*. Sara inhales, letting the air rest in her lungs while her stomach gives a hungry lurch. She's missed Oma's cooking fiercely—has ever since she moved away for college —but the past week she's been surviving almost solely off meals from the hospital cafeteria and protein bars. Neither provided anything more than calorie intake and wishes for something that didn't come prepackaged.

Sara slides her phone into the back pocket of her jeans and closes the car door, leaving her keys in the ignition and her purse on the passenger seat. There's no fear of theft when the only neighbors for miles are corn and cattle.

When she opens the front door, she calls out for her grandmother despite knowing where she'll be. Oma answers back, confirming her suspicions, as she slips off her sandals.

"In the kitchen!"

Despite her exhaustion and heartache, Sara's lips tilt into a smile. It's weak and frayed at the edges (the very action makes her realize how unused those muscles in her face have been lately) but it's sincere. "It smells great in here."

Oma's hands are bowl deep in dough, her aged fingers reaching in and plucking a golf ball sized piece and rolling it smooth between her palms. Behind her bifocals, her blue eyes spark with laughter. "Well, I heard my favorite granddaughter would be coming to visit," she winks; a flash of shimmering blue eyeshadow that has always reminded Sara of those tropical butterflies—the ones that live on the edges of wishes and reality. "So I decided to make her favorites."

Sara leans in and kisses her cheek. "Sorry it took so long."

Oma's smile falters, dimming into something more sympathetic than soft. She reaches, crossing the short distance between them, but stops short when she remembers the dough in her hands. "I'm so sorry, sweet girl."

It's like there's a vice around her neck, growing tighter and tighter the longer Oma's words sit between them. If she were to open her mouth, Sara's certain the only thing that would claw its way out is a sob. She bites her lip, focusing on the pain in a poor attempt to distract herself from the tears burning behind her eyes. The only thing she can manage is a jerky nod of acknowledgment.

Oma mimics the motion with far more grace, before she flicks her eyes toward the shallow bowl of cinnamon sugar. "Why don't you roll the cookies for me? My old eyes can hardly see well enough to make sure I get full coverage anymore."

Sara releases a shaky breath, eyes closing briefly to compose herself. Never has she been more thankful for her grandmother's lack of prying. "Sure." The word is ragged and raw—snagging in her throat before she forces it out—but Oma doesn't call her out on it.

There's something therapeutic about rolling the balls of dough until it's evenly coated in cinnamon and sugar. The simple, repetitive motions. Mindless. It feels like the first time in weeks that she's been able to breathe without every worry invading her thoughts. Beside her, Oma hums some old song that Sara recognizes but doesn't know the words to, her hands molding the dough in time with the rhythm.

For the first ten minutes, no words pass between them, and the world seems a little bit calmer for it. Sara feels the coil in her chest loosen, the tension in her shoulders pulling away like a tide and (even though she knows the waters will rise again) she can't help but embrace the reprieve.

Oma hands her another ball of dough, the song she was humming ended. "How are things with Roy?"

She never refers to him as 'your father'—only by his name. There's years worth of bad blood between them, but Oma has always refrained from pointing out her father's (obvious) flaws. Sara suspects that calling him by his name is her grandmother's way of passive aggressively downplaying the role he has in her life. Her father has never been as considerate, and the older Sara becomes, the more she appreciates her grandmother's discretion.

"The usual," she says, shrugging. There's a tension in her neck she's been unable to stretch out; a hollow ache at the base of her skull she can't escape. She's tried to rub it away for days with no relief, but the temptation to knead at the muscle remains. It's only the dough and sugar sticking to her fingers that stops her now. "He wants me to stay with him for the rest of the summer, but once David's released, he's going home with his parents while he recovers."

Sara winces, heart aching. "And I still need to figure out what to do about the apartment."

The one-bedroom apartment David and her signed for. The one they were supposed to move into next week—together. The one she can't afford on her own.

Oma's hand rests on hers, a comforting weight. The oil from the dough has softened her grandmother's lined palms. "Things will work out, my sweet girl. Everything happens for a reason."

Sara says nothing. Once, *maybe*, she believed that. Never with the same conviction as her grandmother, but with the same half-hearted hope that one wishes on a shooting star. Now, she struggles to even listen to the words without openly flinching.

A final pat on the back of her hand, and Oma gives her a smile wide enough to *almost* make her hope. "You'll see."

THE PLATE OF COOKIES FEELS HEAVY IN SARA'S HANDS AS SHE RIDES THE elevator up; they stare up at her with swirls of cinnamon and chocolate chip eyes. They hadn't stopped baking after the Snickerdoodles. Maybe it was because Oma sensed she needed the distraction, or perhaps she was serious when she accused Sara of "needing more meat on her bones", but they had gone straight to the family Chocolate Chip Cookie recipe as soon as the last batch of cinnamon-sugar cookies made it into the oven.

It's not the first time she's brought David food, but it is the first time it hasn't come from the fast food or grocery store around the corner. Sara wonders if it even matters, or if the batch of cookies will end up in the trash, too.

She sighs. The elevator dings, doors opening to the fourth floor. She pulls her shoulders back, straightens her spine, and masks herself in a confidence she doesn't really feel. The nurses give her pitying smiles as she walks down the hall; Sara can feel the whispers —a prickle at the nape of her neck—the moment she crosses the threshold to Room 432.

David is alone today; the seat his mother usually occupies is empty. He takes one look at her, a fleeting cursory glance, before rolling his eyes. "You again."

Sara swallows down the hurt, knuckles as white as her grandmother's china.

*It's not his fault,* she reminds herself, *he doesn't remember.*

Be patient.

23

"I brought some of Oma's cookies," she offers, setting them on an empty corner of his hospital table. The small shrug she gives is as weak as her smile. "You always liked them more than the ones I made."

"Whatever."

Her teeth sink into her bottom lip, rubbing her arm in a self-conscious effort to have *something* to do with her hands. "Is... is there anything else I could bring? To make you more comfortable? I know your parents—"

"Look, don't you get it?" he sneers. Sara has never seen his expression look so ugly. "I don't *want you here.*"

Sara stares at his hands, fisted and white-knuckled, in the crisp sheets. She remembers how those same fingers used to lace with hers on the center console with the sun streaming in the windows and the local country station coming in staticky on his old truck speakers. The pain in her chest doubles. "I'm just trying to help." Her voice is small, rough. It feels like she's speaking around gravel.

"Yeah, well, who asked you?" he snaps. "I don't want your pity!"

Her stomach sinks. "It's not—"

David doesn't let her finish, his face is flushed with a rage she doesn't remember. "Just leave me the hell alone!"

His nurse is at her elbow, coaxing her out of the room. Sara barely feels her hands on her shoulders, barely registers her words (come with me now, honey). There's a buzzing in her ears, a numbness in her bones, but she still recognizes the sound of her grandmother's china shattering against the wall.

Oma knows the moment she opens the door. Even through the burning of her eyes, Sara can see the way her face falls, the sympathetic drawing of her brow. Her grandmother folds her into her arms, hand stroking over her hair, just as Sara's knees go weak and the first broken sob bursts from her lungs with a violence that leaves her trembling.

"Oh, my dear sweet girl," Oma croons, holding her in the open doorway—moths fluttering around the porch light overhead. Sara sobs harder, the force of it ripping through her chest in a keening howl. Oma holds her, soft shushing sounds emitting from her aged lips, as she rocks her. After a few minutes, she gently guides her to the couch; her arms holding her together the entire way.

She tells Sara stories about the grandfather she never got to meet —how she would help him sow the seeds and tend the stalks until the corn grew taller than he was. She tells of how he'd strip the husk from the first corn harvested, breath it in, give Oma a tobacco stained smile, and say, "Look at that gold, eh Gertie?"

Oma chuckles, deep and raspy. "Oh, he'd say the exact thing every year. Even the bad ones." She sighs. "Sometimes I wonder... if he had let someone else man the farm sooner, if I could've kept him longer." She tilts up her granddaughter's face, arthritic fingers cupping her cheeks and her wizened stare more gray than blue in the lamplight. "And then I remember, how little good wondering does for us."

"But Oma—"

"My dear, sweet Sara." She sweeps some hair from her forehead, fingers whispering over her brow. "Take this time to mourn—your grief, your sadness, it's all deserved. But when the tears run out, pick yourself up. Keep him in your heart, but let him go and move *forward*."

Sara shakes her head. "It's different, though. David isn't dead, he just—"

Oma's hands grip her shoulders, stern in ways she hasn't been since she was a girl. "Gone. Sara, he's gone."

Fury fills her, hot and aching in her chest; pounding relentlessly in her ears. She pulls away, ignoring her grandmother's level gaze. "How can you say that?! How can you just give up on him?!"

Sara has never yelled at Oma. Never. She expects to see a flash of hurt, maybe even anger, but her grandmother's gaze only holds pity. "Because I love you, and your happiness is more important to me than anything else in this world." She holds Sara's hands in hers, weathered thumbs stroking the backs of her knuckles. "You tried and have nothing but his cruelty to show for it. Helping him shouldn't hurt *you*."

She wants to argue. She wants to *scream*.

Sara thinks of her mother's rusty red sedan, of the beer cans and whiskey bottles strewn across the kitchen countertop at home, and has to tramp down the burning urge to remind her grandmother that *that's* what giving up looks like. Instead, she rips herself from Oma's gentle hands and runs out the door—ignoring the voice calling after her.

# CHAPTER FOUR

S<small>ARA DOESN'T STAY AWAY FOR LONG</small>—S<small>HE NEVER DOES AND SHE WOULD</small> never want to. Even if her father's house *wasn't* her only other option, Oma is one of the most important people in her life and she won't let her fall away because of a disagreement. Especially not one born from good intentions.

Besides… objectively, she can see the wisdom of her grandmother's words even if her heart isn't quite ready to believe them. The reception she received from David the following morning, the frigid silence and refused acknowledgment, doesn't inspire confidence. The way his mother texts her not even half an hour after she leaves, words formal and clipped with a hint of awkwardness, all but buries Sara's weakened hopes.

*'We think it might be better for David's recovery if you stay away for a while.'*

Mrs. Mclintock doesn't say how long "a while" is, but Sara doesn't need her to. She knows a polite dismissal when she sees one —knows that what the older woman is *really* saying is "don't come back".

Maybe it's because the weeks have already beaten her heart so thoroughly that she's immune to pain, but she takes Mrs. Mclintock's words with a numb acceptance that lasts long after the hospital disappears from her rearview mirror. Oma's words ring (*he's gone... move forward*) the entire drive; an echo over her heart. Sara still isn't ready to believe it, not fully, but she's *tired*.

David wants her to stay away, so she will. Perhaps her trying to force it was just making things worse... maybe the time apart will give him room to remember. Maybe, if she can just be patient, she can get him *back*.

It's a tiny thread of hope, but it's wrapped around her heart so tightly she knows it would take months—maybe years—to uncoil. She doesn't breathe a word of it to anyone. It sounds too fragile, too much like false hope, to share. Besides, some wishes won't come true if they're spoken out loud and, while she's never been one for super-stitions, Sara isn't exactly in a position to risk it.

Oma's door creaks a bit when she opens it, the bottom hinge still needing oil. The living room is empty, which is a bit strange. Normally, Oma would be watching the evening news around this time. Taking her shoes off by the door, Sara peers hesitantly into the house as she closes the door behind her. "Oma?"

"In the kitchen!" Her grandmother calls back. There's not a single shred of animosity or bitterness lacing her voice, and Sara feels herself relax. Oma's never been one to hold a grudge, especially not when it concerned her granddaughter, but Sara's never quite went off on her like *that*, either. It's a good reminder that some of the good things in her life haven't been upended overnight.

Now that she knows to listen for it, Sara can hear the water running over the sink. She must be doing dishes. She goes to set her bag at the usual spot on the chair by the door—an old wingback chair whose age has faded the floral pattern over time and has recently seen more use as a dumping ground than a place to sit—but stops at the last second.

On the cushion, blinking up at her with large hazel eyes, is a cat.

Sara blinks back at him, frozen in the entry, until the gray tabby sits up and perches itself on the arm of the chair and gives a trilling meow. A smile, so rare this past week that the action feels foreign, pulls at her lips and she sets her purse on the floor instead.

"Well, hi there," she croons, offering her hand. The cat smells it tentatively, before rubbing its face against her knuckles. "What's your name?"

"I was hoping you'd tell me," Oma says, coming from around the corner with a dishtowel wiping at her hands. She leans against the wall, her smile soft and mysterious. "He's yours after all."

Sara's hand stills, head snapping up. "What?"

"You heard me. He's *yours*."

She swallows, reality effectively crushing the hope rising in her chest. "I can't have pets in the dorm."

"No," Oma hums, eyes bright, "but you can at your apartment."

Shaking her head, Sara scratches the cat behind its ears and earns a full throated purr. The sound fills her with bittersweet longing. "But I can't afford it without—" She doesn't say his name. She *can't*. Speaking it is bound to send another fissure through her already fragile heart. "I can't afford it."

Oma tucks the dish towel in her apron, before taking a seat on the couch. "There's an envelope in the kitchen—one of those big yellow ones on top of this little guy's cat carrier. Be a dear and grab it for me?"

Sara eyes her suspiciously, but does as she's asked. There's an envelope alright: big, mustard yellow, and a lot more official looking than it has any right to be. She picks it up carefully, curiosity stirring despite her apprehension. When she brings it to the living room, Oma waves her hand pointedly. "Well, go on. Open it."

She doesn't need to be told twice—the curiosity is as terrible as the apprehension—but when she pulls the papers from their Manila prison, it still takes her several moments to understand what she's seeing. "Oma, what—"

"It's already paid for," she says firmly; no room for arguments. "So there's no talking me out of it." Her expression softens, so tender and full of love and understanding that it just about breaks Sara's heart all over again. "You have been through enough, sweet girl."

In her hand is a receipt, an itemized bill proving her apartment is paid in full for the next year. Sara's lower lip trembles, a tear slipping past her defenses. She brushes it away with the heel of her hand before it can fall. "Thank you," she breathes, voice wobbling treacherously. "But can you really afford—"

Oma stops her with a look. Money isn't something they ever talk about; it's her grandmother's firm belief that talk of finances belong far, far away from the dining table and even then, only between those paying the bills. Anything else is rude. "If I couldn't, I wouldn't. And that's all I'll be saying on the matter."

Sara nods, sniffing loudly and wiping away another stray tear. She's speechless; there are no words that would encompass the depth of her gratitude. Overwhelmed, she sits on the couch beside her grandmother and wraps her arms around her aging shoulders.

Oma pats her hand; places a kiss on her forehead. "There are good things on the horizon for you, my dear. Good, *wonderful* things." She pulls away enough to hold her granddaughter's gaze, paper thin palm cupping her smooth cheek. "There always is after a big storm, but you need to have faith that your rainbow will come or else you'll *miss* it." Her expression softens, fingers brushing a lock of hair from Sara's forehead. "Do you understand?"

Her throat is packed with gravel. She can feel it rattling around each syllable she forces past her lips. "I understand."

The cat chirps at her from the ground, demanding attention, and Sara gives a watery laugh. "He's really mine?"

Oma chuckles, patting her knee. "He's really yours. I'm too old to be cleaning up cat shit."

Sara coughs on a surprised laugh. She's probably only heard her grandmother curse a handful of times, and each incident was more accidental than intentional. "Oma!"

She winks, flashing her signature blue eyeshadow. "Betty is a terrible influence. You know, last week she brought whiskey to our poker night?"

Sara smiles, leaning down to scratch the cat's ears. "Whiskey, huh? Was it good?"

"It was a great time until the next morning."

They both laugh, and for a small, immeasurable moment, Sara feels at peace. Everything in her world is far from right, but here in the warm glow of her grandmother's living room and her new room-mate purring at her ankles, she can see a glimmer of hope.

Sara names him Ansel. It's fitting, what with his grayscale coat and her penchant for photography. Sara likes to think Mr. Adams would approve.

# CHAPTER FIVE

S<small>ARA HATES MOVING.</small>

The packing, the coordinating enough help to transport everything. All of it. Now, she's staring at her small apartment, the living area a maze of half filled boxes, and finds herself exhausted all over again.

Beside her, Jen reties her ponytail, dark hair still swaying well past her shoulders when she's done. Setting her hands on her hips, she eyes the boxes warily. "You sure you don't want help unpacking?"

Sara sighs, running a hand through her hair—flinching at the amount of sweat beading on her scalp. It's hot—muggy in ways that make her want to just curl up on the floor and lay there, but she knows she'll probably hate herself later if she turns down the help. Classes don't start for another two months, but she knows Jen has her hands full with wedding planning—particularly since her mother and her have been butting heads on everything from the color of the invites to the dates. Jen handles it in stride, but Sara suspects Mrs. Foster's real problem is with having a black man for the groom.

"Yeah," Sara says, dread dripping from the word. "Ok."

"Well, don't sound so excited about it," Jen teases, bumping her shoulder playfully. "You ready to introduce Mr. Man to his new place?"

Sara looks at the (suspiciously silent) cat carrier at her feet. Ansel had yowled pitifully the entire drive, only quieting the moment they parked. Even with Jen borrowing her dad's truck, it had still taken two trips to get everything. Not for the first time, Sara wishes Miles wasn't away visiting family the one weekend she needed his help moving into her apartment.

Fiddling with the latch, Sara wonders how long it'll take her to earn Ansel's forgiveness. When she finally gets it open, he merely stares at her from the back corner.

"Come on," she coaxes. "It's not much, but it's still a lot better than in there." Ansel stares, unblinking, but doesn't budge. Sara sighs.

"Just leave it open," Jen suggests. "He'll come out when he's ready."

They shove two of the boxes labeled 'kitchen' closer to the cabinets. Sara can hear her grandmother's old set of dishes rattling between the thin sheets of newspaper and says a small prayer that nothing broke during the move. It may all be a mishmash of donations Oma collected from her friends, but she's thrilled to have something to call her own. The 70s poppy themed stoneware dishes may be outdated, but they hold a soft spot in Sara's heart... they're the same ones she grew up with. The same ones she and Oma shared slices of cake over. She has no plans to replace them (even *if* she had the money for it).

Feeling her phone vibrate, Sara reaches into her back pocket. The number on her screen is unfamiliar—she almost lets it go to voicemail—but knowing her luck it would be someone from the college. She accepts the call, bringing the phone to her ear as she cuts into another box. "Hello?"

The answering silence is broken by the occasional rasp of static. Sara frowns, suspecting an automated call, but it doesn't stop her from repeating, "Hello?"

Frowning, she glances at the screen only to realize the caller disconnected. Huffing on a sigh, she rolls her eyes and puts it back in her pocket.

"Scam call?" Jen asks.

"I guess. They hung up."

Jen rolls her eyes with the same level of annoyance Sara feels, her hands going back to work unfolding the newspaper wrapped around her Dollar Store drinking glasses. "So… how are you doing?"

Sara freezes, eyes closing. She'd known the question was coming —it had been sitting between them, the elephant in the car, all day. Still, she wishes it could have stayed that way. Under wraps and undiscussed. Talking about it just makes it feel more real; more permanent. Shaking, she tries to busy her hands with unwrapping another mug—the unicorn one she had gotten as a joke last Christmas. "I'll be fine."

Jen leans against the counter, eyes dark. "You know, it's ok if you aren't. Right?"

Sara swallows hard, teeth indenting her lip. "I—honestly? I just really don't want to talk about it."

Jen nods, the action somehow free of disappointment. "Ok." She opens another box, the edge of the scissors sliding effortlessly through the tape. "Do you remember that first year? In second grade?"

Sara breathes a sigh of relief at the change in conversation. "Yeah, I remember."

Honestly, it was hard to forget. Their small town didn't get a lot of newcomers—most of the residents were made up of the same people that were born there—but even Sara remembers how everyone was all abuzz the summer before school started.

It was rare to get a newcomer, but someone foreign? The town just about tore itself inside out with gossip when the Foster's decided to adopt outside the country. They all assumed it would be Russia—tons of babies there, she remembers overhearing, no need to look anywhere else. So when Jen—Zhen before her adoptive parents twisted it into something else, something more *American*—arrived with her dark hair and tan skin, speaking Cantonese instead of English, she was all anybody talked about for weeks.

Most of it wasn't good.

Sara always thought it was funny—adults were always so careful to censor their language, but never their prejudice. If not for her father's influence, she wouldn't have known any curse words despite being seven, but that summer she learned just about every racist, hate-filled term for Asian from the community's lips.

She doesn't remember what she said, only that it was something terrible and parroted, but she can recall the way Oma's face darkened and the shame she felt vividly. She remembers the feel of her grandmother's hands, palms still dirty from weeding in the garden, pressed against her cheeks and the way she knelt in the grass so they were at eye level. Sara remembers realizing how grave it all was; how the tears started falling as fast as the apologies.

"Listen to me, Sara. This is something you need to understand. People can be ugly and terrible to one another," Oma said, thumb brushing away a tear. "But no one, and I mean *no one*, deserves your ugliness just for being who they are."

Sara had nodded, blubbering, but hadn't fully understood. Then school started, and she saw Jen for the first time, scared and alone at the corner of the playground. She heard the scathing words—the same ones she learned from the adults—being tossed her way by the other kids. She could see by the look on Jen's face that she didn't need to know English to understand the hate in them.

Sara started sitting with her after that. They made up games that didn't require words; found ways of communicating with just gestures and smiles. That year, Jen learned basic English and Sara learned that the world was so much bigger than the little corner she grew up in.

She stares at the mug in her hand, eyes tracing the animated unicorn's grin with a smile.

"There were a lot of days I couldn't tell you how horrible it all felt," Jen says softly, fingers picking absently at the cardboard. "But you sat with me anyway, and honestly? That made all the difference." Her eyes, dark in ways Sara has always found intensely beautiful, lift. "I just want you to know, I'm here. I'm sitting with you. Ok?"

Sara's throat tightens, her eyes brimming with emotion. "Jen," she laughs, a wet sound, "that's got to be the sweetest, *cheesiest* thing you've ever said to me."

Jen waves her hands under her eyes, her smile watery. "I know, I'm sorry." She runs the tips of her fingers under her eyes, careful to avoid smudging her winged eyeliner.

Sara hugs her. "Thank you."

"Don't mention it," Jen sniffs against her shoulder, returning the hug. "Seriously, don't though."

"Don't worry, I won't tell anyone," Sara assures her, giving her another squeeze before letting go. Aside from Oma, Jen has the kindest heart she's ever met—naturally empathetic in ways that Sara (admittedly) has to work for.

She wipes her eyes with the heel of her hand, not bothering to be discreet. "I promise, if I need anything, you'll be the first to know. Ok?"

Jen nods. "Deal." She looks around at all the remaining boxes. "Do you want to finish? We could just binge on some Netflix on your laptop? We could even watch that one you keep bugging me about. That ghost one."

The fact that Jen, who absolutely *hates* anything remotely scary, is offering to binge a series about a haunted house is more telling than it should be. "Jen, I'm fine. Honestly."

"It's just, with you and—" She almost says his name—Sara can see it, the vowels flirting around her lips—before she catches herself. "And, well, *this*." She gestures to the apartment. The one they both know she was supposed to be sharing. "I just, I know I would feel really sad spending the first night alone."

Honestly, the aspect of what would come after Jen left hadn't even occurred to her. For the past two weeks, her life has been an impossible blur of planning and packing. She hasn't had the chance to stop and think about what her life would look like after the list of to-do's were done. Hasn't thought of the silence, or the loneliness, that would fill the voids that David left behind.

Sara looks around the apartment, at the barren walls and stacked boxes, and feels her stomach sour. It's not home—not yet. Maybe in a week or two, when her life isn't hidden behind cardboard, she will be able to call the little one-bedroom apartment *hers*, and it will ring more true than hollow. Maybe then, the emptiness of it will be more comfortable than lonely.

"Actually," she says, fingers rubbing circles over the ceramic mug in her hands. "Let's do it. It's been a while since we were able to have a girls' night, anyway."

THEY UNPACK FOR ANOTHER HOUR AND A HALF BEFORE BINGE WATCHING four episodes. Sara's mattress is on the floor, bare except for the two pillows and two of the crocheted blankets Oma sent with her back when she started her freshman year at college. She doesn't have a bed frame (or a table, or nightstands, or any other furniture other than the old wingback chair Oma donated from her living room) but, for now, they balance her laptop on a stack of old textbooks and it all works out. And even though Jen jumps at every little sound the entire night, Sara's glad she stayed.

# CHAPTER SIX

SARA STARES AT THE REMAINING BOXES IN HER LIVING ROOM, A MUG OF chai tea cradled in her hands. Her finger taps against the ceramic, a rhythmic reminder of each second she wastes procrastinating instead of just getting started already. It's already past noon, the tea in her hands is the third that morning and already more warm than hot.

She takes another sip; breathes a promise against the rim. The boxes can wait a few more minutes, but her tea is cooling (and she'd hate to waste it).

Leaning against the kitchen counter, she tries to imagine how different it will look—how it will *feel*—once her treasures fill the space. She's glad Jen stayed long enough that morning to at least get her room looking in order. The bed's still on the floor, but at least there's sheets and a quilt tucked around the mattress, Oma's crocheted blankets folded neatly at the foot. In the closet, her clothes hang neatly from their bargain store hangers; the pine dresser she (permanently) borrowed from her childhood bedroom is lined with everything else. They even reused one of the plastic milk crates she used to pack clothes as a makeshift nightstand.

It's not much, but it's hers. Somehow that brings equal amounts of pain and pleasure. *Mine*, her heart whispers, one traitorous second before reminding her, *but it was supposed to be **theirs***.

Sara flinches, forcing a shaky sigh from her lungs. It would be easy to crawl into bed, to throw the covers over her head and spend the rest of the day letting out all the tears she's been holding back, but she won't. She *can't*. If she falls apart now, she's not sure how long it will take to piece herself back together. Her life is strewn across the living room, unlabeled boxes staring up at her like headstones—the items inside begging to be brought back out into the light. If she doesn't do it now, before classes start, Sara knows it will take her five times longer to get it all sorted.

Movement from the living room catches her eye—Ansel sniffs one of the boxes cautiously, his lithe body taunt and his ears pinned back. He's been weaving through the mess like it's his own personal labyrinth, exploring between the niches and scaling up the sides. Last night, she overheard him knock something over, but still hasn't been able to figure out *what*. She takes some comfort in the fact that the sound was more of a thud than a shatter.

He gives a trilling mewl, jumping up onto a stack of boxes, tail swishing. Sara smiles, pushing herself off the counter to close the distance between them. "Enjoy it while it lasts, buddy," she says, scratching under his chin. "We need to get through at least half of these today, so no dilly dallying, alright?"

Ansel answers with a purr, his back arching as he pushes his head more firmly into her hand. Sara laughs under her breath. Living here won't be what she imagined when she signed for the apartment three months ago, but at least she won't be alone. She should text a picture of the both of them to Oma; it would make her smile. Sara owes her that and more.

She pivots, intending to grab her phone, but freezes mid-turn.

There's a man in her apartment.

A shadow of pale skin and charcoal finery. Hands in his jacket pockets, his eyes survey the mess with a casual grace that is in direct opposition of the terror seizing her heart. "My, quite a bit of work to do, hm?"

Sara can barely hear him over the drumming pulse in her ears, numb panic twisting into *fear*. Her eyes dart, searching for something to defend herself with, but she has nothing. Anything she could possibly use as a weapon—her kitchen knives, the expired pepper spray she never managed to shove back in her purse—all of it is still packed away in the sea of boxes littering her living room. The only thing in reach is the mug in her hand and, in a panic, she throws it at him—tea and all.

He dodges it easily; liquid splattering on the floor and the ceramic shattering against the kitchen cabinets—pieces raining down like sharp-edged confetti.

Frowning, he pins her with a reproachful glare. "Honestly, I grant you a miracle and your response is to attack me with stale tea?" He tsks. "Incredibly rude, even for an American."

In her chest, Sara feels her heart skip a beat as realization dawns. "You—you're that guy!" She had written him off as a bad dream—a figment of a man born from exhaustion and gut-wrenching worry in her darkest of moments. To see him, standing in her kitchen, is almost as horrifying as the realization that she hadn't just *imagined* him.

"That *guy*?" he echoes, voice flirting the line between amused and offended. "Of all the ungrateful—"

"Have you been *stalking* me?!" Her gaze flits over the room, but there's no open windows, and she knows she locked the front door after Jen left. "How did you get *in here*?"

His lips tilt, a shadow of laughter dancing across his eyes. "Stalking? My, someone thinks highly of themselves, but no. I said I would leave you be for a time, and I was nothing if not true to my word. As for getting in," he waves a flippant hand, "I wished it, so it was."

"What does that even—"

"You're welcome," he cuts in, fingers curled under his chin, "by the way. Since you seem to have forgotten yourself in all this excitement, I will assume your gratitude is implied. But, please, feel free to thank me. I do *love* validation."

"Thank you!?" she repeats, temper rising. The sarcasm is thick, dripping from each syllable like tar. It is impossible for him to misunderstand her.

He tips his chin, looking entirely too pleased with himself as he gives a mocking bow. "You're most welcome."

"He doesn't remember me!" she hisses, fury overriding the fear.

His eyes darken, lips twisting into something teetering the impossible line between feral and composed. "Well, I certainly didn't hear you making any specific requests for otherwise."

She gapes at him. There is something strange about the way he moves, the way he speaks. Goosebumps dot her flesh, a warning ringing in her skull that *something isn't right*. Sara sucks in a breath, drawing courage into her lungs and willing her voice not to tremble. "I don't know why you're here, but *get out*."

He tilts his head, a slow smirk curling his lips. "Tell me, is it that you didn't understand the terms or that you've forgotten them?"

"Terms? What are you—"

"A life for a soul. A soul for a life." His eyes are feral. "You're *mine*, Sara."

Her stomach drops, the blood draining from her face as she remembers her last words to him.

*Fine. It's a deal.*

Her vision swims, her hand reaching out to steady herself against one of the boxes. The air she's dragging into her lungs in rapid gasps feels thin. "I, wait, no. I didn't—I thought you were just a crazy person!"

"Again, terribly rude. Also, not at all my problem." He pushes himself away from the counter's edge, stalking closer. Sara backs away, pulse hammering so loudly in her ears it's a small miracle she can hear his words. "A deal is a deal, after all."

She takes a step back, then another, and another. He matches each and every one. A glance shows only one escape—the narrow pathway between the countertops and her boxes—but she doesn't dare waste it. She turns on the ball of her foot with every intention of getting the hell away, but she doesn't make it out of the kitchen.

Her slippered heel catches pieces of broken ceramic, sliding her foot from underneath her with a screech against the tile. She throws her weight, tries to regain her balance, but it's too late. She's falling, the ceiling staring up at her in mocking indifference. A crack, a burst of pain, and things go black.

⁕ ⸻⸻ ⁕

When she wakes, the first thing she notices is the throbbing pain in the back of her skull. She groans, shifting, and finds that her spine doesn't feel much better. Opening her eyes, her ceiling stares back at her—pristine white with the beginnings of a cobweb in the corner.

"Ah, sleeping beauty awakens."

It takes her pain-fogged brain a second to recognize there's someone else in her apartment, and another two before remembering there *shouldn't be*. She scrambles up, vision swimming and hands grasping at the counter for support. It doesn't take her long to find him. He's lounging in Oma's floral wingback, his long legs draped over the arm and her traitor of a cat purring in his lap.

His fingers scratch behind Ansel's ear—his eyes dark and fixed entirely on her. "We were wondering when you'd join us."

Ansel gives a trilling meow before jumping from the stranger's lap and padding over to his rightful owner. He gives a mewled grunt as Sara hastily scoops him up, cradling him protectively against her chest. "Get out."

He raises an eyebrow. "I do believe we've already danced that dance. Now, why don't you get that distracting bit of cereal out of your hair and we can have ourselves a civilized conversation." His gaze drops, head tilting as he adds, "But first, perhaps take care of that nasty little cut before you bleed all over the carpet."

Sara chances a glance. The bare skin of her right knee is covered in blood; punctured by one of the ceramic shards littering her floor. Now that she sees the proof of it trailing down her calf, her brain registers the pain. She's none the happier for it. "Seriously. *Get out.* I want nothing to do with you. I don't care about whatever deal you think we made, but—"

He groans, hand dragging down in his face. "You really are the slow sort, aren't you? Very well. Let's speed things up, shall we?" He raises his hands, snaps his fingers with a level of exaggerated drama that would make her theatre friends jealous.

And he's gone.

Blinked out like a bulb.

Her breath comes faster, vision swimming. She grasps for the stack of boxes to her right, her knees weak. It's impossible. She can't —no—she couldn't have imagined him. There's no way—

She blinks, and in the space between one breath and the next, he appears a mere foot away from her face.

Her heart stops.

He smirks. "Are we beginning to understand now? Or would you like a repeat performance?"

# CHAPTER SEVEN

It can't be.

There's no way.

Ansel's claws prick her bare skin as he struggles out her grasp and leaps from her arms—sprinting behind a stack of boxes in the living room. She takes a step back, then another. The edge of the countertop digs into her lower back. "This can't be real."

"Can't it?" His eyes flick to the blood running down her leg. "I suspect it must, at the very least, *feel* real." When she doesn't answer, he rolls his eyes. "Come now, you're acting quite ungrateful."

She trembles, the shock of it all settling into her bones like ice. Her sock is becoming warm and sticky, saturated with blood.

"Honestly," he grumbles. Another snap, another blink, and he reappears in her wingback—leaning his pale cheek against the heel of his hand. "I'm not here to hurt you. What would be the fun in that?"

Sara finds her voice, tucked somewhere between her hammering heart and the ball of lead in her stomach. "Why are you here?"

He shrugs, gesturing to the room with an open hand. "This is home sweet home now, is it not?"

A small laugh, as manic as she feels, leaves her. The shock thinning into disbelief. "So, what? You broke into my apartment to congratulate me?"

He holds up a finger. "Ah, no, actually. I invited myself into *our* apartment. I'm sure you can spot the difference."

Her breath leaves her. "*Our*?!"

"That's how this works," he hums. His arms spread in a wide, grand gesture. "Your home is my home. I go where you go, more or less." He nods toward her leg. "Now, honestly, will you please take care of that? I don't fancy stains."

"Wait, you can't be serious! I never agreed to this!"

"You did, actually. It's hardly my fault you never requested details."

"But—" A knock sounds on the door, interrupting her.

"Police. Is anyone home?"

The man draped over her armchair hums. "My, isn't that inconvenient? Perhaps you can convince him you spotted a spider? Something big and hairy."

"Hello? We've had some noise complaints from your neighbors. We're just here to make sure you're alright."

Sara slides along the wall, towards the door—mouth opening to call back.

"Ah, I wouldn't." He places a finger in front of his lips. "Tell him something, but say nothing about me. Unless, of course, you'd like your little life to go sideways in a hurry."

Sara licks her lips, heart pounding against her ribs. "I'm coming," she yells, backing towards the door. Her fingers fumble with the deadbolt, hand turning the knob.

The officer looks old enough to be her father; salt and pepper hair buzzed short. He's already glancing over her shoulder. "One of your neighbors called saying they heard screaming. Is everything ok in there?"

The source of her troubles walks up beside her—in full, unapologetic, view. "Why yes, officer. Everything is lovely. Thank you terribly so for asking." His voice, the way he rocks back on his heels, is mocking.

Sara waits for the obvious, but the officer doesn't spare him a glance—gives no indication that he's even heard him. In fact, if anything, the stare he pins her with only grows more suspicious. Sara's stomach sinks.

"Miss?"

She swallows thickly, a sad attempt to control the bubbling anxiety rising in her throat. "I, um, yeah. Yes. I just, I thought I saw someone else in the apartment and got scared."

It takes every ounce of willpower to keep herself from looking when the man—no. Not a man, she reminds herself. He's something else. Something *inhuman*. "Should have gone the spider excuse," he admonishes. "Honestly, who taught you how to lie? You're abysmal."

The officer's expression hardens. Apparently as unimpressed by her poker face as the devil at her back. "Why don't I come in and take a look for you?"

"Sure." Numbly, Sara opens the door wider. From the other side of the narrow entry, her intruder gives an I-told-you-so smile as the uniformed man walks past them.

Sara waits, pulse erratic, as the officer checks every room. She doesn't dare take her eyes off the grinning face across from her.

"It's good to see you have *some* sense," he hums, his hands planting in his pockets as he leans against the wall. "There have been a handful of others who proved to be rather lacking in that department."

Sara's thoughts stall.

*Others?*

"Everything's clear," the officer says, confirming what Sara already knows. His posture is more relaxed now, his hand at his side instead of hovering over his gun. Sara wishes his eyes would focus on the smirking man standing mere feet away from her. Then his gaze snags on the blood staining her leg—drying now that the wound has begun to scab—and he frowns. "What happened there?"

"Oh, um, I broke a mug."

He must have noticed the pieces of ceramic littering her kitchen floor, because he nods without questioning her further. "If anything happens, or if you feel like you need help, don't hesitate to call us back."

She nods, her blood humming with what feels like the beginnings of shock. "Right. I will. Thank you."

He tips his head and gives a practiced "anytime" before walking out the door. Sara closes it behind him, staring at the wood grain and trying to grasp the reality of her situation. She can feel her heart battering rhythmically against her rib cage.

"Well, I thought he would never leave."

Her blood boils. "How do I get rid of you?" she hisses.

"Lovely question," he hums, distractedly. "But I'm afraid past experience leads me to believe that you *don't*."

Impossible. He said there were others, which means they had to have managed to escape him somehow. "How'd the other ones get rid of you?!"

A brow—infuriatingly well-shaped—arches. "Considering they *died*, I do believe that makes *me* rid of *them*. But, to each their own, I suppose." He waves a hand dismissively. "It's all just semantics, really."

She pales, her anger cooling into fear. "Are—are you saying you *killed* them?"

"I said they *died*," he scoffs, mouth twisting into a frown. "Honestly, there is a *vast* difference."

His answer does little to ease her fears, and he must notice because he rolls his eyes. "I believe I already confirmed there is nothing for me to gain by hurting you. So you can stop looking at me like that. I'm hardly planning your murder."

When she still refuses to let her guard down, he sighs. "So timid. I expected more, to be honest. Particularly after that brave little face you put on at the hospital."

In the narrow hall, he still feels too close, but she's afraid if she moves he will follow. "You—I thought you were human."

He waves a hand. "Details." Head tilting, his stare is piercing in its intensity. "Perhaps some introductions would set you at ease? You may call me Seth."

The bridge of her nose creases skeptically. "Is that actually your name?"

"It *actually* is. Should I be concerned about your, increasingly apparent, trust issues?"

"I don't have trust issues," she snaps. "I have *you* issues."

"Oh look, your spine has grown back. Splendid news." His arms cross under his chest, a smile teasing at the corners of his mouth. "This is, however, typically the part where you offer your name in exchange."

Her eyes narrow. "What if I don't?"

"Well, I suppose I will be forced to inform you of how incredibly ill-mannered you are and proceed to find out anyway?"

Somehow, she doesn't doubt that he *would*. "... Sara." Never has she said her own name with such grudging reluctance.

"Sara," he echoes, a strange sort of half-smile playing at the corner of his mouth. Sara has the distinct feeling that he's laughing at some joke she's not in on. "I suppose it will do. Now then, clean yourself up, Princess. I was rather serious about blood stains. They're right irritating to get out of upholstery."

Sara doesn't ask how he knows—or about the odd nickname, despite the way it makes her bristle. Instead, she takes it as an opportunity to escape; the wall sliding against her back as she moves away from him before bolting to the bathroom and locking it behind her.

# CHAPTER EIGHT

IT'S HOURS BEFORE SHE OPENS THE DOOR. HOURS OF SITTING ON THE bathroom floor, her back against the tub, with her eyes flitting between her phone and the locked door.

Her search history is a horror show—a mismatch of supernatural and things like, 'where can I buy sage in bulk' and 'how to disconnect fire alarms'. There's no one-fits-all answer to her (very real) problem. Especially since she doesn't really know *what* he is, but one thing stands out.

Salt.

It's an easy remedy, and a hell of a lot cheaper than hiring an exorcist. She knows she has a large container in her cupboard—she remembers unpacking it—but she also has to get to it.

Sara doesn't really know if she believes in God, but as her hand folds around the doorknob, she mutters a quick prayer under her breath, anyway. Just in case. There's a creak of the hinges when it opens. It's tiny, barely noticeable, but every sound feels twice as loud as it is, despite being masked by the drumming in her ears.

The kitchen. She only has to make it to the kitchen. The apartment is silent as a grave—he's probably not even there. What kind of lunatic would wait hours for her to come out of the bathroom?

Two steps into the hallway, she stills—heart in her throat. He's still in her apartment, studying the framed pictures hanging over the couch.

Before she can quietly retreat, he spots her—his dark eyes pinning her in place. "Ah, I wondered how long until you came out of hiding." The corner of his mouth twitches. "I admit, I hadn't expected you for a few more hours yet. Bravo."

Sara swallows, eyes flitting to the kitchen and back. The temptation to make a run for it is heavy on her chest, but she quells it with the memory of how he effortlessly blinked from one end of the room to the other. Outrunning him would be impossible.

She moves around him until the kitchen is at her back, each step measured. Careful. His brows raise, and she realizes he expects a response. She scrambles to find something to say, but the only thing that falls out of her mouth is, "You're still here."

"How terribly perceptive of you."

Her face burns. At her side, her hands fist—nails imprinting crescent moons on her palms. "I thought you left."

He hums, appraising her. "Yes, I'm sure you hoped for as much."

"I'm boring," she blurts. "You should find someone else."

"Come now," he croons, his crooked smile dimpling in the corner. "Don't be so hard on yourself. I'm certain you will prove quite entertaining."

"You should find someone else anyway."

"Souls are a tricky business, I'm afraid. The deal is done. There are no refunds, returns, or exchanges." His eyes gleam, wicked and dark. "You are *mine*, Sara. That truth will stand until you draw your very last breath."

She stiffens, hands trembling as she stares at him. "I'm not yours."

Seth's head tilts, his gaze traveling the length of her before meeting her eyes. "You truly have no concept of the value of what you've bartered, do you?" He shakes his head, smile cold—cruel. "Tell me, what do you think a soul *is*?"

Sara doesn't know. She has absolutely no idea what souls are, what they mean. Before today, she wasn't even entirely sure she believed they were real. But she isn't *anybody's*. Let alone some supernatural jerk that has the audacity to not only twist a flippant dismissal into acceptance and gift her with a curse instead of a miracle, but to insert himself into *her* life uninvited. She feels cheated. Used. "I hate you," she hisses, eyes burning with frustrated tears she refuses to let fall. "I'll never *stop* hating you."

It's supposed to be a threat; a reason in a long list of reasons for him to just *leave her be*. He only smiles as if it were a challenge.

"Oh, Sara," he soothes, a false pity curling around the syllables of her name like smoke. "That isn't the threat you think it is."

A retort—a *scream*—rests in her throat, burning hot, but before she can spit the words, he disappears. Gone between blinks without ever even having to raise his hand to snap.

SARA DOESN'T KNOW WHERE HE'S GONE, OR WHEN HE'LL BE BACK, AND the anxiety that comes with not knowing is almost as bad as him *being* there. She scrambles for the kitchen, pulling the container of salt out of the cupboard. It's full, only just opened to fill the little salt shaker on her little two person bistro table. She thanks whatever higher power that might be listening for small miracles (before cursing them for putting her in the situation to begin with).

Muttering under her breath, she takes the salt and lines the thresholds and the windows with a trembling hand. She has no idea what she's doing, not really, but she's careful to make sure the lines she pours are straight and uninterrupted—wall to wall, frame to frame—before pouring a fistful into her palm.

In theory, the salt should be enough to keep him from entering the apartment, but (in theory) none of this should be possible *at all*, so Sara doesn't push her luck. Pulling the ratty wingback chair into a corner where she can easily see the rest of the apartment, she sits. Her fingers close around the granules, adrenaline making her pulse thrum as she waits.

And waits.

And waits.

She doesn't dare move, doesn't dare let her guard down for even a second, because she knows the moment she does is the moment he'll appear.

When he finally arrives, it's hours later and the sun is just beginning to descend over the horizon, casting long shadows across the apartment. He appears, back to her and fingers straightening his cuff, in the center of the living room.

Sara doesn't give him time to turn around.

With a shrill cry, she throws the salt at his back—

And watches as the fistful of tiny crystals bounce right off him.

A moment of pause—so still, Sara can feel each trembling beat of her heart as her lungs burn for the breath she doesn't dare take.

Slowly, his hand drops from his sleeve. His body turns. The smirk he wears is as dark—as challenging—as the gleam in his eyes. "And here you worried our time together would be dull."

She says nothing. Her hopes are as small and dashed as the salt littering her living room.

Hands in his pockets, he steps toward her—towering over her. Sara's too numb to move as he leans down, snaring her wide, panicked gaze with his dark one. "You will have to try much, *much* harder than that, Princess."

SHE TRIES THE SAGE NEXT.

Smoke fills the rooms, coiling and swirling from the bundled leaves in her hand like snakes. Seth sits in the wingback, his chin resting against his palm and a subtle smirk playing at the corner of his mouth. His eyes are dark, gleaming wickedly as they follow her from room to room.

By the time it's burnt to the stems, her apartment is filled with enough smoke to make her eyes water and her lungs itch. She tosses the remains in the sink, dousing it in water. Before she turns around, she closes her eyes and mutters one final prayer under her breath.

When she looks, he's in the exact same place with the exact same infuriatingly smug expression.

"Well," he hums, "you've made a right mess, haven't you?"

Chest heaving, she drags in a breath—fury fueling her—but the smoke triggers a coughing fit before she can spit out the first word.

His amusement is as obvious as her anger.

"Leave," she rasps between coughs, the venom in her voice clear despite her wheezing. She's not sure if she's commanding or begging —at this point she doesn't even care so long as he gets the hell out of her life.

His eyes gleam. "No."

SHE TRIES EVERYTHING.

Nails cheap wooden crosses over every door. Plants (suppos-edly) purifying crystals in every room. The silver necklace she never really liked but could never manage to part with, finds a home around her neck despite the way it burns with memories of her mother. Before she left, she used to wear the matching heart-shaped pendant daily. When the crosses don't work, she nails up iron horse-shoes next to them and kisses the deposit on her apartment goodbye.

Pentagrams drawn in chalk.

Holy water tossed at his chest.

Chants and prayers in several languages, she just *knows* she's butchering.

Even the priest she convinced to come bless her home (and herself) only succeeds in drawing a snicker from Seth's pale lips.

Nothing works. Nothing helps.

She wakes up each morning teetering between stubborn hope and crushing despair, sometimes swinging between the two so quickly it makes her dizzy. Meanwhile, the days keep slipping by— time unmoved by her struggle to regain her balance. Oma calls at least three times a week, and Sara only just manages to sound convincing as she picks apart her day and shares the bits and pieces that don't include the uninvited guest shadowing her.

Jen and Miles aren't as easy to fool. Sara can read the worry in their voices each time she cancels and avoids making plans for the remainder of the summer.

Jen's voice is soft, free of judgement but brimming with concern. "Are you sure you're ok? I hate thinking of you being alone right now with everything that's happened…"

Sara bites her cheek, glares at the man/demon lounging on *her* living room furniture and coaxing *her* cat into his lap as if he belonged there. Either he can hear Jen's voice through the receiver or he can feel her stare, because the grin he gives her is mocking.

She wants to scream that being alone is the exact *opposite* of her problem. Instead, she tries to sound convincing when she says, "I'm fine, Jen. Promise. I just need a bit more time to figure everything out."

The beat of silence, the thread of doubt lacing her voice, makes it clear Jen's not convinced when she responds, "If you're sure…"

Sara's so far from sure it's laughable, but she assures her anyway. "I am."

Scratching under Ansel's chin, Seth's smile only sharpens. "Liar," he says, the single word dripping in approval. "Perhaps there's hope for you yet."

It's in that moment, more than any of the others, that Sara believes what he's told her from the very beginning.

She's never getting rid of him.

He folds himself into her life.

Tears apart the seams of her routine, stitches it back into something she can only barely recognize. She's constantly looking for him, nerves singing as she expects to find him around the corner, across the street, lounging in her chair. It's been weeks, but she still isn't numb to the way he can blink in and out of her life—can't shake the way her heart jumps in surprise every time she turns around to find him close.

She pulls the cork out of the bottle of wine, forgoing the glass to take a deep drink. It's cheap—cheaper, even, than what she usually buys—but right now she doesn't even care. Her nerves are wound so tight, she's afraid she'll snap. Just one night, she prays. Let him stay away for just one damn night so she can drink and pass out and—

"Having a party for one, are we?"

She jumps, the bottle slipping from her fingers and landing with a clunk on the floor. It's a small miracle it doesn't shatter, but she's dismayed to see the red wine spilling across the floor.

"Damn it!" she hisses, grabbing the bottle by the neck and mourning the loss. It was just some cheap wine, but it was *hers*. But of course he just had to ruin that, too. She's too angry, too tired, to remember to be afraid. The blood is roaring in her ears, the aftertaste of the wine sharp and bitter on her tongue. "What the hell is wrong with you?!"

Seth raises a brow, leaning against the counter. It's the first time she's seen him without his coat—the white sleeves of his shirt rolled up to the elbows, flashing the pale skin of his forearms. She misses the coat. Without it, he looks too casual. Too *at home*. "Far too much, I'm afraid." His eyes flit to the bottle in her white-knuckled grip. "Though, I'm sad to say alcoholism isn't one of them."

She stills, the echoed memory of clinking glass bottles ringing like an accusation in her skull. "I don't have an alcohol problem," she says, the words hissed between her teeth.

"And yet you were eager enough to skip the glassware entirely." His fingers curl around the edge of the counter at his back, his gaze dangerously intense. "It must be a truly special occasion."

He's wrong—she knows he is—but the accusation is a well-aimed blade striking one of her deepest fears. There's a reason she doesn't keep alcohol in the apartment; a reason why she will only buy one bottle of wine, one six pack of beer, at a time and only occasionally. She won't risk letting herself trip into her father's mistakes.

His gaze flits to the clenched fists at her sides, understanding darkening his eyes. "Ah, I see I've found a nerve." He meets her glare, the corner of his mouth twisting into a cruel, teasing smirk. "Tell me, is it your mother or father you're so terrified of becoming?"

*Both*, she thinks. She's so furious she's shaking. The glass neck of the bottle in her grip grows hot. "*Shut up.*"

His head tilts, smile sharp. "My, haven't we grown brave?"

His words are a gunshot, her anger dropping from the sky like a bird full of lead. The tightness in her chest becomes a cold weight. The being in front of her doesn't play by mortal rules—can travel without taking a single step, is invisible to all eyes but her own. Who knows what else he's capable of?

Sara pales, taking a step back even though she knows it doesn't matter. There's no escaping him—she could run to the other end of the world and he'd only be a blink behind.

The serrated edge of his smile softens into a frown, irritation pulling at his brow. "Your fear is wasted."

"I don't believe you."

He stalks toward her, and it's only her stubbornness that keeps her feet planted. Sara has never felt short, but when he stands this close—when the space between them is inches instead of feet—he towers over her. In his shadow, she tilts her head up, refusing to drop her gaze even as her heart tattoos a warning against her ribcage.

He stares down at her, brow raised and hands sinking into his trouser pockets. "Have I not upheld my promise to bring you no harm?" he coaxes, the timbre of his voice an oil spill—suffocating and slick.

She grits her teeth, each word an enunciated hiss. "I. Don't. Believe. You."

"Stubborn thing," he chastises, but there's approval laced in his voice. And Sara realizes he *wants* her to challenge him. It's not as comforting as it should be. "Very well. Hold out your hand."

Her fingers clench the bottle, ready to swing. "Why?"

Seth huffs. "Because seeing is believing, and a sharp tongue is far more entertaining than a dull one."

There's an innuendo there, one that she absolutely refuses to acknowledge.

He raises his hand, palm facing her, and motions for her to do the same. There's nothing threatening about it, but she still hesitates a few seconds before raising a trembling hand.

He smirks. "Now, was that so terrible?"

She bristles, biting her cheek. Whatever point he's trying to make, he hasn't finished making it.

Tsking, he shakes his head. "So serious." When her glare doesn't falter, he chuckles—that damn smirk of his widening. Then, before she can register his intentions, he presses his open palm against her own.

She stares at the way their hands are pressed. His fingers are long and tapered, his larger hand dwarfing her own, but it's neither of those things that make her blood run cold and her body freeze.

She can't *feel* him.

The bottle slips from her fingers, wine spilling out over the floor. She can feel it saturating the soles of her socks.

He leans down, mouth hovering beside her ear. He's too close, she should feel warmth from his body, hear the whisper of his clothing, but there's nothing. "Well, Princess?" he murmurs, a breath that's not a breath. "Do you believe me now?"

# CHAPTER NINE

THE AIR IS THICK, SO HUMID SHE CAN FEEL THE MOISTURE STICK TO HER skin and coat her lungs with every labored breath. Leaving her air-conditioned apartment feels like stepping into a sauna. Sara casts a resentful glance skyward. They've been issuing warnings about thunderstorms all week; one look at the dark, gunmetal clouds over-head is proof enough that it's only a matter of time before the first clap rattles the city.

She walks a little faster.

"Honestly, Princess. Your *hair*."

Sara curses under her breath, casting him a glare as hot and bitter as the weather. His grin is wide and teasing. She hates when he does this. It's bad enough when he taunts her in private, where she can at least snap back. In public, she has to bite her tongue till it bleeds or risk looking insane.

A few drops of rain dot the sidewalk, her only warning before it comes faster—harder. Sara can feel it sliding down her neck, soaking her clothes, and she closes her eyes with an agitated prayer for patience. When she opens them, Seth stands in front of her—grin-ning and infuriatingly dry. Yet, by some magic she still hasn't wrapped her head around, there is no dry spot on the cement at his feet. The rain passes right through him as if he really was no more real than her imagination.

His gaze flicks pointedly to her hair. "Suppose that's one way to tame that mess of a mop."

"I hate you," she hisses.

He blows her a mocking kiss. In her peripheral, she catches a warning flash before the thunder.

She pulls her messenger bag in front of her, fighting off the urge to glare at him. There's already been a few passerby shooting her odd looks.

Get to school. She just needs to get to school, make it through class, and go have lunch with Jen and Miles so she can convince them she's *fine*.

Rifling through her bag, she finds an umbrella wedged under her textbook and murmurs a quiet, "thank god."

"Well, I rather doubt he has anything to do with it."

Ignore him.

Ignore him, ignore him, *ignore him*.

She opens the umbrella overhead, the rain tapping eagerly at the fabric. Sara keeps her bag at her front to avoid the runoff. There's still plenty of time before her class starts, she can probably manage to grab a much needed coffee beforehand. The promise of caffeine is enough to make her walk just a little bit faster.

She hasn't slept well in weeks. Aside from being a snarky asshole, the devil at her back apparently comes with a tv addiction. The murmured voices from the old tube television is tolerable—more white noise than anything—but the sound of his voice, too clear and too real, through the apartment's thin walls is almost unbearable. The one night she refused to turn it on, he retaliated by singing operatic nonsense (she's still not convinced the gibberish coming out of his mouth was a language, despite his claims) at the top of his lungs until she caved.

Seth follows; he always does. Hands tucked into his coat pockets, he flirts at the edges of her vision. The ghost she never asked for. The shadow she can't escape. Sara wishes she could say the last month has made her used to it, but she still catches herself slipping. The first week, she told him to shut up in front of the cashier at her local grocery. She hasn't been brave enough to go back since.

"Art Appreciation today, yes?" he asks. Sara knows better than to believe he doesn't already know. His lips curving into a goading smile. "I'm rather looking forward to it. Last week was more entertaining than I expected."

Her teeth grind, groaning in her skull. Last week he had spent the entire class mimicking her professor's every move and flooding her ears in a never-ending commentary of mundane details Mr. Kent failed to mention. She can feel her blood pressure rising thinking about it.

Pulling her phone out of her pocket, she brings it to her ear without hitting call. Still refusing to look at him, she hisses into the receiver. "*No.* Stay out of my classes."

Seth huffs, blinking in and out around the various people filling the street. For a ghost, he doesn't really *act* like one. No floating, no phasing through walls (or anything for that matter), and it's been agonizingly clear that no one else can see him.

Come to think of it, the only ghost-like thing he does is *haunt* her.

"You're *mine*, Princess. I'm not terribly invested in heeding your demands, petty as they are. Besides, would it kill you to lighten up? Your attitude is terribly depressing."

Sara *hates* that nickname almost as much as the reminder. Loathes it with an intensity that's as physical as mental—she can *feel* her blood pressure rising every time it passes his stupid lips. She'll be damned before she lets him know it, though. The one time she mentioned it, he took it as a challenge to weave it into every sentence.

*"Lovely weather today, Princess."*

*"Princess, your cleaning habits are appalling."*

*"Tell me, Princess, what were you thinking?"*

Sara's lips purse, her steps growing violent. Her foot lands in a puddle, splashing her jean-clad calves with dirty water, and she feels her fraying sense of control *snap*. "Would it kill you to leave me alone?"

"Possibly. Terribly kind of you to ask. And here I was beginning to worry you didn't care," he mocks, laying a splayed hand over his chest.

"I *don't*," she snaps, voice as tight as her grip. Her phone case groans under the pressure, knuckles white.

"So cruel," he sighs.

She almost laughs. Almost. She can feel it, cutting and dark, clawing its way up her throat. Sara swallows it down, lets it settle in her chest like a stone. She refuses to let him goad her into embarrassing herself in public (again). "Feel free to go sulk somewhere."

"Don't be ridiculous, I rather like our walks." He smiles, curved and wicked. "I find them incredibly entertaining."

She fights the urge to run back to her apartment and crawl into bed just to bask in the silence. Aside from bathrooms, her bedroom seems to be the only place he won't enter. Whether it's because he has at least some small amount of decency, or because he doesn't want to face her wrath should he cross that line, she's not entirely sure (though she has her suspicions).

He seems more amused than cowed by her temper.

Sara shoves her phone in her pocket, determined to give him nothing but a cold shoulder. It's taken weeks, but she's realizing that's the only leverage she really has on him. She's not half as "entertaining" when she doesn't speak back.

From the corner of her eye, she catches sight of his pout a second before his lips curl into something smug. "Oh, are we giving the silent treatment another go? Pity." He blinks in front of her, so suddenly it nearly makes her stumble to a stop. The glare she sends him is edged with threats, but his grin only widens. "I suppose I'll have to take it upon myself to speak for the both of us. It has been such a long time since I've had the opportunity to discuss the Baroque period."

Her teeth clench, jaw aching, as he falls in step beside her—filling the silence with droning facts about Bernini and Rubens. She tries to tune him out; ignore the lilting rise and fall of his voice.

It's insult added to injury that he makes the topic almost interesting. Even more so, when she goes to her art appreciation class and has to listen to the same lesson in her professor's dull voice.

THE LITTLE CAFE AROUND THE CORNER FROM HER APARTMENT IS BUSY AS always, but meeting late morning means she's avoided the majority of the nine-to-five crowd. From a table in the corner, she spots Jen waving to catch her attention. Sara plasters on as wide a smile as she can manage, waving back as she weaves through the sea of bodies and chairs.

She sees a shadow in the peripheral, feels her heart drop, but when she looks it's only a stranger in a charcoal coat. Sara feels as relieved as she does silly. Seth has never followed her here—he avoids any and all cramped and crowded places if he can help it. She suspects it has less to do with her comfort and more to do with his. Once, she caught his shuddered expression after a child ran through him quicker than he could blink away. A place like this—brimming with bodies and furniture—it would be close to impossible for him to avoid all contact.

She wonders, quietly and only to herself, if it hurts him.

Jen hugs her in greeting, firmer than usual, but no less comforting. "How are you?" Only Jen could ask that and mean it. It's never just an effort to make polite conversation; she sincerely wants to know.

Yet, still, Sara can't bring herself to burden her with the truth. "I'm holding up."

Jen's face falls, just a fraction, and Sara knows her best friend has seen right through her. The shadows under her eyes probably don't help. "You look tired."

The truth is she looks like shit and still smells a little like sage (she can't, for the life of her, seem to be able to get it out of her clothes). "I've had trouble sleeping lately. Probably just nerves, you know, with classes having just started." She gives Miles a half-armed hug before sitting across from him and sending him as honest a smile as she can muster. "Hey."

"Hey," he echoes, but behind his thick-rimmed glasses, he raises a dark eyebrow.

Sara knows he's not fooled, either.

Jen sits beside her fiancé, hand linking with his under the table. "It's the Literature class isn't it?"

Sara appreciates that Jen understands her well enough to give her a sympathetic wince. "*British* Literature."

"It'll be fine," Jen soothes, her nails tapping on the table. They're teal today. "Just, maybe, *actually* read the assignments this time. That usually helps."

"Jen, I *do* read the assignments," Sara insists, but the look Jen sends is weighted and knowing. "Except for maybe that one time freshman year."

"Yeah, ok," she says, teasing. "Well, I got you an ice water, but I'm going to go get a parfait," Jen says, pulling out her chair. "Do you want anything?"

Sara chances a glance at the line, cringing. It's long enough for her to know Miles definitely won't be letting her off the hook. But, if she has to suffer through his interrogation anyway, she might as well get food for it. "Can you grab me a cheese danish?"

Jen nods, turning to Miles expectantly.

He shakes his head, leaning further into the chair. "I'm good."

Lips thinning, Jen's eyes narrow pointedly as she adjusts her purse over her shoulder. "You need to eat something."

It's enough to make Sara pause, but Miles only rolls his eyes—a tiny smile tucked in the corner of his mouth. "Yes, dear. I'll have a breakfast sandwich."

She nods approvingly, giving Sara another soft smile. "I'll be right back." Then she's wading through the crowd and leaving them behind.

Sara hangs her messenger bag over the back of the chair. "Hurting?" Jen only ever bugs him about eating when there's a possibility of him needing his pain meds.

Miles sighs, hand rubbing his thigh. "Just aching. Been running around the ER probably more than I should. But I gotta make this last year count if I'm gonna land a job there after I finish my residency."

Sara frowns, leaning her elbow on the table. "Do you have your meds?"

"You're as bad as Jen. *Yes*, I have them. *No*, I don't need them." He looks over his shoulder, making sure his fiancée is well out of hearing range before he leans forward. "Now cut the crap. How are you, really?"

Sara flinches, hating that he can tell. Her gaze drops to her drink, stirring with her straw and watching the ice clink against the sides of the glass. "I said I'm fine."

"Yeah, right. You and me? We speak the same language. You saying you're fine is the same way *I* say *I'm* fine." His finger taps emphatically against the table. "Which means you're *not fine*."

"I just don't want to talk about it, ok?" she hisses. "It's hard enough without—" She doesn't finish that sentence. She can't. "I'm just... struggling to adjust. It's no big deal."

"You lost your boyfriend to a traumatic brain injury," he says, voice soft. "I'd say that's a pretty big deal."

"I didn't *lose* David. He's just, he's just a little lost right now. He'll come back." She wishes she sounded more confident, more convinced. The doubt threading through her voice is as obvious as the pity in Miles' eyes.

"Either way, he ain't here." He lays a hand over his chest. "Now, personally? I think you're gonna be better off without his pasty ass—"

"I'm pasty."

"Yes, but I *like* you. And I know you love him, but he was always going to hold you back." His brown eyes, a handful of shades lighter than Jen's, pin her to her seat. "You are going to move *mountains* without him dragging you down, girl."

"Look, I know David wasn't your favorite—"

"Understatement."

Sara sends him a dry, unamused look.

Miles matches it. "Dude never wanted for anything in his *life,* and it *shows.*"

"That's not his fault!"

"Oh, so his daddy making a donation to the school had nothing to do with David pulling a passing grade out of his pampered ass? That wasn't on him, *at all*?"

"We can't control what our parents do, Miles."

"Really? Because an honest man would have taken the failing grade and repeated the class like everyone else."

"It was one class."

"He's going to be a *lawyer*. His daddy buying him a winning grade in legal ethics would be like me sleeping through *pharmaceuticals* and passing anyway."

Miles' brows arch, challenging her to disagree. "He got a pass freshman year, but three years in the real world should be enough to make a guy realize he's a pampered brat." He lifts his mug, sticking his pinky out mockingly. "And that's the *tea*."

Sara's lips purse, irritation growing when he takes a loud, slurping sip without breaking eye contact. "Sometimes, you're kind of a jerk."

"*No*, sometimes I'm brutally honest. There's a difference. And if you weren't my friend, and I didn't care about you, I wouldn't bother."

"Whatever. Point is, I'm fine. So shut up about it before Jen gets back. You know how she is."

"Wonderful and caring, sometimes to the point of suffocation?" he says, eyeing his fiancé fondly from across the shop. "Yeah, I know."

"No cold feet then?" Sara jokes. If she wasn't so happy for them, the moon eyes they make at each other would be borderline nauseating.

"Only the one," he says, patting his left thigh with a wink. "And it hasn't stopped me from doing anything else, so I think we'll be ok."

Sara nods, sobering. "How bad is it, really?"

His smile is sardonic. "I'll live."

It's a thing between them—a hybrid cross between an inside joke and a code word.

Sara's sure he's remembering the night they all got drunk and Jen passed out on the couch. Jen's enthusiasm had ensured that Sara knew all about him before their first meeting—was well schooled about his time in the military and how his career was cut short by an

IED, how the loss of his leg and the hours of physical therapy had inspired him to specialize in emergency medicine—but she hadn't *known* him. Not yet.

He was wearing shorts that day. The intricate lines of plastic and metal, the way it melded into flesh just below the knee, was fully displayed. The booze made her head foggy and her lips loose.

She asked if it hurt.

Miles laughed. "Only every day, but better my leg than my head, right? I'll live." He followed it up with some joke about veteran's benefits after—something along the lines of at least the army was paying for his school even though the VA was doing a shit job of taking care of his leg.

Ever since that night, there had been an understanding between them. Sara knows the truth behind those two words; knows the pain is worse than he would ever willingly talk about. Miles knows it's the same for her.

"You should take the meds," she murmurs, holding his gaze. "At least enough to take the edge off."

He frowns, looking away. "I don't like the brain fog that comes with it," he says, a soft confession. "I'd rather feel the pain."

"But—"

"Look," he says, cutting her off. "I love you like the sister I never had, but please—and I'm begging here—*please*, drop it."

Sara goes quiet, absently tearing her straw wrapper into tiny pieces. "Miles?"

"Yeah?" he sighs around the rim of his mug.

"You have three sisters."

"And they ain't even half as much of a pain in my ass."

Sara smiles, wadding up a piece of the paper and tossing it at him. It hits his shoulder before bouncing back onto the table. "You love that about me."

"I'm pleading the fifth."

# CHAPTER TEN

She hates her literature class.

It's only been two weeks and, really, Ms. Green is nice enough and ten times more engaging than her art appreciation professor, but she *hates* it.

Her pencil taps against the blank page of her notebook, the only writing decorating it being her name and date in the upper corner. It feels like it's been taunting her for hours. The background noise of Seth's newest drama does little to help her concentrate. It's a stupid assignment—one Ms. Green claimed was supposed to just be a fun exercise in how to format their weekly homework assignments. Except, there's absolutely nothing *fun* about having no clue where to start.

Sara glances at the man who's made himself at home in her grandmother's chair. She really shouldn't ask, but she's too irritated with the assignment to care about the consequences at this point. "Hey," she calls, "Which of the seven deadly sins am I?"

He doesn't spare her a glance or a moment's reflection when he answers, "All of them."

She resists the urge to chuck her pencil at his head. Bastard would just laugh as it passed through him, anyway. "Jerk."

He waves her off. "Hardly. It's a true enough statement for most of us." Rolling his shoulders, he casts her a knowing look. "Besides, I'm fairly certain the assignment was for *you* to determine which ails you most."

She runs a hand through her hair, staring miserably at the assignment sheet. "But I don't think I'm any of them!"

Seth's sharp exhale is tinged with laughter, entirely unrepentant when she glares. "Apologies. Only, to deny all of them makes you a little *proud*, does it not?"

"I am not!"

A smug smile touches the left corner of his mouth. "Not the strongest argument, Princess."

Her lips part, ready to argue, but there's a goading glint in his eyes that makes her pause. He expects her to argue—wants it even. She huffs, slouching in her chair with a glower. "Fine," she snips. "I guess you would know, right?"

Smile widening, his cheeks dimple. "Wrong again, I'm afraid. I think you'll find that I'm far too greedy to be proud."

Sara's nose wrinkles skeptically. "How does that work?"

He shrugs, gaze sliding to the window. Outside, a full moon rises over the city skyline. "A greedy man wants everything; a proud man already thinks he has it all." His eyes meet hers pointedly, smile gone. "I assure you, I want much more than what I have."

Goosebumps dot her skin, but she manages to still the shiver threatening to race up her spine.

Sara never forgets what he is—she won't let herself—but she's definitely guilty of overlooking the power hiding behind his childish taunting. Sometimes there's a weight to his stare, though... an intensity that strips her nerves raw. She catches it when his smile slips; when his gaze looks too old to be set in a face so young.

Every now and then, she itches to know how many years those eyes have seen, but she refuses to give into the temptation to ask. She doesn't want him to twist her curiosity into interest. Or worse, *friendliness*.

Seth raises his eyebrows, voice smooth. "You're thinking awfully hard about something. Penny for your thoughts?"

With a jolt, Sara realizes she's been blatantly staring at him and swiftly turns back to her paper. "You don't even have a penny."

"Well, aren't you just the bearer of obvious news?" he hums. The mask he wears—the one of jovial smiles and teasing—is back. Sara wonders if slipping into it is as second nature to him as breathing is to her. "Very well then, I'll happily leave it to my imagination."

He's clearly baiting her (he's *always* baiting her) but Sara stubbornly refuses to play along. "Go for it."

"With *pleasure*."

She frowns, closing her notebook. "Know what? I'll do it later."

"Moving onto the reading assignment, are you?" he hums, a smile twitching at the corners of his mouth. "I suppose that is a touch easier than self-reflection."

Stilling, her eyes narrow. She hadn't mentioned anything about tonight's assigned reading. "You've been spying on my classes, again!"

"It's hardly spying if I'm not hiding. It's not my fault you never look behind you."

The glare she gives him is venomous. She's lost count of how many times she's insisted he leave her campus life alone. "I told you to stay out of my classes!"

"I don't recall agreeing to your petty demands."

A frustrated sound pulls from her throat. "*Why* would you even want to?!"

"I get bored," he says, primly.

"Then why don't you go watch a movie or something?!"

His lips thin. "I *do*."

"Well, go watch another one!" she snaps.

There's a retort ready to be fired—she can practically see the way he chews on it. Sara wonders what holds him back. "I fail to see why this bothers you so much."

"Because it's the only place I can seem to get *away* from you!" She throws her hands in the air.

"Careful, now." His expression darkens mockingly, bringing an elegant hand to rest over his heart. "You'll hurt my feelings."

"Like I care?" she sneers.

"Well, if you'd ever like my assistance with your classes—and trust me, you need an *ungodly* amount of help—you *should*."

"I do not!"

He barks out a laugh, the sound sharp and cruel. "You thought *Romeo and Juliet* was a romance!"

Sara flushes. "It's romantic!"

"It's a *tragedy!*" he shouts, appalled. "There is literally nothing romantic about a story that ends with a double suicide!"

She hates, so much, that she has no counterargument to that. "Fine! Whatever! But I *don't* need your help, especially since I already read the assignment!"

"Did you now?" He actually seems surprised. Sara wonders if she should feel insulted, but the speed in which his mood changes leaves her disoriented. "And what did you think of Rossetti's 'Goblin Market'? Are you a fan?"

She's momentarily thrown by his sincerity. "It was ok, I guess." she offers cautiously. "I liked it better than that Lord Brian guy."

A muscle in his jaw twitches. "Byron. His name, for what must be the umpteenth time, is Lord *Byron*."

She knows, but the level of pure frustration it pulls from him is more than enough incentive to keep getting it wrong. "Same difference."

She can practically hear his teeth grinding. "It's very much *not*, and I loathe that expression."

"Good. I'll make a point to keep saying it."

He glares. "Cheeky."

The smile she gives him is so mockingly exaggerated her cheeks are nearly sore from the strain.

"Ridiculous," he chides, though there's hardly any heat behind it. He tilts his head, considering her thoughtfully. "I must say, I'm surprised. I suspected you to balk at all the ripe sensuality."

Her smile slips. "What?"

"Surely you didn't miss it?"

"Miss what?"

Shaking his head, he brings a pale hand to his temples. "I

expected too much. Tell me, what did you think the poem was about?"

"I don't know! Creepy goblin guys harassing girls on the street."

"That is not only a terrible summary, but a fail-worthy answer. What is it *about*? What are the themes? The lessons?"

"Well, what do you think?!"

His expression is a picture of neutrality; voice deadpan. "Sex."

Sara coughs, a flush rising rapidly to her cheeks as she brings a fist to her chest. "*What*?!" she wheezes. "It is *not*."

"No? Care to share your interpretation of the line, 'Eat me, drink me, love me'? I'm terribly curious."

Heat rushes up her neck. "You're such a pervert," she accuses, hiding her face in her hands to escape his taunting grin. Unfortunately, it does nothing to save her from his amused chuckle.

"Because I know how to read?"

She glares at him. "Because you read it like *that*."

His head tilts, his smirk waning into something contemplative. "You haven't actually *read* it, have you?"

The glare she sends him is swift. "*Actually*, I have."

"Out loud?"

"Does it matter?"

"Yes, in fact, it *does*. It's poetry. It's meant to be spoken—to be *heard*," he stresses. An odd look of determination hardens his gaze. "Pull out your book."

"Fine." She rolls her eyes, but fishes the textbook from her bag and turns to the page. "'Morning and evening,'" she reads, "'"maids heard the goblins cry: "Come buy our—"'"

"What are you *doing*?"

"I'm reading it out loud!"

"That's not a reading, it's a butchery!" He seems legitimately appalled. "Slide it over. Honestly, your subpar education has never been more apparent."

"Feel free to haunt my past English teachers instead," she grumbles, pushing the textbook to the edge of desk pointedly.

"And be forced to correct them all day? Hardly."

"You correct *me* all day."

He brushes her off. "Completely different. Now," he taps a finger to his ear pointedly, "*listen.*"

He reads it, start to finish; his voice a rhythmic melody of vowels and consonants strung together into something even her ears find beautiful. There's a purpose in the way his tongue curls around each word; a reverence. When he speaks the final line, his eyes settling on her, Sara finds her mouth has gone dry.

"Do you hear it?" he asks. "The difference?"

She nods, fingers twisting in her lap. She hates that she has to take a moment to find her voice. "Yeah."

His finger taps, soundlessly, on the page. "It's more than just words on a page. There's music and *meaning* there."

It dawns on her then—the lack of teasing, the brightness in his eyes. "You love it." He withdraws, taken aback, and she shakes her head. She gestures to the book. "The, um, poetry."

That's why he goes to her classes. That's why he refuses to stop. No wonder she never saw him… antagonizing her was never the reason he came. She wonders if he frequents the other literature classes as well.

Glancing at the page, he straightens. "I have... an appreciation."

It's more than that, but she doesn't push. Pushing feels too much like curiosity, and she'll be damned before she lets him think she's interested in anything having to do with *him.*

Chewing lightly on her bottom lip, her eyes scan over the page. The way he read it… it's hard to deny the truth of his interpretation. "It's really about that?"

He shrugs. "Obviously there's more to it—and the case could be made for other interpretations, I'm sure—but sexuality is certainly a prevalent theme."

The urge to ask for further explanation is so real, she has to bite her tongue. He's right, she *does* need help, but the thought of asking for it makes her recoil.

What would he ask for—what would he *take*—in return?

# CHAPTER ELEVEN

Sara's not sure how it's possible, but somehow her art history professor makes the class as boring and tedious as her literature class. Thank god her math teacher was at least entertaining. Which, considering the subject, is both surprising and almost ironic (not that she's complaining).

She tries to focus on what Mr. Kent is saying, but she finds her attention faltering. There's just something about his voice—the listless, steady way in which he speaks—that makes every lesson sound as dry and tasteless as stale bread.

Really, *really* stale bread.

But at least most of the art was pretty.

Painting has never been her thing (she doesn't have the patience for it), but she can appreciate it. The core values of what makes an image great is the same despite the medium—color, composition, lighting, movement. There's a reason this class is a requirement for her Bachelor of Photography degree. Unlike her English and math requirements, Sara totally understands how the material is relevant to her career path. She'd even go so far as to say it's interesting. Or *would be*, if the person teaching it was literally anyone else.

In her bag, her phone vibrates—the sound muffled, but still loud enough for the surrounding students to glance over. Sara wonders if it's just because they're as bored as she is. It's probably a really bad sign that she almost (*almost*) wishes Seth would crash the class like he did the first few weeks, but apparently he finds her professor as dull as she does.

The vibrating stops long enough for Sara to doodle a flower on the corner of her notebook before starting up again. She frowns, feeling her classmates' eyes as she reaches into her bag and silences it. A glance at the screen shows an unfamiliar number, but it's the same as the one that called a few seconds before. It's probably just another scam call—she's been getting a lot more of those lately—but it's weird that they called right back when she didn't answer.

Her professor's voice makes her jump. "I'm sorry. Am I boring you, Miss Bennett?"

*Yes*, she thinks, but the heat crawling up her neck and the weight of her classmates' stares makes her tongue stick to the roof of her mouth. Awkwardly, her fingers fumble for the power button. "Sorry," she mutters, "I was just turning it off."

Mr. Kent looks down his long nose, this thin face pulling into a sneer. "Phones should be turned off *before* class. Not during." How he manages to still sound toneless even while his expression screams irritation is a mystery.

"Sorry," she echoes, shrinking in her seat. Mentally, she adds 'professor is a total dick' to her list of reasons why this class might be just as bad as British Literature.

THERE'S A VOICEMAIL WAITING FOR HER WHEN SHE GETS OUT OF CLASS.

It's still probably just a telemarketer call (they seem to be the only ones that bother with voicemails anymore) but she decides to listen anyway. Part of her is just curious to see what the latest scam is—it's been a while since she got the one about the car payment she didn't have being overdue. Longer still since anyone's called about her "home warranty".

She brings the phone to her ear, dodging the other students as she

78

fights her way through the narrow halls. The voice that plays isn't a recording, but it's unfamiliar—an older sounding gentleman.

*"Miss Bennett? This is Dr. Hastings from Valley Creek Medical Hospital. I need you to give me a call back as soon as you can. It's in regards to your grandmother."*

The chill she gets is instant, heavy on her chest and shattering the breath in her lungs like glass. She's frozen. Students move around her, shoulders checking hers as they dodge her.

Sara doesn't feel any of it.

She doesn't feel anything.

# CHAPTER TWELVE

She runs up her apartment steps, shoes slapping painfully against the aged tile. Sara doesn't care. Her heart is hammering in her chest; a war drum in her ears. A blistering combination of worry and fear that leaves her lungs burning and her skin flushed. In her bag, she feels her cell phone slap against her thigh with every lunging step.

She just needs her car key—run in, run out, drive. It repeats, a mantra to keep her steady. Her hand shakes as she fits the key into her lock, and she nearly breaks it off with how hard she turns it, but she doesn't care. She shoves it open, the adjacent wall saved only by the twang of the doorstop.

The car key should be in the kitchen—it's always in the kitchen, hanging on the hook just beside the fridge.

From his—no, *her* wingback chair, Seth's voice reaches her. "Well now, that was dramatic."

Taunting. Always taunting.

Her blood freezes, face paling. She hadn't even considered the possibility—she hadn't had the time to—but there he sits, elegant and poised, and now she wonders how she could have ever over-looked it.

"It was you." A statement. A *fact*. She won't let him convince her of anything else.

He scoffs, but the teasing glint fades from his eyes. "Was it now?"

"How *could* you?" The words are breathy, barely audible between her heaving gasps, but the edges of each syllable are serrated—Sara hopes they cut him to the bone.

His stare is wary, eyes flitting between her clenched fists and her barred teeth. Slowly, he stands. Sara finds a small amount of satisfaction in the careful way he approaches her—as if she were wild. As if she were *dangerous*. "Princess, I haven't the faintest idea what you're on about."

It's too much. Him pretending not to know is worse than him denying it, and all the fear and anger she's harbored since receiving the call increases tenfold—burning her chest and spilling down her cheeks. The instinct to hurt him is overwhelming.

Her fist flies.

She knows it will pass through him, knows that it won't inflict the pain she wants it to, but her eyes are blurry and the pain in her chest is only coiling tighter. She just wants him to *hurt*. Wants to seek whatever shred of satisfaction she might find in watching her fist pass through his *stupid* face.

Her knuckles meet flesh—cracking painfully against his jaw—and he staggers. His eyes, as wide as her own, are open in ways she won't let herself notice. The wounded expression—the shock parting his mouth—it's either her imagination or a trick and she won't be lured in by it. She *won't*.

He flees, between one blink and the next, and Sara stands alone in her living room with aching knuckles and a hammering heart. Her knees fail her, exhaustion cresting over the anger, and she slides to the floor.

She hates that, even in the midst of her hiccuping sob, she keeps thinking back to the dismay that shone in Seth's eyes the moment before he blinked away.

It takes half an hour before she feels safe enough to drive.

When she puts the key in the ignition, she can feel the hysteria begin to bubble—a pressure in her throat, a hiccup in her lungs—but she forces herself to breathe through it.

She doesn't think about Seth; doesn't think about the emotion in his eyes the split second before he blinked away. She doesn't think about *anything*. Flashing the turn signal, merging onto the freeway, it's all done with a numbness that makes her feel more machine than human.

That's ok, though. Right now, she would rather feel the clicking of gears than the pain in her chest.

It's an hour's drive, but it somehow manages to feel twice as long. Sara doesn't remember any of it; just a blur of asphalt and corn-fields. She's on autopilot until the exact moment when she pulls into the hospital parking lot, and all the emotions she repressed on the drive hits her with a force that leaves her gasping.

Still, she makes it to Oma's room—a mess of tears and heartache. The staff gives her soft, pitying glances as she passes while simultaneously trying to avoid eye contact so they can continue doing their jobs.

It's like David all over again, but worse (so, so much worse). There is no hope hiding away in the corners of her heart, no promise of '*maybe*'. Oma is dying. Soon she'll be gone.

Oma's hand pats her cheek, fragile and weathered. "It's ok, sweet girl. I've made my peace."

The tears come faster. Harder. Sara chokes on a sob, snot running down her throat. Oma shushes her softly, but the sound doesn't soothe the break. Not this time. "I don't want you to go," she whimpers, grasping at her grandmother's hand. She hates how cold it feels against her palm.

"I know," Oma whispers between a rattling breath, "I know."

Sara shakes her head, eyes burning. "There has to be something they can do," she hiccups. "There has to be."

Oma softens, voice strong in a way her body isn't—level in a way that makes Sara's break. "Some things just *are*," she says, hand reaching up to stroke her granddaughter's hair. "I've had a good life."

*But you should have more,* Sara wants to scream. *You should have longer.* But she can't bring herself to say the words, because there is no fear hiding behind her grandmother's blue eyes—no regrets.

Oma smiles, cool hands reaching up to cup Sara's tear flushed cheeks. "Listen to me, sweet girl. When the time comes, you'll need to speak to Janice. She's the executor of my will. She'll make sure everything is taken care of. Do you understand?"

Sara does, but she doesn't *want to.* "But—"

"Sara," she chastises, and for a moment she looks so much like the grandmother Sara remembers—scolding her for stealing an extra cookie from the jar or trying to fib her way out of finishing her homework. "Do you understand?"

The words won't come—they're lodged like a knife between her heart and her throat—so, around another hiccuping sob, Sara nods.

With patient hands, Oma guides her closer until her face is buried in the crook of her neck—her grandmother's fragile arms wrapped around her. Despite her weakness, her hold is strong; a tether in the storm. A lifeline. Sara's terrified of what will become of her once it snaps.

"I know it's hard, and I know it hurts, but all things heal. Even the heart." Oma presses a kiss to her temple, her words a whispered promise against her skin. "I'm ready and, in the end, that is the most any of us can hope for."

TWO DAYS LATER, SARA LEAVES OMA'S SIDE TO GRAB BREAKFAST FROM the hospital cafeteria. She's not gone long (fifteen minutes at most) but when she comes back, the bran muffin she ate weighs like a stone. There are too many nurses going in and out of Oma's room, and when she catches one of their eyes, Sara *knows.* She knows that she missed that last goodbye, traded it away for a crappy muffin that Oma could have made ten times better with less.

The nurse consoles her, hand rubbing practiced circles on her back as she explains that sometimes this is what happens. Sometimes the dying wait until there is no one to watch them go; no one to be haunted by the sound of that final, rasping breath.

Maybe it's true. If it is, Sara finds no comfort in it. She cries until it hurts, until someone comes to take Oma—no. Not Oma. Oma's gone. It's just her body (*a* body, the deceased own nothing). It feels like only minutes, but she knows it must have been at least an hour before they wheel it away to the morgue in the basement. Sara tries not to think of the steel wall of refrigerated, temporary graves—tries not to think of how her grandmother's face is among its patrons— but it presses against the lids of her eyes; a horrible vision she can't shake.

One of the nurses, the one that soothed her while she sobbed, asks if Oma had any family she can call. Anyone she can grieve with.

Sara thinks of the red sedan that drove away and never returned; thinks of the daughter at the wheel. She could find her—she knows she could, if she really tried. Her mother would want to come for the service at least, wouldn't she?

*Shouldn't* she?

Sara wasn't the only one abandoned when her mother left. Oma hadn't heard from her since she drove off. Sara frowns.

"No," she says, voice hoarse. "No other family."

Her mother should be there, she should know, but that doesn't mean she deserves to. She lost that right the moment she walked away without ever bothering to look back.

ON THE WAY HOME, HALFWAY INTO HER DRIVE, SHE STOPS BY A TATTOO shop. The bell rings over her head, a tauntingly merry chime, and she grits her teeth to quell the tears.

The woman behind the counter takes one look at her, eyes softening in pity. Dark hair is swept into a ponytail, the colorful sea of floral ink decorating her arms and neck on full display. "Lose someone?"

Sara nods, voice too raspy to be trusted by itself. "My grandmother."

The artist nods, her smile sweet and knowing. Sara wonders how many others have walked through that same door, listened to that same taunting chime, while carrying the same ache in their heart. "Come on back and we'll set you up, honey."

Numb, Sara follows. Sits on the bench. Reminds herself to breathe.

"Do you know what you want?"

Sara thinks of the springs she spent in her grandmother's flower garden, cutting roses and making bouquets for the table. She remembers searching for ladybugs—how her grandmother would tell her to make a wish every time she found one hiding between the thorns. Sara can only think of one wish now, and it's to remember how Oma looked on those spring days; smiling and happy with her favorite polka dot sundress and an iced tea sweating in her hand.

"A ladybug," Sara rasps, pulling her shorts down to expose her hip. "Right here."

Where only her eyes will see, where her father never will.

She doesn't want to give him the opportunity to tarnish it with his opinions.

SETH DOESN'T RETURN HOME UNTIL THE FOLLOWING AFTERNOON. SARA hasn't left her bed for anything less than pressing, and she curls deeper into her covers when he enters. The tattoo on her hip stings, a physical reminder of the pain in her heart. It pairs well with the bruising ache across her knuckles. Somehow, the pain is grounding.

She can feel him hovering at the edge of her vision; a silent shadow. She hates that he doesn't speak when, before, that's all he ever seemed to do. Hates that he's decent enough to be almost human. It would be easier to suffer his taunts, to be *angry*, than his pitying gaze.

Refusing to look away from the dramatic grayscale of the Half Dome print framed beside her bed, she swallows down the emotion threatening to choke her. She has to ask; she has to *know*. "It really wasn't you?"

A pause, then—in a voice so soft she could hate him for it—he answers. "No."

Sara pulls the comforter over her head, but doesn't bother stifling her tears.

HE DOESN'T COME BACK. NOT THAT DAY, OR THE DAY AFTER. SARA almost thinks she's rid of him, but can't quite find it in her heart to believe it. Whether he's doing it for her benefit or his own, she's thankful for the space. For the quiet.

Ansel follows her like a shadow. If she's in her room, she can find him at the foot of the bed; in the kitchen, on the windowsill. Sara's not sure if it's because he senses how deep her grief runs, or if it's just because he's unused to her being home so much, but Sara's thankful for the company. Though she tries not to think too much about his new favorite spot in the living room. It's hard enough to ignore the emptiness of the old wingback without finding her cat curled up on the cushion.

She can only afford to take a week off from school before she risks falling behind further than she can catch up. What she wants is more time to process, to mourn, but she knows she won't get it. Life, at least her life, doesn't cater to her needs. She drags herself out of bed, turns the shower on as hot as she can stand, and lets the steam fill her aching lungs. She stands under the spray, washing her hair with a numbness that speaks of habit more than thought. Her mind is back in the hospital room, Oma's hands on her cheeks.

*Speak to Janice.*

# CHAPTER THIRTEEN

Janice's home is eclectic in ways that Oma's never was—pictures and artwork lining every available wall, painted murals of flowers dancing along the door trim, the formal dining table covered in half-finished canvas instead of placemats. It should feel claustrophobic, the amount of knick-knacks is borderline hoarding, but somehow there's an order to the chaos that makes it feel full without being suffocating.

Bifocals perched on the bridge of her nose, the attached beaded lanyard glinting in the morning light, Janice spreads documents over the surface of the kitchen table as she explains each one. Sara listens numbly, hearing the words but struggling to register them, until Janice gets to the bank statement. "The savings account was pretty much cleared out a few months ago, but the house—"

Sara interrupts, shaking her head. "Wait, what?"

That can't be right. Oma never spoke about her finances, but she regularly gave Sara advice. Having a healthy savings was one of the topics she exhausted the most.

*A rainy day fund is no good in a flood.*

Janice looks down at the statement, nodding. "Her savings is empty. It looks like she withdrew the balance a few months ago. There's still money in the checking, though."

A few months ago.

Right before classes started.

The apartment.

Sara's vision swims. Janice says something else, but everything is muted. Echoed. It dawns on her then, what she should have probably suspected from the start. "She knew." Sara pins her grandmother's oldest friend with a look, the horror in her heart growing with every trembling second. "She knew she was dying."

Janice pauses, expressions changing so rapidly it's like she's on a skip reel: surprise, regret, hesitance, and, finally, resignation. "Yes."

Sara didn't think there was anything that could make it hurt more, but the sharp pain in her chest proves otherwise. "Why," she wheezes, throat tight. "Why didn't she tell me?"

How much time had she wasted? She would have come to visit more, would have taken her time to enjoy every remaining moment. Why—

"Gertie didn't want you to worry," Janice soothes, taking her hand. "She was adamant that you be able to enjoy your last year without this hanging over your head. She didn't know it would be so quick. No one did. The doctors thought she would have another two years."

Sara knows the words are meant to bring comfort, but they only sharpen the pain. All those months they could have had together, gone. So what if it would have pushed her graduation back? What's a half a year in the face of just a few more months making memories in Oma's kitchen, laughing when the flour smudged their cheeks?

Janice's aged fingers slip away from her own to rifle through the remaining papers. "The house is to be sold, the profits to go to you on your twenty-third birthday."

A little less than a year; just after she's due to graduate. She's not entirely sure how she feels about that—Oma's house has always felt like home. "Does it have to be?"

"Sold?" When Sara nods, Janice sighs. "Yes, dear. Gertie was very clear. She had big dreams for you, honey, and she knew you wouldn't find them in the likes of this place."

THERE IS NO FUNERAL, NOT IN THE TRADITIONAL SENSE, BUT JANICE DOES organize a Celebration of Life.

They set up tables in the garden, drape fairy lights between the house and the gnarled oak. It's smaller than Oma deserves, but the people who come are the people she cherished, and Sara thinks that's just how she'd want it. A handful of people, laughing and toasting a life well-lived under a late summer sky.

Jen hugs her when they arrive, the embrace so tight it's borderline painful. It feels good—grounding. "I'm so sorry." Her voice hitches, cracks. She grew up having play days and sleepovers under Oma's roof—shares many of the same fond memories that Sara holds dear. The grief she wears is as real as her own. "Oma was an amazing lady."

Sara tries very, very hard to resist the instinct to flinch at her use of past tense. She nods, throat tight. Over Jen's shoulder, Miles greets her with a sad, empathetic smile, and Sara is reminded that it was just last year that she joined him on the grass for his brother's funeral—the ritualistic rifle fire loud and the folded flag heavy in his mother's arms. She remembers the bitterness Miles spat later, fueled by whiskey and grief, that the army had some nerve to take his brother after taking his leg.

Then, Sara couldn't find the right words to help him. Now, she understands that there are none. The truth is that none of it is fair.

It's not fair that Miles lost his leg in a war he had only agreed to serve in as a medic, only to lose his only brother six years later to the front lines.

It isn't fair that she lost the love of her life to a freak accident and a miracle turned sour, only to lose her grandmother to death just when the tear in her heart was beginning to heal.

That night, Sara sleeps in the spare bedroom Oma always called hers. Her dollhouse, built by her grandfather's careful hands when she was born, sits in the corner. Tomorrow she'll have to sort through Oma's life, treasure by treasure, and decide what she can keep and what she'll have to let go.

The digital clock on the nightstand illuminates the room, the numbers changing faster than she can find sleep. She stares at the dollhouse, admiring the tiny shingles and hand painted shutters, and knows there's no space for it in her tiny apartment.

(It doesn't stop her from wanting it anyway.)

She takes as much as she can, unwilling to part with all of it. The bed frame from her old room, the mustard velvet couch from the living room—but it's not the large items she finds herself in danger of taking too much of, but the seemingly infinite amount of odds and ends she has a memory attached to. She combs through the house with a diligence that borders on frenzy, her pile of treasures growing faster than she can box.

Here is Oma's favorite pie plate she would use almost exclusively despite having three others; there is the embroidered artwork that hung in the bathroom for as long as Sara's been alive. She takes the bundt cake pan, the faded coffee tin full of tea bags. Sara's never crocheted in her life and has no use for her grandmother's hooks, but she takes those too—the wooden handles shiny from use. It takes her at least five minutes to talk herself out of taking the yarn as well.

She packs up every single one of the photos; strips them from the frames and presses them neatly between the pages of Oma's albums for safekeeping. All in all, the pictures take up two moving boxes. Sara knows they will likely take up a cringeworthy amount of space under her bed, but she can't bring herself to regret it. Photos and yarn were the only things Oma hoarded. Sara can't rationalize the second, but she can justify the first.

Miles' hand rests on her shoulder, startling her. She's not sure when she stopped moving or how long she's been staring through

Oma's decorative set of wedding china, but the worry lining his fore-head gives her a pretty good idea.

"You good?"

A question with 'yes' or 'no' answer. Miles has always been good about offering an easy way out of difficult conversations. If he were anyone else, Sara might have lied as easily as breathing, but she knows Miles. Trusts him to know when to push and when to let the conversation die. "No," she says, her smile as weak as her heart, "but I'll live."

Miles nods. Behind the frames of his thick-rimmed glasses, his eyes soften with sympathy. He gives her shoulder a soft, reassuring squeeze before dropping his hand. "Yeah, you will." Miles nods toward the china she had been staring at. "This coming, too?"

Biting her lip, Sara stares longingly at the displayed plates—eyes tracing over the sweeping floral pattern and wondering if she even likes it (or if it's just her love for Oma bleeding into everything she owned). "I have nowhere to put it," she murmurs, regret tightening her chest. She tries to tell herself she won't miss it, will probably never think of it again. It's just that the pressure of knowing what to take and what to leave feels like a game of dodgeball she'll never win. No matter what, she's sure to return home with bruises.

She still hasn't been able to make a decision on the dollhouse.

Wordlessly, Miles opens up the display case, pulling out a plate and wrapping it in newspaper.

Sara watches in painful silence until she realizes he's putting it in one of the boxes labeled as 'keep'. "Miles—"

"Keep it," he says, eyes warm and expression soft. "Keep all of it, if you want. If you don't have space at your place, there'll be space in ours."

Sara shakes her head. "It's not fair to ask you to store all this just because I can't make up my mind."

"So go through it in a month, or a few months. Or a year. Life's too short for regrets, and if you force yourself to leave this behind now, you're going to regret it." He gestures towards the plates, eyebrows raised. "Take it. We already have a spare room full of stuff. What's a few more boxes?"

Her throat tightens and her eyes burn; gratitude as poignant as the loss. Stiffly, she nods. Miles ruffles her hair, the way he knows she equally hates and loves, before reaching for another plate.

THE HOUSE IS BARE, NOTHING BUT SKIN FOR WALLS AND WINDOWS FOR eyes. A corpse.

Everything that made it home is packed up in boxes; some of it for donation (Oma's clothes, some of the furniture, the majority of the kitchen supplies). A lot of it isn't. As she watches Miles load up the dollhouse into the truck, she feels another pang of guilt over how much she's keeping. There's no way she'll be able to fit everything in her tiny apartment.

Jen links their arms, leaning her dark head on Sara's shoulder. "It doesn't feel the same, does it?" Somehow, she always knows exactly what's going through Sara's mind.

"No. It feels…" she trails off. Hollow? Lifeless? Both words fit in ways that make her heart ache, but neither encompass the full scope of it. It's like someone developed the film wrong and everywhere she looks, it's nothing but shadows and static. Sara doesn't have a word for that, though, so she leaves the sentence hanging and unfinished.

Jen doesn't push for more. "Do you want a moment to say goodbye?" she asks, voice soft.

It should sound silly, saying goodbye to a house, but Sara knows it's exactly what she needs. In so many ways, this place was the one she called home. Her measurements are notched in the doorway of her old bedroom—the walls still lavender from when she was ten and begged Oma to let her paint it. In the garden, hundreds of daffodils lay dormant, set there years ago by her and Oma's hands and waiting to bloom come Spring.

Her childhood is cradled in these walls, in the soil… so much of who she was, who she *is*, planted around the property like painted eggs on Easter morning. Sara knows she won't have time to find all of them, but—maybe—she can gather enough.

"Yeah," she croaks. The word feels like sandpaper, all scratch and grit.

Jen gives her a gentle squeeze before unfolding herself from the crook of her arm. "We'll be outside finishing up, but Sara? Take however much time you need, ok?"

She's tempted to ask if forever would be too long, but her throat is still so tight she doesn't want to risk the words cracking, so Sara nods instead. Jen gives her a final pat on the shoulder—her touch lingering—before she pulls away. Behind her, Sara hears the front door softly shut.

The house is so still, so empty, she feels like a phantom drifting from room to room. It's only the occasional creaking of the floorboards under her feet, the feel of the wallpaper sliding under her touch that ground her. She goes through every room, every closet, with a diligence she's never had. There's a fear prodding her heart, a whispered command to commit as much as she can to memory before she forgets.

She saves the kitchen for last, her fingers tracing the grout lines over the counter. The ceramic feels cool against her palms. Most of her memories were made in this kitchen—Saturday morning banana bread steaming, fresh and soft out of the oven. The sink overflowing with dishes and flour streaking their hair when Sara would help bake and assemble plates of Christmas cookies.

How does she say goodbye to a lifetime in the meager span of a few minutes?

Silently, she shakes her head because she knows the answer is *she can't.*

Her eyes drift to the kitchen window. Sara's always admired how it looked over the garden—a living picture framed by wooden trim. She steps closer, for a better look, and her heart plummets.

Surrounded by the vibrant colors of Oma's garden, bathed in the golden light of dusk, a charcoal shadow is wedged between the color. He reaches for one of the wine colored roses as if to skim the petals, to feel the velvet texture slide beneath his fingertips. When his hand drops, there's a softness around his eyes and a tension highlighting the sharp line of his jaw. On him, the expression is foreign to her, but she recognizes the emotion behind it.

Longing.

She doesn't know why he's there, why he would risk her fury to come, but in that moment Sara knows it wasn't with the intention of being seen. He has always been the picture of composure around her (spine straight, shoulders back) but she sees none of these things now. The line of his body is soft, shoulders bowed in a way that looks more tired than relaxed—vulnerable.

She waits for him to look up, for their eyes to meet, but he never once faces the house. Instead, he turns away—his back to her and the fields of dried corn stalks stretched out before him in a shifting sea of gold. With his hands hiding in his pockets, he is a splash of ink, a colorless silhouette in a warm, vibrant landscape.

Framed by the kitchen window, Sara can't remember standing witness to a more lonely picture.

# CHAPTER FOURTEEN

Saturday morning, two days before she has to return to class, Sara hears the tv click on—Seth's voice a distorted murmur passing through the walls. Her ears strain, trying to catch his words as she lies on her back, breath caught in her chest and eyes staring past the bedroom ceiling, but his voice is too soft.

Then Sara notices Ansel's absence. She can't hear what he's saying, but she can at least guess who he's talking *to*.

Sara rolls onto her side, hugging her pillow to her chest, and closes her eyes. She still doesn't understand how she struck him. She had been so full of anger, the kind of fury that twists pain and fear into something sharp. Something dangerous. It barely feels real, more nightmare than memory, but her knuckles still ache where they connected with his jaw.

She'll have to face him eventually, but for now she lets the sound of the television and Seth's occasional murmur wash over her like white noise.

"I hit you."

It's the first thing she says to him once she convinces herself to leave her bed. Her hair is still greasy—begging to be washed—but suddenly the question burns her. It shouldn't have been possible, but her fists struck him as if he were any other man made of flesh and bone.

"You did," he hums, eyes fixed on the television. Sara vaguely wonders how he was able to turn it on. "Is this the part where you apologize? If so, kindly hold it in until the commercial break, would you? I believe Maria is finally catching on to Juan's dastardly deeds."

Her face flushes. She had given herself a pep talk before she abandoned the safety of her room—had told herself that she wouldn't let him rile her. She hates that he's able to push her buttons without even really trying. "That's not what—how is that even possible?!"

"Well, he certainly would be hard pressed to make it any more obvious. Last episode, he—"

"How did I hit you?!" she snaps, and for a moment the only sound that breaks through the tension is the swelling music from the television.

Seth sighs, finally giving her his full attention. Behind him, Maria is shouting, and it dawns on Sara that the soap opera he's watching is in Spanish. "It's not that complicated, Princess. You wished to hurt me, so you did."

It sounds like a copout, a simple answer meant to appease more than educate. She's already well aware of her motives. What she wants to know is *how*. "That shouldn't even be possible! You're—you're not *real*!"

He goes impossibly still. "Not real?" he echoes, tone flirting on the edge of either fury or hysteria. His eyes flash, and Sara realizes it's likely a combination of both. "Is that what you think? That I'm some—*figment* of your imagination? Something to kick at when the guilt comes round to play?" He stands, towering over her. Sara hates how small he can make her feel by simply existing in her space. "Let me be perfectly clear, *Princess*. I am much more than you could dream up."

Sara swallows, pulse thrumming in her ears, but she tilts her chin defiantly—refusing to break eye contact. "What, did I strike a nerve?"

"You bloody well struck more than that, didn't you?" he sneers. "Tell me, should I expect a repeat performance? Perhaps you would care to punish me for whatever other traumas you have rattling around in that skull of yours?"

The angry retort, prepared and ready, withers on her tongue. There is a regret souring her stomach. No matter how many times— how many ways—she tries to justify it, she can't shake the guilt lodged in the space between her lungs. The problem is, she believes him. Not *in him*, but she trusts that he enjoys her misery enough to celebrate when he's the cause.

He still deserved it. If not for herself, then for every other bit of pain he's no doubt orchestrated for others, but not for Oma. Not for what she was accusing him of.

Accepting his innocence (at least in this one instance) cools her fury into bitterness. She is the ember after a wildfire—snuffed of a flame but still hot enough to burn. "I hate you."

He snorts, arms folding over his chest. "And yet, I rather like you. Most of the time, anyway."

Her fists clench, crescent moons imprinting on her palms. She still carries bruises on her knuckles. "You're not funny."

"I am, actually," he says, offering a skeletal smile. "Your sense of humor is simply lacking."

The sound of smashing glassware mingled with the actress's screaming in rapid-fire Spanish emits from the tv, and Seth's entire body pivots toward the screen. "Damn it all! You see? You've gone and made me miss it." He gestures to the television, movements wide and exaggerated. "Rewind it!"

Sara balks. He can't *possibly* be serious. "*What?*"

"You bloody well heard me! Rewind it! I did not suffer through an ungodly number of Fanta commercials just for you to ruin the riveting finale of *Amor Prohibito*'s eleventh season!"

"You want me to rewind your Spanish soap opera."

"For the love of—*please*. Please, rewind the blasted thing and I will try my damnedest to forgive you? Yes?"

The breath leaves her, a resigned huff, and she grabs the remote left on the sofa. "You are so weird, I can't even," she grumbles, hitting various buttons. "How did you even turn it on?"

"Ansel was of great assistance."

"That... doesn't really answer my question."

He sneers. "Of course it does. Use your imagination."

She rewinds it five minutes before selecting pause. "Do you even know what they're saying?"

"Why *wouldn't* I?"

Sara raises her eyebrows, gesturing pointedly to the tv. "Because it's in *Spanish*?"

"My statement stands," he quips, sinking into his chair. "Now either turn on the subtitles or hush."

She has no interest in watching a soap opera in a language she can't understand, and even *less* interest in voluntarily sitting in the same room as him... but she's tired of being in her room, staring at the same four walls. Sara sits on the couch, pulling the crocheted blanket—one of Oma's she notes with a pang—around her shoulders before turning on the subtitles.

Juan begs for forgiveness, the camera zooming in on Maria's torn expression before going to another pop commercial. From his chair, Seth curses the world's obsession with soft drinks.

Pouting, he looks more human than ever, and Sara remembers the slump in his shoulders, the isolated smudge of shadow against a landscape of color, and feels her stomach churn.

She doesn't know how Oma would feel about any of this, but if there's one lesson she stressed, it was to admit (and apologize) when you're wrong. Somehow, Sara suspects the circumstances would do little to change her opinion on the matter.

Still, it takes her another two commercials before she works up the courage. "I'm sorry." The words are soft—strained—but she knows by the way his attention pivots to her, eyes wide and mouth parted in surprise, that he's heard. She pulls the blanket closer, looking away. "I shouldn't have hit you."

The show returns, the music swelling as Maria's face returns to the screen. Seth is silent for so long, Sara begins to suspect he won't answer at all. She's not entirely sure she deserves one.

"You didn't know you could," he says softly. When she looks, he's watching the tv without really seeing it.

Sara closes her eyes, breathing shaky. "But I wanted to." She wished so desperately for him to hurt, she managed to do what should have been impossible.

"Yes," he murmurs. "But given the situation, I can hardly fault you for it. Let's just consider ourselves lucky you didn't feel the urge to go to any more drastic measures, shall we?"

They both fall into silence. On the television, Maria takes her cheating husband into her arms and forgives him and (despite not having watched any of the previous episodes) Sara finds herself as disappointed as Seth is.

# CHAPTER FIFTEEN

Sara hates that her first day back to school is literature.

She's dreading the make-up work with a fierceness that leaves her equal parts nervous and resigned. Her professors have already agreed to give her two weeks to catch up, no points docked, but Sara suspects her grade will suffer despite their kindness. Math is one thing—it's all just numbers—but the reading and essays from the other two classes are going to bury her.

So, when Jen suggests they meet for lunch after class, Sara accepts. Not because she needs a Vietnamese coffee (she does) but because maybe, just maybe, the promise of hot noodles and a sugared dose of caffeine will be enough to get her through her class in one piece.

When her alarm goes off, she flirts with the idea of begging for one more day off and canceling her plans for lunch. Her eyes itch and her limbs feel heavy. A glance in the closet mirror proves that she looks as much of a mess as she feels. Sara stares at her reflection a full five minutes before the alarm goes off again and she groans.

If she cancels, Jen will worry. If she cancels, she might show up *here*.

She doesn't need to look around to know her apartment is unsuitable for company. There are dirty dishes scattered like landmines throughout, the carcass of a rotisserie chicken still sitting on the counter, and the litter box so overdue for cleaning she cringes every time she walks into the bathroom. It's easier to make herself presentable.

She drags herself out from under the covers, one grudging limb at a time. At the foot of her bed, Ansel twitches; his paw reaching up to cover his face. Sara scratches the top of his head, giving him a soft kiss on his furred cheek, and smiles when he gives a grumbled whine.

At least one of them gets to stay in bed.

THE PHO IS HOT; THE BROTH WARMING HER STOMACH AND DRAWING A contented sigh from her lips.

Jen reaches for a spring roll, glancing up at her carefully. "So how was class?"

Sara finishes slurping up her bite of noodles before answering. "Do you want to do my make-up work? I'll pay in love and affection."

Jen gives a sympathetic twinge. "That bad, huh?"

Sara doesn't justify her question with an answer, but she does drink another spoonful of broth. By far, one of the best things about living in the city is having access to the types of food she'd have to drive over forty minutes to an hour for back at home.

She stills at the thought, heart cringing at the reminder that she's supposed to visit her father in a few days. "I'm going to see Dad this weekend," she says, because as much as she's dreading it, she'd rather talk about him than Oma. The tattoo on her hip is healing nicely, but the scars on her heart run far deeper. She's not ready for those wounds to be prodded.

Jen's answering smile is awkward—a strange mix of sympathy and hope that only she's ever been able to pull off. "Maybe it'll be ok?"

"Yeah," Sara mutters, "Maybe." She stirs the soup, watching the noodles swirl in the bowl. "How's it going with your family?"

Jen rolls her eyes. "Oh, you know. My mom still hates my future husband. So that's been great. I told her I wasn't going to do a bridal shower, and she flipped her lid."

Sara stills, eyes darting to Jen's face. "You don't want a shower?"

"With my *mom*? There, in a confined space, with Miles' family?" She shakes her head, leaning into the back of her chair. "Yeah, no. I'd never put my in-laws through that. I love my mom, but she's a straight-up Karen. Which is hilarious because," Jen gestures pointedly to herself—sculpted eyebrows raising. "Not like she adopted a baby straight out of China or anything."

Sara cringes. She doesn't disagree. Mrs. Foster is the type of woman to sing her daughter's praises one moment and then condemn immigrants the next. "Yeah, I see your point."

Jen sighs, raising her cup of coffee mockingly. "Yay for problematic parents!"

"We should start a club."

"Who should be president?"

Sara pretends to think about it. "Well, your dad is pretty chill, so I guess I win with two for two."

Jen snorts on a laugh, a delicate hand covering her mouth. "God, it would be the most popular club on campus."

"No kidding. Too bad Miles won't be able to join." Both his parents are as wonderful as he is—still married, still in love. There's no wondering how he grew up to be an upstanding human being.

"Oh!" Jen gasps, grinning wide. "He can hook us up with some therapy!"

"Our club's patron saint of counseling," Sara laughs.

Jen joins her, earning them both some annoyed looks from the older couple sitting at the table to their left. It only makes them laugh louder and, for a brief moment, Sara doesn't think about the missing piece of her heart or the itch of the tattoo on her hip.

WHEN SHE GETS HOME, SETH IS ALREADY THERE—HOVERING OVER THE small kitchen table and staring at the stack of mail she's left there with a frown. He makes no indication that he's heard her come in, but Sara knows he must have. Even if she'd been trying to sneak up on him, she doubts she'd succeed.

Dropping her bag by the front door, she crosses her arms under her chest and walks past him without greeting. He's continued to keep his distance the past few weeks, which she appreciates, but she refuses to offer any kind of interaction he could misinterpret as friendly.

They aren't friends.

"There's no 'h'," he murmurs, a thread of a question underlying the statement.

Sara pauses, hand on the fridge handle. "What?"

"Your name. There's no 'h' at the end."

She stares, a little perturbed by his open curiosity. Since Oma's passing, he's been more careful in his taunts—slowly reintroducing them and studying her reactions. It reminds her of the way her town would test ponds in the winter—measured step by measured step—before clearing it for the kids to skate.

Still, his innocent statement feels like the beginnings of a trap. Sara narrows her eyes, waiting for the ice to crack beneath her feet. "Yeah, so?"

"I hadn't realized," he says, shoulders shrugging. "It's an uncommon spelling, is it not?"

"I mean, having the 'h' is more popular, I guess. But I've met a few others with my spelling."

"How strange," he mutters, but before she can take it as an insult, he adds, "Is there a reason?"

"Um, no? Not really." At least, not one that she'd ever heard, but she doesn't exactly hear a lot about that sort of thing. Anything that involved her mother, any stories that couldn't be told without erasing her, weren't told at all. Sara strongly suspects that the choosing of her name is one of them. "My dad used to joke it was one less letter to learn to spell my name."

Seth's scoff is haughty, his expression twisting into a scowl. "How… thoughtful."

She'd be deaf to miss his blatant sarcasm, but Sara doesn't reward him with a response. Instead, she opens the fridge and pulls out her water pitcher. The tap is probably fine, but the city water has always tasted odd compared to the well water she grew up on.

"I hear I shall have the honor of meeting the man in a few days?"

The pitcher slams on the counter. A small part of her takes a fraction of a second to be thankful it's made of plastic instead of glass, before she whirls on him. "*No.*"

"Well, I'm certainly not going to be left behind."

"You're not invited."

"Come now, if that's your only qualm, I'm sure it can be remedied easily enough."

"You know it's not," she snaps, teeth groaning in her skull. "I don't want you there."

"You don't want me at all," he corrects, hands sliding into his pant pockets and leaning against the table. "Shall I remind you of how little your wishes sway me?"

She screams, the air hissing through her teeth like a growl, before she stomps away from him. It's only after she's slammed her bedroom door, her chest rising and falling with each angry breath, that she realizes she never grabbed a glass of water.

# CHAPTER SIXTEEN

S<small>ARA PULLS INTO THE DRIVEWAY, KNUCKLES WHITE ON THE STEERING</small> wheel. Her foot releases some of the pressure off the pedal—a vain attempt to stall the inevitable. A glance in her rearview mirror proves that her backseat is empty, but she knows he can't be far. He never is. "Seth?"

She doesn't jump when his voice materializes behind her; eyes meeting hers unflinchingly in the mirror. "Princess?"

Her teeth sink into her tongue, stilling the half-hearted protests that sit there. The house she grew up in is just ahead, silhouetted by the evening sun, and there isn't much time. "I know you live to make my life hell, but can you please, *please* just shut up while I'm visiting my father?"

There's a long pause—enough to make her glance to check that he's still there. She barely catches his clouded expression before he shifts into one more mocking and familiar. "Worried I might poke fun at his bald spots, are you?"

No. She's too busy stressing over the consequences of letting her defenses fall; too aware of how quickly the conversation can turn from casual pleasantries to mocking each of her life choices. She swallows, wishing she could blame the dust kicking up from her tires for the dryness. "Just promise to be quiet. Please."

He huffs, eyes sliding to the horizon. "Very well, then."

The relief is so great, it's physical—the flutter of eyelashes and a knot unraveling in her chest. "Thank you."

Seth doesn't respond, but she can feel his questioning gaze lingering the entire ride up the long driveway—only breaking away once the house comes into view.

Her father's house hasn't changed. The gabled roof, the rockers on the front porch, all give the impression of a picturesque country home. Sara knows better. The closer they get, the more the disrepair becomes apparent—chipping paint, broken and missing rails. She steels herself as she exits the car, knowing the inside is bound to be worse, and sends Seth one last warning look before heading up the front steps. He huffs in response, rolling his eyes and murmuring "so dramatic" under his breath.

When she opens the front door, it still smells of stale beer and spilled whiskey; still lacks the warmth that Oma's home had in abundance. No pictures on the wall, no cookies in the oven... the collection of bottles is absent from the coffee table, at least. Sara tries to give him credit for making at least that much effort. "Dad?"

His voice comes from the back of the house. "In the kitchen!"

She finds him in the fridge, fishing a bottle from the lower shelf on the door. Sara looks around, frowning. "Where's Belle?"

"Kennel. Got tired of her getting underfoot while I was cooking," he gruffs, grabbing the magnetic bottle opener from the side of the fridge and popping off the cap to his beer. "You want something to drink?"

Sara eyes it warily, wondering what number it is. "No thanks. It's a long drive." She doesn't bother asking if he has anything that doesn't come with a percentage on the label. Sitting at one of the counter stools, her attention flits to the adjacent living room where Seth is sneering down at the ancient blue and green couch.

He glances up at her; his expression saying everything his mouth doesn't.

*Plaid.*

Sara smothers a smirk.

"Bob's been asking after you. Wants to know if you'd be interested in some work over break at the Christmas tree farm."

"Oh." Bob was always looking for people to work, because no one ever stuck around. *Mostly* because he was a penny-pinching ass that liked to pay under the table so he could skirt under the minimum wage. "Thanks, but I actually have plans over break."

"Oh yeah? What plans are those?"

Her mind scrambles for an excuse, but the first and only thing that comes to mind is also probably one of the worst things she could bring up. "Jen needs help getting stuff ready for the wedding."

It's a mistake.

She knows the moment she sees her father's shoulders stiffen. "That right?"

Teeth sinking into her bottom lip, Sara says a mental prayer. "Yeah. Just a few things."

"Didn't even know she was getting married."

"It hasn't come up."

"Who's the sucker?"

It takes everything she has to resist correcting him. "You don't know him."

Roy sneers. "You tell him there's still time to run?"

"No," she says evenly, "because they're very happy together."

"For now."

*Ignore it*, she tells herself—a familiar mantra. *Ignore it, ignore it, ignore it.*

From the living room she hears a quiet scoff—Seth is staring at her father, lip curled in distaste. It isn't entirely unlike the look he gave the sofa.

"What's for dinner?" she asks, eager to change the subject to just about anything else.

Her father sees through her (he usually does) but lets it go. Sometimes, Sara wonders if he tries even half as hard as she does to keep the peace. "I got some Tri Tip and corn on the barbecue." He nods toward the fridge. "And some of Phylis' mashed potatoes."

Phylis is the owner of the diner in town. When her mother left them, Roy quickly became one of her regulars. Her cooking is as familiar to Sara as Oma's was, but never preferred. Her mashed potatoes weren't bad, though. Sara suspects she would probably find them a lot more appealing if they weren't served straight out of a styrofoam cup.

"Sounds good."

She sets the table with paper plates and silverware—metal but cheap. Sara wonders if he's still buying the Walmart bulk sets so he can use the cheap price to justify throwing them away instead of washing them. The only thing that feels like it's made to last is the steak knives. She puts the potatoes in the microwave while her father cuts the meat.

Seth watches her from a respectable distance—she can see his shadow at the edges of her vision—but keeps his word and remains blessedly silent. Sara hates that the absence of his voice feels foreign. When they finally sit at the table, and she's asked to pass the butter, she's mildly horrified to realize her father's voice inspires more anxiety than Seth's has in weeks.

It takes all of ten minutes before she's reminded why.

Roy doesn't look up from his steak when he broaches one of the many conversational land mines with the subtlety of a bull. "When do you plan on getting a real degree?" The knife in his hand doesn't pause—sawing through tendon and flesh.

The words cut; another scar hidden on her heart. Her hands plant themselves on the table to still their trembling. "It *is* a real degree." She wonders how many more times she will have to come home to this conversation.

Her father doesn't bother to hide his scoff, his fork dragging a piece of meat through a trail of gravy on his plate. "A waste of money, that's what it is."

She bites her tongue, stilling the words that sit—burning—at the tip. *It's not your money. It's not your life.*

"You gotta be able to take care of yourself, Sara." He takes a swig of his cola, ice clinking against the glass. Sara is beginning to suspect it's laced with whiskey. "You ain't got that boy to lean on any—"

She cuts him off. "I don't want to talk about David."

"Well, you ought to," her father snaps. "I told you, Sara. I said you were getting in too deep with that boy and now he's gone and left you high and dry."

"He didn't *leave*, Dad! It's not his fault he can't remember!"

"Bullshit," he spits, an angry flush crawling up his neck and darkening his cheeks. "He's playing you like a fool, because that's what people do when they get the chance!"

She wants to argue—wants to *scream*—there is a lifetime of bitterness ready and waiting to be fired from her tongue. It would feel so good to finally let it go; to let the words fall like bombs from her lips and watch the shock on his face when they land, but she doesn't.

She *can't*.

In a family torn apart by death and abandonment, he's the only one left. As much as she wants to, she can't bring herself to sever that last remaining tie.

At the end of the table, sitting in the empty chair opposite of her father, Seth is silent. With his elbows on the table and his hands folded in front of his mouth, his eyes burn with a stillness that leaves her on edge. She had begged for his silence, but now—in face of her father's judgment—she wishes he would say something (anything) so she might feel just a little less alone.

Sara stands. Her meal's only half eaten, but she's not hungry anymore anyway. Even if she was, starving would be better than staying. "Thanks for dinner."

There's a flash of... something on her father's face. Maybe it's regret, but she suspects that's just her wishful thinking. "Wait a minute, now. Where are you going?"

"Home, Dad." She's already bringing her plate to the sink, her father a shadow at her back. "I'm going home."

When she turns to grab her purse from the counter, whatever softness she thought she glimpsed in her father's face is gone— replaced with something pinched and painfully familiar. "So, that's how it's going to be, then? I say something you don't like and you're just going to up and leave?!"

She's so, so tired. The anger she felt earlier has cooled into apathy. "Yeah, Dad. That's how it's going to be."

His sneer is ugly, fueled by a cursed combination of beer and bitterness. "That's what's wrong with your generation! Thin skin!"

Sara stares at him—the red creeping into his cheeks, the dilated pupils of his eyes—and knows the argument he's goading her into won't be won by anything she says. "Goodnight, Dad."

He keeps talking; more insults hurled at her back as she leaves. When the front door closes behind her, she can still hear his muffled curses from the porch step. Sara ignores it, feeling numb as she settles into the driver's seat. She can see her father's silhouette through the thin curtains, feet pacing and hands wild.

She turns the key in the ignition.

As she pulls onto the gravel drive, Seth speaks—a phantom voice from her backseat. "You failed to mention the part where your father is a complete arse."

She fights the urge, the *instinct*, to defend him. "Do you have to sit back there? It's weird."

A blink later and his form fills the passenger seat, the dim light from the console casting shadows over his features. "Does that mean we're not talking about it?"

"There's nothing to talk about," she snaps. She hates that her voice is as rough as the gravel crunching beneath her tires. She hates the burning in her eyes even more.

Seth is silent, but Sara can feel his gaze. They pass the mailbox, and she turns off the driveway onto cracked asphalt. In the distance, she can see the faint glow of the highway. Minutes pass, and Sara thinks he may (for once) leave it alone.

She always has given him too much credit.

"You know, I had a dear friend with a similar situation once. His father was a right piece of work."

"Good for him."

"I'm doing my very best to do the empathy thing you lot prattle on about. Do you mind?"

"Yes, yes I do. I mind. Can you please just drop it?"

"Well, I suppose since you asked so nicely," he grumbles.

A moment of silence, and then it spills out of her like a flood. "God, he's just such a—and it's not like he's even paying for it!"

Seth tsks, voice dripping with disgust. "Deplorable."

"Why does he even care?! He's never cared. *Never*. Now, suddenly, he's all invested in what I do with my life?" She shakes her head, fighting back the tears threatening to spill. "*God*, he's such a, a—"

Seth cuts her off, his words strained. "Sara, pet, perhaps you should pull over."

The glare she sends him is swift, but sharp. "You're the one who—"

"Yes, but you're damn near double the speed limit, and I'd rather prefer you stick around a bit longer."

Immediately, her foot relieves pressure off the gas—her mouth going dry when she catches sight of the speedometer. "Oh. Thanks." Then, his words registering, she adds, "And I'm not your pet."

He chuckles, but Sara doesn't dare take her eyes off the road to read his expression. "Course not, Princess."

Sometimes, she swears she could strangle him. "I'm not *that* either."

"Sure you are. It's in your name."

"In my—what are you even talking about?"

"*Your name.*" Sara can practically hear his eyes rolling. "Honestly, have you never looked it up?"

His meaning strikes her, and she can't suppress the groan that leaves her lips. "Oh. My. God."

"Ah, there it is. The sweet sound of understanding."

"How do you even *know* that? Like, do you just browse baby name books for fun?"

She can see him shrugging from the corner of her eye. "Live long enough and you pick some things up."

"Like baby names?"

"Like *languages*," he snips. "Honestly, did you think I've been hanging around your flannel loving lot this entire time? The world is a big place, seeing it has been one of the few upsides to my irritatingly persistent condition."

Sara turns onto the highway, checking over her shoulder as she merges. "I *really* don't understand the vendetta you have against flannel."

"Simple. It's *flannel*."

"It's comfortable."

"It's *hideous*."

# CHAPTER SEVENTEEN

*S*HE *IS SURROUNDED BY TALL, DRIED STALKS OF CORN—SO TALL THAT every direction looks the same as the last. Instinctively, she knows there's a place she needs to be hidden somewhere through the mismatched rows, but the more she looks the dizzier she becomes. So she stands, feet rooted in the tiny clearing, unwilling to go forward blindly.*

*A smooth, accented voice to her left—one she already knows the face to, "What are you waiting for, Princess?"*

*Sara frowns, looking at him. He's always the same. Same eyes, same clothing. "I'm lost," she admits. Somehow, it's easier to confess her weakness in this strange world of dreams than when she's awake. Perhaps honesty has its own place in dreams. She frowns, head tilting. "Why are you here?"*

*Seth blinks. "I'm not."*

*"Oh," she breathes, not really understanding. "Ok."*

*He nods toward the maze of corn to her right. "The sunrise on the other side is quite extraordinary. You should capture it."*

*There's a familiar weight across the back of her neck. Sara glances down, finding her camera. Yes, that's right—she is supposed to be taking pictures. The rows of corn feel tighter, more impassable, when she looks up. "I don't know how to get there."*

*The smile he gives her is soft, unfamiliar, as he holds out his hand. "Close your eyes, then. I'll lead you through."*

*She hesitates, looking over her shoulder at the motionless scarecrow watching them. "But I can't leave him. He'll get lonely without me."*

*Seth shakes his head. "He's just a scarecrow. He doesn't have a soul."*

*A soul? Sara frowns. "I thought it was a brain the scarecrow wanted?"*

*He smiles, but there's no warmth to it. It's sad—knowing.*

*Pitying.*

*"Only in fiction, Princess."*

*Sara nods, even though she still doesn't understand. The scarecrow stares back at her, black button eyes swallowing the light and its painted mouth a neutral smear of red paint. She places her hand in Seth's waiting palm, his fingers curling around hers with a gentleness that makes her feel found. "I'm scared," she murmurs, a soft confession.*

*He squeezes her hand, a promise in his smile. "Trust me. Close your eyes and I will lead you."*

SARA WAKES SLOWLY, HER EYES FLUTTERING OPEN AND TAKING IN THE light streaming from her window.

Groaning, she props herself onto her elbow and runs a hand through her hair—fingers snagging on the tangles with a wince. Ansel sleeps, undisturbed, at the foot of her bed; curled so tightly he resembles a throw pillow more than a cat. When she shifts her weight, he releases a whining, drawn out sigh at the slight disturbance. Sara stares at him, her mind slowly adjusting to the realm of reality.

She had been dreaming—she remembers she had. Her gaze lands on her camera bag across the room, and her eyebrows pull into a frown as she tries to piece together the hazy bits of remembered dream. There was a corn field and a scarecrow—the kind her hometown used to have at their Harvest Festival in the fall—and a patient, upturned palm...

The pieces fall into place, a sledgehammer to her heart. "Seth," she breathes, pulse jumping. She had dreamed of Seth.

She dreamed of him, and it hadn't been a nightmare.

Oh *God*.

"You called, Princess?"

His voice materializes beside her, and she feels a sinking dread in the pit of her stomach. Slowly, she turns to meet his gaze. He must read the horror in her eyes, because his bored expression tightens into something serious—something *concerned*. "What's happened?"

No, she's imagining it. She has to be. Sara swallows, tries to still the trembling of her hands by fisting them in her comforter. Then her gaze snags on her reflection in the mirrored closet doors and she stills. Her hair is a wild nest of frizz and tangles, complexion pale and hazel eyes wide, but it's not her reflection that startles her, but the absence of *his*.

Seth follows her gaze, the tension in his jaw—the hard line of his shoulders—relaxing. "Ah, yes. It's a trifle disconcerting at first, isn't it?" He regards the mirror thoughtfully. "I haven't had a good look in a few hundred years, but if memory serves I'm *quite* handsome."

She shakes her head, determined to get her thoughts back on track. No way in hell was she going to comment on that. "Do you manipulate dreams? Do you have that power?"

He frowns, eyes narrowing. "Not that I'm aware of... why?"

"Are you sure?"

He scoffs, almost insulted. "I can't say I've ever tried." A thought must dawn, because his head tilts and his stare sharpens. "Would you *like* me to?"

She chucks a pillow at him—he doesn't even flinch as it sails over his shoulder and into the closet doors behind him. A flush crawls up her neck, hot and prickling. Sara pulls the comforter up to her chin to hide the worst of it. "*No!*"

There is a grin flirting at the corner of his mouth, growing with each step, until it becomes almost predatory. A cat playing with a field mouse. "Well, you *are* in a state this morning. Aren't you?"

"Shut up," she hisses.

"What could you possibly have been dreaming about, I wonder?" He leans over her, eyes dark and teasing. "Was there a bed involved?"

The entire room feels hot, and she can feel herself sweating beneath the blankets, but she doesn't dare lower them. Sara sends him her sharpest glare and, because she's flustered and an *idiot*, blurts, "It was just a cornfield!"

His leer falters, coughing on a laugh. "You Iowans and your *corn*." He shakes his head. "I suppose there was flannel involved as well?"

"I *hate you*."

He doesn't even flinch. "Yes, you love to remind me." Straightening his cuffs, he gives her a roguish grin. "It's still rather early. Shall I leave you to try and revisit those sweet dreams of yours?"

She chucks another pillow at him, with the same results as the last. It only fans her fury. "**Get out!**"

His snicker echoes long after he blinks away. Sara stays in bed, the comforter pulled up to her ears as she watches the morning light shift and change. She wishes she could forget the pieces she remembered—wishes she could forget she had dreamed any of it at all—but she can't unsee the scarecrow's crude, painted face or unhear the tenderness in Seth's voice—the promise in his words.

*Trust me.*

# CHAPTER EIGHTEEN

Sara puts the dream to the back of her mind, shoves it so far away that it settles beside all the other trauma she wishes she could forget completely.

That is, if he would *let* her.

"Any good dreams last night, Princess?"

The hand holding the handle of her mug tightens as she closes her eyes and reminds herself not to take the bait. Instead, she finishes stirring the creamer into her coffee and places the spoon in the sink. "Yeah," she lies, "I dreamt that I lived alone. It was great."

Seth grins, his ankle hooking over his knee as he leans into his chair. Sara wonders if the antiquated floral print is as old as he is. "'The lady doth protest too much, methinks.'"

Glaring over the rim of her mug, Sara tries to concentrate on the bittersweet taste of coffee instead of the sugar in his smile. "No."

"No?"

She settles in her usual spot on the couch across from him, feet curling under her. "It's Saturday."

He raises a brow, eyes glinting in amusement. "Indeed it is."

"There are no literature references on Saturdays."

"Oh? I wasn't aware."

"It's a house rule."

The sound he makes is half laugh, half scoff. "You wish me to speak plainly?"

"I wish for you not to speak at all," she retorts, her second sip of coffee interrupted by the ringing of her phone.

"Such a cruel girl," Seth admonishes, his eyes curious as he watches her pull the cell out of her hoodie and bring it to her ear.

"Hello?" she answers, frowning when there's nothing but silence in response. Sara sighs, rolling her eyes as she disconnects the call and tosses her phone onto the cushion next to her. "God, that's annoying."

Seth's gaze seems pinned to her phone, head canted and brow furrowed in thought. "Been getting much of those lately?"

"Too much," she grumbles, returning to her coffee. In truth, they haven't been coming too often—every two weeks or so—but it was enough to be irritating. Sometimes she didn't bother to answer, only for them to call a second time. At first she thought it was a prank, but the number keeps changing. She's written it off as an out-of-country scammer with a shitty connection.

There's a thread of tension in Seth's stare, though. It's unlike him.

Raising her eyebrows, she meets his gaze pointedly. "Why?"

The thread snaps, his shoulders lifting into a shrug that somehow still manages to look more prim than casual. "Curiosity, I suppose. The amount of telemarketer calls you lot receive is nothing short of horrifying."

Sara's laugh is breathy but honest. She can't say she disagrees.

SETH LEAVES SHORTLY AFTER. SARA STRONGLY SUSPECTS IT'S BECAUSE she's turned on *Ghost Hunters* (the level look he shot her made it pretty clear that he didn't appreciate her humor). She binges on the fourth season before catching up on the dishes and making spaghetti for dinner. The entire time, she basks in the lack of commentary— revels in the silence as she twirls the pasta around her fork—and makes a mental note to turn on *Ghostbusters* the next time she's desperate for some time alone.

Except, dinner is cleaned up and the sun has dipped far past the horizon, and there's still no sign of him.

Sara frowns, trying to still the anxiety coiling in her chest. Seth has never left her alone this long—especially when she's staying in—but that's not a *bad thing*. Maybe he's learning some boundaries, or maybe he was just bored hanging around her all day. Either way, *she* benefits. So what if it's weird?

Her fingers tap against the ceramic of her mug, chewing her bottom lip and glancing at the time. It's past midnight, and she's fast approaching season five.

Maybe, just maybe, he's gone for good?

Somehow, the thought isn't as welcome as it should be.

A loud pounding on her door startles her from her thoughts with such ferocity that she nearly drops her mug. Her free hand goes to her heart, releasing a shaky breath as she sets her tea to cool on the counter. In her chest, her heart beats against her ribs as she inches toward the door—trepidation growing with every striking knock.

"Hey! I know you're in there! Open up!"

Sara stills, stomach dropping. The voice is slurred, but she would recognize it anywhere. Shaking, she takes another step forward—hand rising to the lock.

Seth's voice materializes behind her. "Don't."

Jumping, she snatches her hand back to her chest—tries to calm the racing of her pulse. "It's David."

"Not the one you remember."

The pounding continues, in time with her heartbeat. The door rattles in the frame. On the other side, David continues to utter slurred commands.

Sara shakes her head, gathers her courage. "You're wrong." She reaches toward the deadbolt, but Seth blocks her path.

"I'm not."

He isn't solid, she reminds herself. She can reach right through him if she chooses to. As if he can read her thoughts, Seth's expression shifts—the warning edge softening into something pleading.

Something desperate. "Please, *please* listen to reason." His hands rise, hovering between them. If he were real, Sara would think he meant to touch her face. So close, she can see the way they tremble before they drop back to his sides. "If you let him in," he breathes, a storm of warnings and prayers, "I won't be able to help you."

Nervously, she licks her lips. Her voice, less than a whisper, wavers. "Help me?" David's fist is still hammering against the door, the rhythm drunken and sloppy. He would never hurt her—never. He probably needs help or, maybe, he's finally remembered?

The thought alone is enough to bolster her courage, and her spine straightens with resolve. "Move."

Seth's face twists into a grimace. "Sara, please—"

It's the sound of her name on his lips that does it, heat prickling her palms. "*Move.*"

He stares down at her, eyes searching her own with a terrifying intensity. "No."

"You can't stop me," she reminds him.

His eyes close—pained. It's enough to make her confidence shudder, and when his eyes reopen, she's rooted by the honesty she sees in them. "No, I can only beg you to see reason. He's not in control of himself. If you allow him in, he *will* hurt you. Do you understand?"

She doesn't—she *can't*. Behind him, she can hear the door handle shake violently and her breath catches in her throat. Something cold coils in her gut as she recognizes with growing horror the amount of force on the other side of the door. "David would never hurt me," she whispers, but her voice is as wavering as her faith. The sound changes—he's switched from fists to feet. Sara wonders how bruised his hands will be in the morning. "He just wouldn't..."

For a long moment, Seth is silent—David's drunken curses slipping through the silence like a knife. "Ask him, then."

"Ask him?" The words feel heavy, cloying and awkward as stale taffy on her tongue.

"Before you open that door, ask him why he's here."

Sara swallows, throat tight—raw. David tries the handle again.

She can't. Something in Seth's eyes, in his voice, rings true enough to make her afraid of what answer she would receive if she found the courage to ask. "I hate you," she whispers, eyes burning.

The tension in his shoulders eases, melting under her scathing words as if they were balm. "I know."

The softness in his expression, the gentle acceptance, only serves to make her hate him more. Angry tears roll down her cheeks, blurring her vision, but she gives him the darkest glare she can muster before retreating to her room—the door slamming behind her.

She screams—crying—into her pillow until her voice goes hoarse, and the insistent pounding on her door goes quiet.

THERE'S NO MISSED CALLS WHEN SHE WAKES UP. NO VOICEMAILS. SHE wishes she could claim to be surprised, but the truth is she's just numb. Seth gives her space. For someone who exists to annoy her, he's shockingly adept at making himself scarce when she needs him to. Sara thinks of the bruises on her knuckles, the feel of his jaw beneath them, and tries to convince herself he does it for his sake more than hers. But then she remembers the openness of his expression, the softness, when she told him she hated him.

*"I know."*

Sara wraps Oma's blanket around her more firmly, warding off the chill.

# CHAPTER NINETEEN

She doesn't tell Miles, or even Jen, about David's late night visit. She doesn't tell *anyone*. Sometimes, it feels more like a bad dream than a memory; a trick of her imagination to keep her nerves strung tight. Sara knows the moment she puts what happened into words, is the moment it will all feel real.

Which, with finals and the holidays looming around the corner, is literally the last thing her sanity needs.

Shockingly, Seth doesn't push it. Perhaps—no. He *must* see the way she jumps at every sudden sound. He has to. Seth sees her flaws and vulnerabilities as easily as if she were wearing each one pinned to her sleeves.

She tries to push it to the back of her mind, bury it under all the things she needs to do and the tests she needs to study for, but it keeps wriggling free. Teasing her until she surrenders and finally brings herself to ask, "How do you know?" It had been bothering her all day, a thought she couldn't escape no matter how much she tried to swat it away.

"I'm old and therefore know a lot of things," he drawls. "I'm afraid you'll have to be a touch more specific." His chin rests on the heel of his hand, expression bored as he watches the tv. It's a hot dog commercial; Sara wonders how many times he must have already seen it today.

"That he—" she stops, forces herself to say his name, "that *David* would hurt me."

He stills, his gaze piercing. "Be careful of what you ask, Princess."

She stands, temper rising, and turns the tv off before setting her hands on her hips. "Why? Because you don't want to talk about it?"

Seth's glare is equal parts annoyed and exasperated. "Because you won't want to hear it." His voice is smooth but firm; leaving no room for her arguments. "Some things are better left buried."

"Yeah, well, David isn't buried," she snaps, hand gesturing to her front door. "He's very much alive!"

Seth's lips parts, a retort ready on his tongue, but he closes his mouth before it can escape him—his jaw straining from the effort of holding it in.

"What? What were you about to say?"

His jaw works, a grimace tightening his features as his words hiss past his lips. "His body is alive," he says. The syllables sound forced, as if they're being ripped from his throat. "There is a difference."

Sara stills, heart stuttering in her chest. "What does *that* mean?"

A growl, deep and guttural, slips between his teeth—knuckles white as his hands clench over the upholstery. Suddenly he's standing, towering over her and way too close for comfort, but the look in his eyes—the manic gleam—pin her in place. "It means we are more than just flesh and bone," he snarls, lips pulled back and teeth gleaming in the light. His long, tapered fingers splay over his heart. "It isn't our bodies that make us, you foolish girl. Just because that, that *thing*, wears your dear David's face doesn't mean they are one and the same!"

His words strike like a blade, cutting sharp and deep. "That *thing*?" she echoes, voice as thin as the air feels. She takes one breath, then another, but each one feels more empty than the last. Swaying, her hand reaches for the wall to steady herself, shaking her head. What he's suggesting... it's too terrible to believe. "No. You're *wrong*."

The curled sneer shaping his lips softens; melting until it looks more like a grimace. "Maybe," he murmurs, but the shape of the syllables are too soft, too heavy. Pity masquerading as acceptance.

"No," she snaps, finding her balance. "Not maybe. *You're wrong.*"

Seth says nothing, but the expression he wears—the pity darkening his eyes—gives him away.

He doesn't believe her.

What he thinks shouldn't bother her. She should walk away, forget this conversation ever happened, and move on with her life. But she can't shake the heat in his gaze—the conviction—when he spat David's name like a curse.

"Take it back," she says, trembling with a level of fear and fury she can't find a name for. She wants to hear him say it, wants to hear the words from his own lips, so she can cover up the memory of the ones barbed in her heart (*that thing*). "You're *wrong*, so take it back."

He openly flinches; the muscle in his jaw straining. "You're asking me to lie," he says, the statement hissing past his clenched teeth. "So, terribly sorry, but no. I won't."

"Why?!"

"Because I refuse to lie to you for the sake of your feelings," he snaps. "If you don't wish to hear my opinion on the matter, then *don't ask.*"

It strikes her, as quick and as devastating as lightning. She thinks of the way he twists everything, how every answer he gives is as convoluted and vague as possible.

It's not that he won't take back the words.

It's that he *can't.*

The implication of what that means makes her stagger. She sinks onto the couch, her hand covering her mouth and heart hammering against her ribs. Her mind scrambles to recall his words, to catch some hidden loophole, but everything is blurring together and she can't recall his exact phrasing. And, with how carefully he words everything, she gets the sense that—if she wants a true answer—hers must be too.

"Do you really believe it's not David?" she asks, voice soft. *Believe*, because to exclude that one word would be to open herself up to certainties and she just *can't*. No matter his answer, even if her suspicions are right and he's forced to tell her only truths, she doesn't want to be left without hope.

Belief isn't the same as fact.

"Yes." The word leaves him in a hiss, as if it physically pains him to say it. If Sara had any doubts about her theory before, she doesn't now.

"You can't lie, can you?" The question is little more than a murmur, but his reaction is jarring.

He stills, face twisting into a soundless snarl and his hands, fisting, tremble at his sides. "No." One word, one syllable. It lands between them, heavy with bitterness and edged with fury. It clangs, metallic and sharp, in her ears, and Sara realizes what that one word has stripped him of.

His *armor*.

He can't hide behind twisted half truths if she knows how to ask her questions. Form them right, and there is nothing he can hide from her; no secret safe so long as she knows what words to wield to pry it from his lips.

Seth seethes, and it's the first time Sara has ever seen him without his carefully arranged mask of control and composure. The heat in his glare is savage. Feral. Sara has never seen a wolf in the wild, but she imagines this is what it would look like—this untamed storm of fury and fear—if she backed one into a corner.

It's at that moment she realizes what it means to hold power over someone. She's already drunk off the potential of it—of knowing she can find the truth so long as she listens for it. But there's a grimace, a vulnerability, hiding behind his sneer, and it's enough to make her stomach churn. "You have to answer."

A statement, not a question, and his answering silence is proof that whatever magic forcing his tongue has rules. Sara licks her lips, pulse fluttering in her throat. She rearranges the words, asks again, "Do you have to answer?"

Maybe it's the sympathy weaved into her voice, or maybe he's simply resigned himself to the situation, but he wilts. The hard line of his shoulders, the knuckle-white clenching of his fists, loosens.

The jagged edges of his snarl softens until his expression is more frost than fire. "*Yes,*" he fumes, looking away.

Sara expects him to blink away, to run—she knows she would—but instead he sits, slouching in his chair and cradling his temple with long, pale fingers. He looks defeated, and she realizes that she probably isn't the first (or last) to have figured it out. Still… she shakes her head. "I don't understand."

Seth scoffs, not bothering to look up. "Shocking."

"Shut up," Sara murmurs, without any heat. Her mind is still strung up on the implications. "Why do you have to tell me the truth? What's the point?"

A muscle in his jaw jumps. From where she's sitting, she can almost imagine the groaning of his teeth. "Why," he spits the word as if it's poison, "must you insist on asking questions I have no answer to?"

"That doesn't—"

"It *does,*" he snaps, "If you would just *listen.*"

Her breath leaves her. "You… you don't *know*?"

"Does that surprise you?"

"I mean, you're kind of a know-it-all. So, yes?"

He huffs, gaze sliding back to the window. He must hate it, being nothing but honest all the time. Suddenly she has a newfound understanding of why ninety percent of the things that come out of his mouth are steeped in sarcasm.

Sara shifts, hands twisting in her lap. "It's… kind of backwards, isn't it? You having to tell the truth?"

He frowns, his hand lowering as he sends her a baffled look. "I beg your pardon?"

"Just, I mean," she stumbles, face flushing the longer he pins her with that stare. "I just thought lying would be part of the whole demon thing."

Seth's laugh is sharp. "First, I'm a figment of your imagination and now I'm a demon." He shakes his head, a sardonic smile twisting the corners of his mouth. "You certainly know how to give a man a complex."

"But if you're not…" A thought dawns, her stomach sinking like a weight. "Oh my—you're not the *devil*, are you?!"

He slouches further into his chair, hands cradling his temples. "**No**."

The idea is stuck now, though. Snared in a way that's hard for her to untangle. She remembers the darkness surrounding him, the lure in his voice, when he offered to save David's life. "But the deals and, and the souls!"

He groans, eyes disappearing behind an elegant hand. "I can assure you, I am not nearly old enough to be considered *biblical*."

The knot in her chest loosens, unwinding the longer she measures the resigned slump of his shoulders. Of course he's not. That would be insane.

Except this whole thing *is* insane. How else could she possibly describe living with a man only she can see? That blinks in and out of her life like a ghost, but has the power to pull David away from Death's door? She swallows, mouth dry, because she knows now that so many of her answers are only a question away. "Then what are you?"

His hands slide away, and he casts a praying glance to the ceiling. "At the moment? A man sitting in a chair. Now, would you kindly turn the television back on? I'm looking forward to hearing how Juan plans to explain his illegitimate child."

It's not an answer or, at least, not the kind she was looking for. Maybe, if she wasn't aware of the power her questions held over him, she would let it go—turn on the tv and let him deflect their conversation. But she *does* know, and this isn't an answer she's willing to give up. Not so easily. Not yet.

"Are you human?"

He stills, his words careful. "I was. Perhaps I still am."

God, he makes her want to scream. "What does that even mean?!"

His expression hardens, a subtle warning written in the line of his jaw. "I was born human," he hisses. "Whether I still qualify is up for debate."

His anger is palpable—like smoke—filling the room and burning her lungs. A warning, maybe even a threat, darkening his gaze. Sara doesn't care. The weight pressing on her chest is nothing compared to the questions clawing at her heart. Somewhere, David is living a life without her in it and she has to know *why*.

She swallows, wets her lips. Finds the right words in the lines of his scowl, pries them from him like a secret. "Why aren't you human?"

Suddenly he's in front of her, so close she could feel the heat of him if she wished it—a towering form of fury and resentment. Teeth bared, the words hiss past his sneering lips. "I was *cursed*."

Sara's lips part, eyes wide and chest heaving. He doesn't wait for her to blink before disappearing.

# CHAPTER TWENTY

Sara stares at the screen, one hand rubbing her temple while the other continues to scroll down the webpage. There's a headache brewing, a tension spanning over both her eyes, telling her to rest. She ignores it, instead.

The library is only open for another hour and she plans on using every minute. After that, she'll go to the coffee shop across the street and continue searching there. Somewhere, in some dark corner of the web, there has to be the answers she's looking for. There *has* to be. The thought of Google failing her now, when she *really* needs it, is nothing short of horrifying.

Finding nothing of use on the page, she closes the tab with a little more force than strictly necessary—frustration pulling at her chest. She huffs, her eyes leaving the bright screen to trace over the rows of books to her left. The library was blessed with large windows, and the evening light casts warmth over the little nook she's chosen for herself. If her reason for being there hadn't been so daunting, Sara suspects she would find it beautifully romantic. A perfect picture. She makes a mental note to bring her camera next time.

"A library, Princess? I never thought to see the day."

She stills, lips parting around a curse. Of course, Seth would find her. *Of course.* Despite the fury in his eyes when he blinked away last night, he has been nothing but civil since reappearing this morning. Still, in every interaction there's been a shift Sara can't quite shake… a reserved hope, an anticipated dread, hiding behind his candid smile.

She hates it almost as much as the idea of being stuck with him for the rest of her life. So here she is—at the library with a stack of books at her elbow and a slew of webpages on screen. Incriminating her. Seth hovers over her shoulder, no doubt scanning the titles of the multiple tabs she has running. All of them centered on one thing:

How to break a curse.

Sara closes her eyes, mouth dry, as she waits for the inevitable.

"Ah… I see." She refuses to look at him, but she senses him shift. Leaning against her desk, his stare is uncomfortably focused on her face. "Dare I bother asking?"

Sara glances at him before she can remind herself to resist. His eyes are dark—knowing—his left brow quirking towards his hairline. She tears her gaze away, chewing on her bottom lip and fidgeting in her seat. Her name escapes him, a breathy admonishment, and she gives up on ignoring him.

She pulls the laptop closer and opens a word document. The library isn't all that busy, but it's quiet enough for her to be wary of speaking out loud. Her finger taps against two of the keys.

'No.'

The corners  of his mouth curling into a sardonic half-smile. "Cheeky." His fingers drum, obnoxiously silent, against the edge of the desk. "As… flattering as your concern is, you're wasting your time."

She frowns. *'How do you know?'*

He gives her question only the briefest of glances before shaking his head, a dark chuckle escaping his lips. "Honestly, Princess. Do you think I never looked?"

*'How?'*

He rolls his eyes. "Little miss expert now, are we? Have you considered, perhaps, that my time is limitless?" He gestures, flippantly, to her screen. "What you're reading is second hand information that I've already collected straight from the source."

She flushes, typing, *'Have you considered, **perhaps**, not being an ass?'*

His grin dimples. "Only on very rare occasions." Standing, he adjusts the collar of his overcoat. "Now that we have that sorted, I do believe it's time to toddle on home. I have it on good authority that someone's been putting off their reading assignment. *Again.*"

Another day she may have scolded him for spying on her classes, but today she finds herself nodding instead. Silently, she closes her laptop and slides it into her bag, before stacking the books she pulled and depositing them on the designated library cart.

During the walk home, her mind buzzes with questions—her eyes flitting to him between each thought. There is so much she doesn't understand, but she *wants* to. Somewhere in the last few weeks, Seth has become less of a burden and more of a—

She can't bring herself to finish the thought.

Chewing her bottom lip, she stifles the questions burning at the tip of her tongue until the exact moment she closes her apartment door behind them. "Do—" She swallows thickly, a sour attempt to sound confident. Ansel meows at her feet, rubbing himself against her ankles. "Do you know why?"

Seth scoffs, collapsing in what is slowly (but surely) becoming his chair. "Why?" He makes a motion with his hand—his eyes staring unseeingly up at her ceiling—and Sara realizes her folly.

"Why you were cursed," she elaborates.

Something in his expression shifts. Ansel, seeming to realize that he isn't going to be immediately fed, abandons her to rub his face against Seth's draped hand. His fingers curl, scratching against the cat's cheek, until a rumbling purr breaks the silence. "I refused to marry."

"Oh." That *definitely* wasn't one of the (many) answers she had envisioned on their walk home. Tentatively, she sits on the couch across from him, fingers drumming on her knees. "That... doesn't really seem like a good reason to curse someone."

He mutters something incomprehensible under his breath.

"What?"

"She was with child," he grumbles, still refusing to meet her eye.

Her thoughts grind to a halt, face paling. "You had a kid?!" she blurts.

He goes silent for so long, she wonders if he will refuse to answer. "No. No, she—she lost it." His exhale is a shaky, bitter laugh —tainted with self loathing. "She lost it, and my first reaction was to uncork a bottle and celebrate. Thank the universe for letting me off the hook." His eyes meet hers, dark in ways Sara can't name. "My miracle, her curse. Do you understand now?"

*My miracle, her curse.*

The words echo in her ears; a cacophony of painful understanding. Her stomach sours, bile rising in her throat until she can nearly taste the acid on her tongue. "That's why there's a price," she murmurs, barely audible over the rushing in her ears.

Seth's jaw clenches. "Yes."

She hugs her knees to her chest, resting her chin there. "That... that was pretty terrible of you."

His eyes close, pained. "I'm aware."

Sara looks at him—really *looks*—and wonders. "Do you regret it because of what happened or because it was wrong?"

A long moment passes between them, Seth staring upward as if the answer were hidden in the shadows playing off the ceiling. Ansel jumps into his lap, offering a demanding mewl until Seth's fingers scratch behind his ears. "Both," he confesses, turning his attention to her. "I'm... not sure if I would have arrived at one without the other."

"Then... at least you're a better person because of it. Right?"

The laugh he gives is short and breathy. "If you consider me a person at all."

"You are," she says, surprised by her own conviction.

The smile teasing his mouth is soft—sincere in ways that make him look painfully human. "Thank you."

"You're welcome," she murmurs, hugging her legs tighter. There's an odd feeling curling in her chest, coiling dangerously around her heart. It sets her on edge. "So," she says, desperate for distraction, "was it your, uh, lover? That cursed you?"

"No." Seth shakes his head, both hands now working under Ansel's chin. "Her grandmother." He frowns, lips pursing as if tasting something bitter. "The crotchety old bat."

"How do you know?"

"She spent her last five years on this earth rubbing my face in it," he grumbles. "She was the only one who ever saw me despite never having struck a deal."

Sara stares, eyebrows raised. "And?"

"And *what*?"

She can't tell if he's being purposefully dense or not. "How do you break it?"

Seth snorts. "As much as I appreciate your optimism, I'm not entirely sure it can be."

"She—the grandmother never told you?"

He goes quiet, gaze drifting to the window. "I asked once, if it was possible. Do you know what she said? *'Time will tell.'*" His eyes are like flint—sharp at the edges and ready to strike. "As if that's any answer at all."

"Well, it could be worse. She could have just said no."

Seth looks at her, his gaze piercing. "If the doctors told you, with certainty, that David would never regain his memories, would that truly be worse than never knowing? Doesn't it hurt?"

Sara sucks in a breath. Her first instinct is to lash out, to let the pain sharpen her answer to a point, but there's an openness in his expression that makes her pause. There's no mocking smile, no cruel edge in his tone, and Sara knows his question was an honest one.

*Doesn't it hurt?*

Every day. The thread of hope she carries is so thin, it cuts. When she's alone and things are quiet, she feels like she's drowning—clawing for the surface, for the light, when it would be so much easier to let go. To *sink*.

"I don't know," she murmurs, but she can't meet his stare while she says it. When she looks up, his eyes are too deep. Too knowing. Curses weren't the only thing Sara looked up at the library. Judging by his clothes he's had over two hundred years experience with tentative hopes—has had to face them every time someone looked through him, every time he spoke, knowing no one could listen.

Sara wonders how deeply the thread he carries cuts; if there are scars left over or if it's still bleeding freely.

The way hers are.

S ARA TAKES HER TIME.

Scouts out the best hill to plant herself on, sets up the tripod, measures the light. Sunset is still an hour and a half away, but she doesn't mind the wait. Here, overlooking the city, the quiet almost matches the fields surrounding Oma's home. The wind whistles a bit through the trees, and the grass doesn't share the same nostalgic rustle of thousands of swaying cornstalks, but the feeling of solitude —of peace—is the same. Both are things she's been sorely missing lately.

"You know," Seth says, slanting her a look. She hates that he's followed her here, but she can't even summon the energy to tell him to buzz off. "You should really be spending the evening catching up with Mr. Darcy and Miss Bennet. I do believe  they've been rather neglected by you as of late."

'Neglect' is probably a lot kinder than she deserves. She hasn't made it any farther than the fifth page, and the deadline for the exam has only been creeping closer. Still. "There's always the movie," she quips, trying to sound more confident than she is.

"And here I believed you to be above cheating." Sara can't tell if he sounds disappointed or impressed. "You don't know what you're missing, truly. Miss Austen is a treasure."

She hovers over her camera bag, rifling around for her case of lens filters. "I'll take your word for it."

Seth chuckles, hands disappearing into his pockets. "Honestly, it wouldn't be half as terrible as you make it out to be if you'd take a moment to stop *griping* about it."

Rolling her eyes, she pulls out the desired filter, perched between her thumb and forefinger, and carefully places the case away. "Look.

Just because boring old books are your happy place doesn't make them mine. I'm *never* going to like it."

"Well, not with that attitude, you won't."

Sara could argue, remind him that she'd hate literature even if she was all sunshine and rainbows, but she screws the filter onto her lens with a quiet shake of her head. The last thing she wants to do is taint the peaceful atmosphere with his literature obsession.

She expects him to fill the silence (he always does) but his hands are tucked in his pockets, his posture so relaxed he'd *almost* be slouching if he didn't somehow manage to still look elegant doing it. His face is turned toward the horizon, the evening light casting a glow on his pale skin and the shadows highlighting the cut of his jaw.

For a second—only a second—she thinks it's a shame he can't be captured on film.

Swiftly, before he can catch her, she turns away. Finds reasons to fiddle with the shutter speed and aperture even though she knows it's fine. She holds her breath, presses the release, listens to the sound of the shutter closing, and pulls up the preview to inspect it. It's good, but not perfect. A little bit longer on the exposure and—

"You must love it."

Her head snaps up. "What?"

Seth must be gesturing to her camera, but somehow she feels like she's included in that fluid flick of his hand. His head tilts. "You have this terribly odd look on your face when you're clicking away."

Sara frowns. "Gee, thanks."

He makes a disgruntled sound in the back of his throat, as if he has the nerve to be irritated with *her*. "You're at peace, doing this. Open. Vulnerable." His brow furrows, chin raising as he regards her. "As if everything else just… disappears."

Sara stares, her heart twisting in her chest. Seth turns back to the horizon. She can hear the strain in his voice when he admits, "I envy that look."

Releasing a shaky breath, she forces herself to stop searching for answers in his face and turn her attention back to her camera—gaze caressing the familiar curve of the lens, the fading labels on the body.

"Every time I release the shutter I feel..." she trails off, searching for the words in the shifting colors painting the horizon, fingers twiddling with the camera strap. "It's like I'm taking a single moment in time and I'm... I'm *immortalizing* it. Making it stay." She smiles, a sad and wistful tilt of the lips. Photography lets her take a beautiful moment and make it last forever. She lowers her face to the viewfinder, adjusting her settings.

Seth scoffs, but the sound is more sad than cruel. "Immortality isn't half so romantic as it sounds." He drinks in the view, head tilting. "But I understand your meaning. Moments are fleeting. Particularly the beautiful ones."

She thinks of the day she brought home the doves; of carefully chewing around BBs while she ate with her parents on the back porch. Sara remembers her father laughing, amused by her expression when she found one. Pulling away from the viewfinder, she swallows—willing the tightness in her throat to ease. "When I was little, I used to wish I could make the days last longer. Sometimes, I thought if I wished hard enough I could keep the sun up for just that much longer."

The corner of Seth's lips curl into a minuscule smile, one she may have missed had she not been looking for it. His eyes, which had always looked black to her, are transformed to a warm chocolate by the sun's lingering touch. "Even you can't stop the sun, Princess."

For once, she sees no trace of his usual taunting. There's a fondness in the curve of his mouth; a softness in his gaze. Both terrify her. She hides behind the viewfinder, heart fluttering anxiously in her chest. The light—it has to be the light. Nothing more.

Silence hangs between them, broken only by the occasional click of the lens, until the world turns more silver than gold. Packing up her equipment, Sara chances a glance at her forced companion. Only a quick look, but enough to convince herself that he belongs in this landscape. His eyes are meant to look black, and his smiles are supposed to be cold, because there is nothing warm about him. Nothing at all.

LADYBIRDS

She heaves the camera bag over her shoulder and grabs the tripod with her free hand. There's foxtails sticking to her socks, pricking at her skin, but she's too eager to leave to think about pausing to remove them. Sara only makes it a few yards before his voice stops her.

"Might I ask why you never come for the sunrise?"

For a moment she is perfectly still, a statue in a landscape of tall, swaying grass. The sun was the closing of the day—an ending to a chapter. The sunrise was the opening scene for something *new*. New and entirely unknown, when all Sara ever wanted was to remain in the comfortable embrace of the familiar. She licks her lips, tries to ignore the pressure on her chest.

"It's too early," she murmurs, hating that it's only a fraction of the truth.

# CHAPTER TWENTY-ONE

SARA SWEARS THE WEATHER WAS BEAUTIFUL WHEN SHE WALKED TO class.

Crisp on the side of cool, but not enough for her breath to fog. Now though, there are gray clouds darkening the horizon that hint at the possibility of rain. Sara knows they only have a couple more weeks (at best) before the frost, then the snow, settles in. Some of the trees have already started to change, red haloing the edges of their leaves. Thanksgiving will be here before she knows it—Christmas after that. The thought makes her chest ache.

She can't imagine either without Oma.

There will be no homemade gravy. No lovingly iced sugar cookies. The mugs of hot chocolate won't warm her the way Oma's did; imbued with happy memories and laced with a magic that was all her own. Her father's version of celebrating is to splurge on a fancy bottle of whiskey—Sara can't remember the last time he bothered to put up a tree. It never really bothered her that much before. She had Oma and, in the last few years, David's family to celebrate with. Now, both of those options are gone.

If it weren't for Miles inviting her to his family's Thanksgiving, she would have spent it alone. She's already resigned herself to going home for Christmas, but she would have lied through her teeth to avoid spending Thanksgiving there too. Her father's given her no apologies for the way he acted at her last visit and she knows better than to expect one. Sara has the sinking feeling that the holiday spirit won't be enough to save her from a repeat performance.

Experience has taught her as much.

The sound of scraping chairs rips her from her thoughts. Somehow, class has ended. Sara looks down at her notebook, flinching when it confirms that the only thing she's written is the date.

She's not even sure which old British guy they were talking about today.

Discreetly, she glances around the room as she packs away her things. She's almost disappointed to find Seth absent. Maybe he looked in long enough during the lecture to at least tell her what to google later.

Her professor stops her before she can follow her classmates out the door. "Sara, could you stay for a moment?"

"Oh." Sara fidgets, adjusting the bag on her shoulders. "Um, sure Ms. Green."

Sara likes her despite hating her class. She's young, damn near close to being fresh out of college herself, and it shows. She's easier on the homework load, more forgiving of tardiness and real life's penchant for getting in the way.

Ms. Green waits until the last student files out, the door closing behind them. She sighs, removing her reading glasses and pinning Sara with a knowing (pitying) stare. "How are you?"

The answer is so ridiculously transparent, Sara has to smother the urge to laugh. Everything is so far away from being fine. "I'm ok."

Ms. Green nods, a softness around the edges of her eyes that speaks of sympathy. "I know how hard it is to lose family, and I'm so, so sorry for your loss."

Sara's throat tightens. The sentiment is sweet, rife with good intentions, but it still makes her stomach churn. This is the last thing she wants to talk about, and certainly not with her professor. Still, she forces a strained "thank you" past her lips.

Another nod, and Ms. Green leans against her desk. "Sara, I want to be honest with you. It might be in your best interest to retake the class in the Spring."

Sara stills, breath burning in her lungs. "What?"

"You're struggling. And, at the rate you're going, I'm worried you're going to fail the class." She folds her hands in front of her, face pinched in a way that suggests the conversation is painful for her, too. "We're getting to the point where you need to start acing these tests if you want any hope of passing."

Sara pales, her breathing weak. She's pretty sure she thanks her professor (she hopes she does) but she's so numb she can't be sure. There's a pressure on her chest, a burning in her lungs. Turning to leave and seeing Seth sitting in the back row—his eyes soft with knowing—only makes the pain sharper.

⁕ ⸺⸺⸺ ⸺⸺ ⁕

IT'S RAINING, BECAUSE OF COURSE IT IS.

Sara huddles under the metal awning of the bus stop around the corner from campus, waiting for the steady drizzle to stop and cursing her luck. She doesn't dare try to walk home in this weather —not with her expensive textbooks and not without the umbrella she (conveniently) left at home.

She pulls the hoodie further over her head, sniffing and wiping at her eyes with the heel of her hand. The stores are already boasting Christmas decorations in the windows, their merry lights blinking tauntingly from across the street. Sara glares at the overly cheerful Santa grinning through the glass.

She really wishes they would at least wait until after Halloween.

Seth appears at her side, the way he always does. She doesn't jump—she's come to expect no warning. "Come now, it's not so terrible." His hands sink into his pockets, rocking back onto his heels as he stares up at the sky. "So you have to repeat a class? At worst, it'll only delay your plans a handful of months."

She sniffs, wiping her nose on the sleeve of her sweatshirt as discreetly as she can manage. "Can you not?" she says, forcing the words around the gravel in her throat. "I'm not in the mood."

She can feel his stare, but she refuses to meet it—pulling her knees up to her chest a little tighter.

He hums, "Ah, I see. You'd rather sulk."

"You know what?" she snaps, "Maybe I *would*." Her arms cross over her chest, hands fisting in the fabric at her elbows. "Oma's dead, my boy—my *ex* would rather die than remember me, my dad can't look up from the bottle long enough to support me in *anything* I do. And now, just to top everything else off, I'm probably going to have to put my entire life on hold because of this *stupid* class."

There's no way she'll be able to juggle four photography classes *and* literature next semester. There's not. She missed three more months at her grandmother's side, three more months of happy memories, all because Oma hadn't wanted her to delay her gradua-tion. Now, knowing that it doesn't even matter is crippling. It *hurts*. It hurts so terribly and he can't possibly understand. Couldn't possibly care.

A bitter laugh escapes her. "But you don't care about any of that, right? As long as you can say you own me, nothing else matters, right?"

He shakes his head. His skin is pale—ghostly—under the humming fluorescent light. "If you truly believe that nonsense, then you're more foolish than I gave you credit for."

"Nonsense?" she hisses. Inside her pocket, her fists clench—nails biting into her palms. "You remind me *all the time*. How—"

He cuts her off, voice sharp. "*Never.* I have never *once* claimed to own you." His eyes close, facing skyward as if praying for patience. "People aren't possessions, regardless of how many men throughout history have claimed otherwise."

Her lips part, ready to argue—always ready to argue—but the fight leaves her as quickly as it came. He's right. He's never said it in those exact words, but the implication had been there. Heavy and without any room for misunderstanding. "But you—"

"I said you're *mine*." His voice is dry in the wet weather, but there's a sigh hiding behind his eyes—a fatigue. "That won't change, regardless of your pitiful whining."

"Ok, but you see how that's just as bad? Right? It literally means the same thing!"

"But it doesn't," Seth hisses, eyes flashing. "To say I own you is to say I hold power over you." He shakes his head, a bitter laugh falling from his lips. "No. You are *mine*, Sara, but only because I am equally *yours*."

Sara gapes at him, outraged. "But I never—I didn't. You are **not** mine."

She expects his taunts; a smooth, dark chuckle. Perhaps even his scorn. She receives none of it. Instead his lips pull into a sneer, bitter at the edges. "Not yours? I've been yours from the very moment you bargained for David's life." His eyes slide to meet hers, mouth softening into something resigned. "I have to answer your every question; forced to speak only in truths. You're the only one who can see me. The only one who can *touch* me, but only if you wish it. I may as well be chained to your wrist."

It feels like he stole the breath from her lungs, leaving her empty and lightheaded. "I—but you never..." she trails off, trying to find her bearings. Her hands grip the bench, bile acidic in her throat. "I don't understand."

"What is there *possibly* to misinterpret?"

She stares at him. The sneer, the callous set of his shoulders. He's the same as always, but there's an exhaustion hiding in the shadows of his eyes—a resignation—she had never cared to notice. "Why?" she whispers.

"I beg your pardon?"

"Why," she repeats, louder. "Why would you pretend?"

The laugh that leaves him is cold. "Tell me, would you have seen me as anything else? Had I... tossed compliments and condolences at your feet, would any of it have made any difference?" He sighs, staring listlessly at the rain-soaked street. "I am the villain in your story, Princess. I never held any expectations of anything different."

There's a lump in her throat, an anxiety tightening her chest, that renders her speechless. Silence stretches between them, filled only by the steady tapping of rain on the aluminum awning sheltering them. She doesn't know what to say to break it, except maybe... "You're right." The startled look he gives her is swift, sharp with reluctant hope. "I... I wouldn't have. I'm sorry."

He softens—mask melting away like wax under heat—and for the first time, Sara recognizes him for what he is.

Tired.

The smile he wears at the corners of his mouth is fragile. "No need to apologize, Princess. There have been far worse heroines to suffer through."

Sara thinks of the day she struck him—the edge of panic in his gaze the moment she discovered she had the power to hurt him— and feels sick. How many others came before her? How many found his weaknesses and chose to exploit it? She doesn't have the courage to ask. "Was it... have you always had to? Be the villain?"

"No," he confesses, as if admitting a past sin.

She nods, hands twisting in her lap. "What happened?" His eyes close, jaw tightening, and Sara realizes her mistake. "I'm sorry, you don't have to answer that."

She doesn't want to force an answer from him, not this time. Not for this.

The rain continues to fall around them—the only sign he heard her is his continued silence. It isn't until the headlights of a passing car light up the wet landscape that he speaks. "Her name was Mary. Mary Jacobs." He pauses, eyes darkening. "An ordinary name for an ordinary woman. Her young son was dying in her arms—pneumonia. She hadn't the money for a doctor. Even if she did, she certainly wouldn't have been able to afford the treatment. She wanted him to live."

Sara's lips twitch into a sardonic smile. "So you gave her a miracle."

Seth snorts. "By the time the deal was struck, he had already passed." His eyes meet hers, painfully serious. "There's always a price, Sara. *Always*. The man that wishes for riches, sacrifices happiness. The woman who prays for someone to love her unconditionally, receives it from a person she finds repulsive." He shakes his head, expression softening. "The girl that wishes for her boyfriend to live, finds herself alone because he doesn't come back the same."

She sucks in a breath. "It's just because he doesn't remember."

He watches her, eyes bottomless. Sara hates that he doesn't assure her. Hates that he *can't*.

"Do you know?" she asks, words trembling on her tongue. "When you make your deals. Do you know what the price will be?"

"No." He gazes up at the rain. "I don't."

"What was the price for—"

He doesn't let her finish. "Please, don't ask me that. You will hate the answer nearly as much as I would telling it."

His voice is curt, but Sara can see something unsaid dancing in the empty space between them. Perhaps it had always been there— twisting and turning just on the edges of her vision. "You regret it."

Not a question; a truth.

He doesn't bother pretending otherwise. "He's the only one I ever tried to take from Death. I've been very careful to make sure it stays that way."

"That bad?"

"Worse." He laughs, the sound dark and hollow. "It was supposed to be a mercy. I thought—I truly, *truly* believed there could be no price worse than dying. I was wrong. Obviously."

Sara wants to ask why he bargains at all, but she's afraid she already knows the answer.

"Was it ever worth it?" she asks softly.

"Once," he says, voice teetering on the thin edge between bitterness and apathy. "Only once."

"Will you tell me about it?" The look he gives her is questioning —baffled by her curiosity. She shrugs. "I could use some happy."

He scoffs. "You asked if it was ever worth the trade, that hardly qualifies it as *happy*."

"Do you ever get tired of being so melodramatic?"

"Don't be ridiculous, of course not." His lips purse; the faintest echo of a smile. It disappears as quickly as it came. "She was in pain —agony, really. Every minute of every day. When she spoke, when she smiled... the slightest brush of wind against her face." His eyes close, mouth twisting into a grimace. "She begged me to make it go away."

"So you did."

He nods, the corner of his mouth lifting into a self-deprecating smile. "So I did."

"What was the price?" She almost doesn't want to know, but she can't keep herself from asking.

"She stopped feeling anything. Not the heat from an iron, or the chill from the snow."

"That... doesn't seem so bad."

He shakes his head, a sneer twisting his mouth. "Then you're a fool. *Nothing*, Sara. She could feel *nothing*. Not the embrace of her child, or the kiss from her husband. She died, starving for touch, from a heart attack because she couldn't bloody well feel the symptoms. She was the only one, in a long list of victims, that thanked me. Even on her deathbed, she *thanked me* and I... I never wished, so fervently that she wouldn't." He meets her gaze, more open and vulnerable than she's ever seen him. Pained. "I did nothing but trade one Hell for another."

"Oh," she breathes. It feels like the air has been sucked from her lungs, leaving her chest hollow—starving. "Is...is that how it is for you?"

His brow creases. "What?"

Sara swallows, bolstering her courage. "The touch starved thing. You said you traded one Hell for another. Is that how it is for you? Is it Hell?"

He stares at her, a manic laugh escaping him. Sara hates how brittle it sounds; how fragile. She can almost hear him breaking around the edges. "How can it be anything else?"

# CHAPTER TWENTY-TWO

HE'S DIFFERENT, AFTER THAT.

Maybe she is, too, but she's definitely not imagining the change in him. The edges of his taunts have been filed down; his cutting remarks softened until they feel more teasing than cruel. Sara wonders if it's because she's earned a degree of trust, or if he simply has no other secrets to guard. She's not even sure if the reason matters, because the end result is the same: Seth has become infinitely easier to live with.

They're teetering on the line of friendship; each more considerate of the other. Seth stops watching tv when she goes to bed; Sara makes sure to turn it to his favorite channel come morning. He stops baiting her in public, makes an effort to stay in her line of sight so she can see him without looking crazy. Sara wears her earbuds faithfully– perfects the faux answering of her phone just so they can speak freely on the streets, in the laundromat, between classes.

She tries not to evaluate how much time she spends talking to him; tries to push it to the back of her mind with the justification that it's only natural when he shadows her the way he does. She, under no circumstances, will admit that she kind of enjoys having someone to listen to her complain about why art appreciation is eighty percent essays and why can't every teacher be like her Algebra professor who only grades on tests and never homework.

Perhaps the most surprising development is Seth actually *does.* He *listens.*

He chimes in when she leaves an opening, engages in the conversation without ever dominating it. He is free with his opinions, but even when they disagree, he never dismisses her own. It takes her a week before she recognizes that (for him) the friendly debates are more about the conversation than the outcome. She wonders, guiltily, how many of the others before her treated him with the same silent apathy as she had only a month ago—wonders how many of them never stopped.

Then she thinks about the time between, the years he's spent with no one to see him, no one to *hear* him, and feels her heart twinge. She makes a small promise to herself, that she won't punish him with silence again (no matter how he may press her buttons). She won't scream at him to leave her classes, won't demand his absence in her life.

Growing up under her father's roof, she knows what it's like to feel invisible.

Sara stares at the exam questions, knee rapidly bouncing under the desk. Between her heartbeat drumming in her ears, the scratching of her classmates' pens fill the silence. Mouth dry, she glances at the clock and feels herself pale. She's already used up a quarter of her test time and has nothing to show for it but a blank page.

Turns out, the movie doesn't cover everything.

She swallows thickly, the questions on the page blurring as her eyes water. So much for graduating after next semester—she'll be too busy repeating this stupid class and cursing GE requirements.

Someone stands in front of her; a familiar charcoal shadow she doesn't need to look up to name. "Pick up your pen."

She gives the tiniest shake of her head she can muster. Even if there wasn't an audience, she's not sure she could trust her voice.

Seth sighs, lowering himself until his eyes are level with hers. "Pick up your pen and write exactly as I say. Do you understand?"

Hope flares, bright but short-lived. Things have been good between them lately, but does she dare trust him? With *this*? Her future?

He must see the hesitance in her expression, because he sighs. "Honestly, a little trust wouldn't go amiss. What could I possibly gain by misleading you?"

The enjoyment of watching her fail. The goading I-told-you-so rights for the entirety of next semester (at least).

She looks at him, gauging his expression. There's no hint of deception, but Sara's not entirely convinced there would be. Still... her blank paper glares up at her, a daunting reminder of the alternative. With a bracing intake of breath, she picks up her pen and sets the ballpoint tip to the page.

Seth shifts to her side, his voice soft and measured despite her being the only one capable of hearing him. She transcribes each word, fills the lines and then the pages. When she turns it in with five minutes to spare, it's with a silent prayer.

"I GOT AN A MINUS," SHE MUTTERS NUMBLY. SHE ALMOST THINKS IT'S A mistake, but the numbers on her laptop screen stay the same no matter how many times she double checks them.

Seth huffs. "Well, you couldn't possibly expect me to get you full marks. You passing at *all* is suspicious enough."

Pulse racing, her hand shakes as she clicks for her overall grade.

C minus. A passing grade. Barely passing—but *passing*.

She slumps in her chair, relieved laughter shaking from her lungs. Glancing over, she catches the tail end of Seth's smile before it recedes. "Thank you," she breathes.

"Don't make a thing of it. Witnessing you make a butchery of our language was becoming more wearisome than amusing." He folds his arms over his chest. "Besides, there's still plenty of time for you to fail, yet."

He's right. If she wants to pass this class, it isn't going to be by getting an A on just one exam. She needs to do enough to hold the grade.

Pensively, she chews on her bottom lip. She remembers he had offered his help once, in that twisted half-mocking sort of way that he has. She had declined purely out of spite before, but she can't deny that she needs the help. "Would you—I mean, do you think you could help me study for the next one?"

His head tilts, dimples flashing. He looks positively delighted. He crosses his legs, fingers laced over his knee. "I believe I can carve some time out of my busy schedule."

"Are you sure you want to do this?" Jen asks, voice low. Her eyes flit between the picture on Sara's screen, to the hair stylist finishing up another customer, and back to her face. "You hate it when they take off more than two *inches*."

Sara shifts in her seat, the hard plastic chair a far cry from comfortable. The picture on her screen is definitely shorter than she's ever even *considered*, and she had really only decided to do it on a whim, but she feels no apprehension. In all honesty, she *isn't* sure. The idea only dawned on her a few days ago, a stray thought that nudged its way into a decision as she combed through her wet hair —playing with the ends and eyeing her reflection in the mirror.

It's been years since she's changed her hair; years since she embraced something new. Her life has become unrecognizable. There are more scars on her heart now, deep and twinging, and she's tired of looking in the mirror and seeing the face of the girl she was before. She's tired of pretending the pain hasn't changed her.

Also… Ms. Green offered extra credit to anyone who came to class dressed up for Halloween—the amount of points a reflection of the amount of effort put into the costume. Sara thinks of the handful of 80's movie posters her professor has hanging over her desk.

She could really, *really* use those credits.

"I'm sure," she says, nodding. "I'm ready for a change."

Jen still looks nervous for her. "Yeah, but this is kind of a *big* change. It's going to take you forever to grow back if you hate it."

Sara shrugs. "It's just hair."

Jen stares. "Ok, who are you and what have you done with my best friend?"

She rolls her eyes. Sara can't even pretend that her friend is wrong for being concerned—she used to swear up and down that she'd never go short. Her long hair was a source of pride, something almost intrinsic to who she was.

But she's not that same person anymore.

Between David's accident and Oma's death, the fights with her father and the recognition of pain in Seth's eyes, the length of her hair feels trivial at best... a painful reminder at worst. She used to love how Oma would braid her hair in the summer, weaving in flowers from the garden as if any ordinary weekend was May Day.

Sara's fingers play with a strand of hair, twisting it around her knuckle before letting it fall. "It's fine—*I'm* fine."

Jen must sense something in her tone, because her expression softens—lips parting around a quiet, "oh." She takes Sara's hand in hers, squeezing softly. "Well, for the record, I think it'll look great on you. You *totally* have the bone structure for it."

Sara smothers a laugh, nudging her friend's shoulder with her own. "Thanks."

Jen nudges back, grin wide. "Anytime, Bestie."

The hairdresser—Natalie, according to her name tag—calls her name, and Sara rises. When she glances over her shoulder, Jen gives her two enthusiastic thumbs up.

"So what are we doing today?" Natalie asks, rotating the chair for her to sit.

Sara shows her the picture as she settles in. "I want to do something like this."

Natalie whistles, the swallowtail tattoo on her forearm winking as she flicks the cape over Sara's front. "Big change!" She winks at Sara through the mirror. "It's going to look great!"

Taking a few minutes to comb through Sara's hair, she works out the tangles before banding it at the nape of her neck. Then she holds up her scissors, offering a final chance to change her mind. "Ready?"

Sara nods, butterflies in her stomach. "Ready." She can hear the scissors slice through the banded strands—three cuts—and then she's struck by a sudden feeling of weightlessness.

The stylist laughs, holding up the ponytail for her to see. "Feels weird, doesn't it?"

Staring at her reflection, a small smile teases Sara's mouth. "Yeah. It does."

It feels lighter.

SARA RUSHES HOME AFTER, THE AIR ON THE BACK OF HER NECK COLD BUT her spirits high. Class is starting in an hour, but she hadn't thought to bring her school bag with her to the salon. Turns out a full cut takes longer than a trim (go figure).

She doesn't think about Seth's reaction to the sudden change, not until she's through the front door and his eyes are on her—pinning her in place.

He blinks, expression infuriatingly neutral. "Your hair."

Instinctively, her fingers reach up to the strands hovering just past her ear. "I, uh, cut it."

He continues to stare. "Yes, I can see that."

"Yeah, I—well, it was time for a change, anyway. And I know Ms. Green really likes those old eighties movies. So, yeah. I'm Claire. You know, from—"

"*The Breakfast Club*," Seth finishes. "I'm familiar."

Oh. "Really?" Aside from a handful of pop culture references, *she* wasn't really well acquainted.

"Time is something I have in excess." He shrugs. "You'll be hard pressed to find a film I'm *not* familiar with."

Sara remembers the way his expression darkened, how the words "*I do*" hissed between his teeth when she demanded he watch a movie instead of attending her literature class two months ago.

"Oh." In that moment, the obvious dawns on her. "You... you don't sleep, do you?"

He smiles, crooked and bitter. "No rest for the wicked, I'm afraid."

There's a pain there, hiding at the edges of the sardonic lilt in his voice. It's hard to imagine a life without rest—without the weightlessness of sleep or the lucidness of dreams. Sara almost pities him.

"Surely you aren't planning to wear *that*?"

Almost.

Her eyes narrow. "Why not?"

"Your shirt is purple."

"So?"

"Claire's is pink. Honestly, it's like you're not even trying."

She stares, dumbfounded. "I *cut my hair*. How is that *not* trying?"

"Yes, but why go that far if not to go all the way? Use that pink blouse—the one you keep meaning to donate but never get around to—and roll up the sleeves." He nods toward her waist. "The skirt will do well enough, but add a belt and switch the black boots for those brown ones."

Sara's stare doesn't drop. "Uh huh... *How* many times have you watched that movie?"

"Far more than I care to count," he grumbles, gaze lingering on her hair. Slowly, a grin spreads across his face—crooked and dimpled. "You do know what they called her?"

"Uhm, no?" Just because she knows about the movie doesn't mean she's in any way ready for trivia.

His smile widens, but it's the teasing glint in his eyes that gives it away.

Sara groans. "*No.*"

"Always, the Princess, aren't you?"

SHE CHANGES. NOT BECAUSE SETH SAID SHE SHOULD, BUT BECAUSE SHE'S desperate to score every single point of extra credit she can get. Sara won't admit it (at least not to him) but he's right—the pink blouse in the back of her closet works a lot better.

So do the brown boots.

And the belt.

Sometimes, she could hate him for being right. Especially when his eyes gleam, his mouth curling at the edges with a reserved sort of told-you-so confidence, when he sees her. "Well, make way for the Princess."

The glare she sends him is weak at best. "Ha ha. Hilarious."

"I *do* try."

Sara grabs her bag off the couch, slinging it over her shoulder and glancing at the clock. She's running a few minutes behind, but a thought nags at her. Shifting her weight, she adjusts the strap of her bag and fights the awkwardness threatening to make her voice catch. "I, uh, won't be home after school."

He perks, head tilting. "Oh?"

She adjusts the bag on her shoulder, shifting awkwardly. "I'm taking some more sunset photos, so I won't be back until after dark. You know, in case you got worried or whatever."

"I appreciate your consideration." He smiles, small but achingly soft at the corners. "Truly."

Sara shrugs, too embarrassed to meet his eyes. There's a prickling heat crawling up her neck that has no business being there. "Yeah, so, anyway. Bye." She turns, silently berating herself as she heads toward the door—her steps a little too quick to come off as casual. She tells herself it's because she's running late and *not* because she's running away.

Seth calls after her. It's only the surprise of hearing her name that prompts her to turn back, to meet his eyes. His expression is soft— sincere. "Your hair, it suits you."

The heat has spread to her cheeks now, but (somehow) she manages to keep her voice steady. "Thanks."

The tiny curl at the corner of his mouth grows into a smirk. "Good luck, Princess. Also, there's to be a surprise essay on one of Shakespeare's sonnet readings today. Do try and brainstorm on those themes we've talked about."

Sara makes a point to slam the door behind her, hoping he didn't catch her hint of a smile.

THERE'S AN EXTRA PEP TO HER STEP AS SHE GOES TO HER CAR.

Ms. Jones had laughed—delighted—when she walked into class and was quick to assure her that the full amount of extra credit would be awarded. Twenty-five extra credit points might not have been enough of an incentive for most of the class, but considering her next semester was riding on her passing, Sara is *thrilled*. Also, she's pretty sure she killed the in-class essay. Seth's warning might have helped. A lot.

So did the quick brush up on Google right before class.

Humming under her breath, she flings her bag onto the passenger floor before reaching for her seatbelt.

"So where are we going?"

Sara screams, hand flying to her chest as she pivots in her seat to glare at him. The wide grin he wears only fuels her fear induced fury. "What the hell is *wrong* with you?!"

"Loaded question, I'm afraid," he says, blinking into the passenger seat. "But in this case, I suppose my fault lies in being prone to boredom. Also, you forgot to turn the telly on."

She runs a hand through her hair, trying to convince her heart to calm. She can still feel it banging mercilessly against her ribs. "You always managed to turn it on before."

"Only with our dear Ansel's help."

She manages to restrain the urge to remind him that Ansel is *her* cat and no one else's. "And today is different because?"

"He's napping."

Sara stares at him, anger mounting, before she shakes her head and starts the car. "You're impossible," she hisses.

A beat of silence. Sara can almost feel the shift in him. "You were actually frightened." A statement, not a question—one Sara doesn't bother responding to. "My apologies, it wasn't my intention."

Gritting her teeth, she turns the key until the engine sputters to life. "Sure."

"I can't lie."

She swallows, chewing on her words until they soften. As much as she hates to believe him, she doesn't really have a choice in the matter. "Just… don't ever do that again."

He nods, eyeing her strangely. "Very well…"

Sara can still feel the question in his gaze after she pulls out of the parking garage, but it takes her another minute before she can answer it. "There's that story," she mutters, feeling silly even as she says it. "The one with the killer in the backseat. It's always freaked me out, ok?"

"Ah," he breathes, "I see." Somehow, she doesn't doubt that he *does.*"Would it be any consolation to know *that* particular story is merely an urban myth?"

"It really wouldn't." Her phone rings, breaking through the silence with a jingled merriment that grates on her nerves.

Seth raises a brow as her hand fumbles blindly through the messenger bag at his feet while keeping her eyes on the road. "*Jingle Bell Rock?*"

"*Jen,*" she growls, ignoring his bark of laughter as her fingers finally find her phone. She pulls it out, glancing at the screen before hanging up and dropping it into the cup holder with a muttered curse. "I swear to god, these telemarketers have it out for me." She turns a corner, glowering. "Also, remind me to take off that stupid ringtone later."

"Not feeling the Christmas spirit?"

"We haven't even made it through *Halloween.*"

"Fair enough," he chuckles, settling into the seat and watching several streets pass as she drives. "I'm surprised you don't plan on joining the festivities," he says eventually, seeming genuinely curious. His gaze snags on a toddling ghost buster and he smirks. "Seems a shame to waste such a delightful holiday."

Sara rolls her eyes, finger tapping on the steering wheel as she waits for the light to turn green. "No."

"But why?"

"Because I'm an *adult*?"

"That's hardly stopping your peers. I have it on good authority that even your BFF Jen is participating."

Sara closes her eyes, sending up a quick prayer for patience before sending him a glare. "How many times do I need to tell you to stop spying on my friends?"

"At least once more, apparently," he quips, unrepentant. "Besides, I would hardly call it spying. I just pop in every now and then to see how they're getting on."

"They don't know you're watching them. It's spying, and it's *creepy*."

"If you'd rather keep me all to yourself, all you need to do is ask."

"That is *not* what I said."

"You're the only one who can see me."

"Why do you keep 'popping in' on them, then? There are literally thousands of other places you could go to do some people watching."

He hesitates. When she chances a glance, his expression is pinched in a way that makes her nervous. It's the same look he gets when he wants to twist the truth, but doesn't know how. "Seth?"

He grunts, looking out the window. "Just to make sure everyone's well."

"Yeah, I'm not letting this one go. I command you to tell me."

"You can't *command* me to do anything," he retorts. "You may have me on a leash, but I'm not your *dog*."

At the intersection, she stops at the red light and faces him fully. "You can either give me an actual answer or I can needle you with questions the rest of the ride. Why do you keep checking on them?"

Seth grits his teeth, jaw straining. "They're your *people*." The words rush out of him, a hiss of breath. "If something happened to either of them, it would crush you." He shakes his head, eyes meeting hers. The depth of sincerity she sees there makes her hands sweat. "You've lost enough."

Sara swallows, breath shallow and eyes blown wide. Behind her, a car honks. At some point, the light turned green.

Taking her foot off the brake, she drives through the intersection; grasping the steering wheel with a white-knuckled grip to mask the trembling of her hands. It's only after she turns onto the highway that she finds her voice. "Why?"

The word is shaky, vague enough that he could easily answer around it, but it's all she can manage. Her heart is hammering in her chest, an echoed beat of a fist against solid wood. In front of her is miles of open road dotted with a spattering of cars, but all she can see is the panic in Seth's eyes when he begged her not to answer the door.

"I don't know what he is capable of." His answer is soft, strained at the edges. "And the firm he's interning at is out of my reach."

Licking her lips, she tries to keep her voice steady. She doesn't need to ask who '*he*' is. "Reach?"

"There are… limitations to how far I can travel."

He doesn't elaborate. Sara doesn't ask him to. A silence falls between them, thick and brimming with tension. Her thoughts a whirlwind of disbelief—David would never hurt *anyone*, let alone her friends—but through it all she can still hear the drumming of his fist against her door, the slurred curses and violent rattle of the handle.

# CHAPTER TWENTY-THREE

THEY DON'T TALK ABOUT IT.

Sara doesn't ask, Seth doesn't offer, and so the conversation dies before it even begins. She does think about it, though. It's in the back of her mind when she drives to class, when she does her grocery shopping, when she faithfully locks her deadbolt the moment she's through the front door.

A week later, Jen invites her out for dinner and drinks, and Sara jumps at the chance to be out of her apartment and out of her own head for an evening. Part of her expects Seth to argue when she asks him to leave her be for the night, but he only shrugs. Then she's stumbling out of the restaurant with Jen, their arms linked and laughter slurred, and she spots him across the street. She's so drunk, she shouldn't have even noticed him—he's a charcoal shadow blending into the building behind him—but, somehow, her eyes find him as easily as if he were the only spot of color in a sea of gray. He stays, stone still and ever watchful, until the very moment Miles pulls up and helps them safely into the car. When she arrives home, he's curled up in his chair with Ansel on his lap watching reruns of *Amor Prohibito*.

"Was it a worthwhile evening?" he asks.

He makes no indication that he ever left the apartment, so Sara doesn't either. "It was fun."

Seth nods. "Good." His eyes flit from her bare feet to the heels in her hands and chuckles. "Get to bed, Princess. The morning will come all too soon."

It's a good suggestion. A great one, in fact. She barely manages to change into an oversized t-shirt before her body hits the bed.

When she wakes up, Sara fully expects her hangover to be the worst of her problems. Her head throbs with her pulse, cotton lining her tongue and her stomach lurching when she stands. It's only after forcing down some pills and half a slice of dry toast that her stomach feels calm enough to trust. Seth watches her, wearing that infuriatingly smug grin the whole time, but he's at least smart enough not to comment.

Then she gets in her car, turns the key, and listens to the engine sputter and whine.

Sara frowns, tries it again. The engine turns over, and she breathes a sigh of relief and chalks it up to the freezing temperatures.

Until she gets about a mile down the street.

"No, no, no!" she mutters, panic rising faster than the smoke from beneath her hood. "Please, *please* don't do this to me. Not today. Please, not today."

The engine responds with a final, sputtering breath before going silent. Sara swears using just about every curse she knows as she drifts to the side of the road, clumsily searching for the hazard lights. Dark smoke leaks out from under the hood, mixing with the steam.

She stares, disbelievingly, before her head drops to the steering wheel with a loud curse.

SHE WAITS TWO HOURS FOR THE TOW TRUCK, AND ANOTHER THIRTY minutes at the mechanic's filling out paperwork. By the time she leaves, it's well past noon, but the mechanic promises to email her a repair estimate before the end of the day. Instead of picking up groceries, she orders a pizza while riding the bus home (and tries not to cringe when they tell her the total).

Three hours later, the pizza sits like lead in her stomach as she stares at the emailed estimate on her phone.

She should have bought instant noodles instead.

"What are you doing?" Seth says, frowning at her. "Don't you have an essay due tomorrow in your art history class?"

The reminder only serves to make her feel even more stressed. "It's half done."

He glances at the clock, his eyebrows raised. "Do you believe the other half will write itself?"

"Shut up. *Please*, just shut up." She rubs at her temples, staring at the numbers as if looking long enough will change them.

She can feel his stare, almost pinpoint the exact moment he recognizes the tension in her. "What's wrong?"

She can't bring herself to explain, so she holds up the repair bill in silent invitation.

A beat, perhaps two. "Ah. Yes, I can see how that would be mildly concerning."

Sara groans, laying her face in the fold of her arms. "I need to get a job."

Seth frowns, and for a moment he looks legitimately troubled. "No, you need these last few weeks to study. Particularly, if you still wish to pass without my interference."

She hates that he's right (she hates that she doesn't have another solution even more).

Seth hums thoughtfully. "You could try gambling."

Sara is in absolutely *no* mood for his humor. "You're not funny."

"I'm not joking."

Her head rolls to the side, temple pressed uncomfortably against the fragile bones of her wrist, as she looks at him. His blank expression instills little to no confidence. "Even if I had money to throw away, I *suck* at gambling."

The exasperated twist in his expression would almost be comical if it weren't for its tendency to make her feel like a child. "You have *me*, Princess. How could you *possibly* lose?"

Understanding dawns. "That's cheating."

"Your point?"

She shakes her head, sitting up and turning until she's facing him fully. "That *is* my point!"

"Please, it's hardly as if they don't cheat themselves. You honestly believe all those pretty machines are random?" When she is unmoved, he rolls his eyes. "Think of it as divine intervention."

"There's nothing divine about you."

"Fair point. Think of how miserable you'll be if you have to repeat your literature class."

Sara blanches, mouth souring at the thought. "Do...do you really think it would work?"

"I suspect you're an abysmal player at best, but so long as you do what I say and at least make an attempt at having a poker face, I suspect we will get on just fine."

Her fingers play with the hem of her flannel shirt, eyes tracing and retracing the numbers on the estimate. "Ok, but, maybe we should test it out first?"

Seth's smile goes wicked at the corners. "I happen to know a fellow."

MILES HAD BEEN THRILLED WHEN SHE ASKED IF HE COULD TEACH HER how to play. Sara hadn't even known he had a love for it (and she's mildly concerned that, somehow, Seth *had*). However, his enthusiasm started to trickle away two drinks and six hands ago.

"You're sure you've never played before?" he asks (again) as he shuffles the cards. Sara notices that he spends way more time ensuring they're mixed well compared to the first hand he dealt.

Jen swats his arm, a buzzed smile curling her mouth. Sara lost track of what glass she's on. "You already asked her that."

Miles grumbles something unintelligible under his breath, but deals out the cards.

Sara shakes her head, glancing at her hand.

Seth hovers over her shoulder, evaluating her cards. "You'll want to hold on to that one, Princess." He's so close; were he anyone else —anyone with physical form—she would feel the heat of his body at her back. She swallows, trying to banish the thought, but his mouth is so close to her ear and— "You're only a card away from a flush."

She feels the last word—an impossible whisper of warm breath against her cheek—and she jumps, cards slipping from her hands and spiraling to her feet.

Seth pulls away from her, casting her a perplexed look that would match her friends' exactly had there been a touch of concern. Instead, he almost seems put out. "What on God's earth was *that*?"

"Uh, Sara? You ok?" Miles asks.

"No, Captain Obvious. She's obviously not. Honestly, what the bloody hell *was that*?! You just wasted a winning hand!"

Jen gives a drunken laugh, waving off his concern before Sara can bother. "She's *fine*," she slurs, before slapping her cards on the table. "I have two three's! Do I win?"

Miles sighs. "Baby, maybe you should sit a few out."

"What?! No, I'm winning!"

He runs a hand over his face, an exasperated (yet fond) smile dimpling his cheek. "Honey, I love you, but you weren't even supposed to show your hand yet."

Jen looks down at her cards proudly splayed across the table. "Oh."

He gives her a sympathetic rub on the back. "Next time, baby." Miles shoots her a questioning look. "You still good to play?"

Sara's sober enough to sense what he's really asking. "Um, yeah. I'm fine. I, uh, fold I guess."

Seth's still staring at her, a frown turning the corners of his mouth. "Well, I should bloody well hope so. I was fully prepared for you to be lousy, but this is borderline embarrassing."

It takes just about every ounce of her willpower to withhold the urge to send him a scathing glare while Miles finishes reshuffling the cards and deals out a new hand.

She gets a bit better at it, though Seth insists that her poker face still needs work. Since he can't lie, she's stuck with no other choice than to believe him. After another ten rounds, she's gathered almost all the chips. When she folds, Miles tosses his cards on the table with a muttered curse.

His three aces would have definitely beaten out her pair of tens.

"Ok, I know there's something to be said about beginner's luck, but this is *bullshit*."

Jen laughs, absolutely thrilled. "She's kicking your *ass*!"

"I thought you said you didn't play!" he accuses. "It's like you know every time I have a good hand." He looks behind his shoulder, searching.

Jen laughs harder, but Sara only finds herself more confused as he leans in his chair. "What are you *doing*?"

"Trying to figure out how your cheating butt is seeing my cards." He points to a picture on the wall—the one of him and Jen from their trip to Texas last year. "It's the picture frame, isn't it? The reflection?"

Seth snickers from behind his hand, looking entirely too pleased with himself. "Oh, don't you dare spoil this for me. This is going to bother him for *weeks*."

Sara rolls her eyes, though she can't really tell which man she's more exasperated with. "I can't see your cards."

"Yeah, uh huh." Miles stands, moving to her side of the table and kneeling until they're at the same eye level. Behind his thick-rimmed glasses, he squints as he searches the opposite wall. "Seriously, though. How the hell are you doing that?"

"She's got skills to pay the bills!" Jen exclaims between giggles.

Sara fights a smile, shrugging. "Maybe I have an invisible friend whispering in my ear."

Miles scoffs. "Hilarious."

"Oh!" Jen gasps, "We should go to the casino!"

Sara catches Miles' pleading look, smiling. "We totally should," she says, watching his face drop before she adds, "next time."

Jen groans. Miles mouths a silent, yet somehow emphatic, 'thank you.'

I T'S FREEZING OUTSIDE, CRISP IN WAYS THAT ARE BORDERLINE PAINFUL. Sara shivers, pulling her coat closer around her neck and stubbornly wills her teeth to stop chattering. Beside her, Seth is completely unfazed—his bare fingers playing idly with the chain of his pocket watch and his eyes distant.

"How are you not f-freezing?" she asks, bouncing on the pads of her feet.

He blinks, regarding her strangely. "Beg your pardon?"

Sara frowns. He's never had to ask her to repeat anything. *Never.* "What's wrong?"

Seth shifts awkwardly, hands disappearing in his pockets, but he meets her eyes. "In there, you said friend."

Sara frowns, trying to figure out what he's referring to. When she does, she fights the heat rising to her cheeks. "Oh. Well, yeah. We're friends." It's not something she ever really evaluated, but it feels right. It feels true. At some point, he's transformed from her personal nightmare to someone she looks forward to seeing. She can't even pinpoint when it changed; each shift a subtle layer of gossamer.

Seth is still staring at her, lips parted and brows furrowed, and Sara feels a sudden pang of insecurity. "Aren't we?"

His lips twitch into a crooked smile, his gaze lowering as he clears his throat. "Yes. I rather think we are."

T HE NEXT DAY, SHE TAKES THE BUS TO THE CLOSEST CASINO. BETWEEN the Blackjack and poker tables, she more than doubles the amount she needs to repair her car.

"Time to go, Princess. The big men upstairs are watching you a little too closely," he murmurs, his grin wide. This time, when Sara feels his breath whisper across her wine-flushed skin, she doesn't jump.

# CHAPTER TWENTY-FOUR

To say she studies is probably one of the biggest understatements of her life.

She's not worried about math (numbers and equations she can memorize) or even her art appreciation final (because despite Mr. Kent's droning, she at least understands the material), but her literature class is close to killing her.

Seth, to his credit, is as tolerant as any reasonable person should be, but the last few weeks seem to have worn away at his patience. "No," he groans, eyes hidden behind his long fingers as he massages his temples. "That isn't even close to accurate."

Sara threads her hand through her hair, ready to pull at the short strands. "You said accuracy doesn't matter as long as I can support it!"

"That isn't support, it's drivel."

She stands, the kitchen chair screeching against the tile. She's too busy pacing the short span of her front room to care. "I hate this. I hate it, I hate it, I **hate it**." Grabbing the throw pillow from the couch, she screams into it before collapsing face-first onto the cushions. From around the fluff, she mutters weakly. "I really, really hate it."

Seth sighs, but the frustration in his voice has at least given way to pity. "I am well aware."

Sara turns her head, eyeing him miserably. "Why am I so bad at this?"

The shrug he gives is small, his hand coming away from his temple so he can face her fully. "Your mind is more suited for certainties—the black and white. Literature is about interpreting the gray areas, not memorizing facts."

"Well, don't hold anything back," she grumbles.

He huffs on a laugh, eyes warm. "You'll get it, Princess."

"No I won't."

"Hm, perhaps not. But, at the very least, we can work on improving your poker face."

She groans, flopping on her back and staring at the ceiling. "What does my poker face have to do with anything?"

"My dear, lie convincingly enough and you can turn any pile of bullshit into a passing grade."

Sara's not convinced (not even a little) but at this point she's got nothing left to lose.

HER HEART IS IN HER THROAT, PULSE DROWNING IN HER EARS AND SWEAT lining her palms. The computer screen stares back at her, a click away from knowing if the last month of Seth's lectures were a waste of time or a saving grace.

Sara swallows down her nerves, wipes her hands on her jeans, and forces herself to click the link.

She passes her classes. All of them.

A strangled sound escapes her—the sheer amount of relief she feels is enough to make her cry. Her last semester would be the last two classes she needs to fulfill her bachelor of photography. No more math and *no* more literature.

She feels Seth hovering behind her, reading the posted results over her shoulder. When she looks, his lips quirk into a smile. "Well done, Princess."

Sara beams, leaning back in her chair to stare up at him. "Thank you. I couldn't have done it without your help."

His grin turns teasing. "*That*, I believe, we can safely agree on. Still, your efforts were commendable. Particularly when considering your complete lack of talent in the subject."

Sara's eyes narrow, trying (and failing) to look offended. "I *think* there was a compliment in there."

"Perhaps if you squint."

She laughs, her day bright, despite the gunmetal clouds gathering outside her window. For the first time in months, it feels like she's outrun her problems. She curls up on the couch, Oma's blanket draped over her lap and a mug of hot chocolate warming her hands as she rewatches *The Princess Bride*.

Silently, Seth's lips move in time with the dialogue. But if he's seen the movie enough times to be sick of it, he says nothing.

The next day she looks at the calendar, registers that Christmas is only five days away, and feels her mood sour.

"I REALLY DON'T WANT TO GO," SHE GRIPES, SHOVING A SET OF PAJAMAS into a duffle bag.

Seth hums, distractedly staring out the window at something she can't see. He's felt distant the last two days—quiet in ways that she might find worrisome if it wasn't for the imminent holiday disaster she was facing. "Then *don't*."

"He's my father. And it's Christmas."

"More's the pity."

She could throttle him. "Are you even listening?"

Rolling his eyes, he gives her his full attention. "You realize we have had this exact conversation more times than I care to count? If you're truly that worried about your father's feelings, then just get in the blasted car and *go*."

She stares at him, momentarily thrown by his abrasiveness. Snarky, she's used to, but the abrupt way he dismissed her... "What's wrong?"

His jaw works, the way it always does when she's asked a question he wishes to avoid. "I have... some concerns," he admits, scowling. "It's nothing I wish to worry you with."

Sara doesn't miss the fact that he doesn't meet her eyes as he says it. "Why doesn't that make me feel better?"

"Perhaps because you have a penchant for worrying excessively over things in general."

She glares, arms folding across her chest. "Ok, seriously. Are you going to tell me what's going on?"

"Not if I can help it," he grumbles, shooting her a dry look. "And I would appreciate it if you'd refrain from asking."

Lips pursing, she regards him carefully. He meets her eyes unflinchingly, but there's a pleading edge in his gaze. Sara sighs, arms dropping limply to her sides. "You'd tell me, right? If it was something I should worry about?"

His expression softens. "Only once I'm sure it's worth worrying over."

"You know, somehow that's not all that comforting."

He doesn't answer and Sara doesn't push, even though she knows she could.

SARA GOES HOME FOR CHRISTMAS. MOSTLY BECAUSE SHE CAN'T FIND A good enough excuse not to. She's ashamed to admit she half-wished for a snowstorm, but only got an inch for her trouble. Hardly enough to excuse her.

When she pulls in, there are no Christmas lights on the house, but she can see a tree through the front window. Sara can't remember the last time he brought a tree into the house, let alone decorated one, but the sight of it in the corner of the living room offers a thread of much needed hope. She grasps it, willing it to be a sign that the holiday with her father will offer more joy than heartache.

Even if things go badly, she tries to console herself with the fact that it's only two days—one night. She'll be back in her own home before Christmas Day is fully over. And, should things get *too* heated, there's nothing but her own stubbornness keeping her from taking her car and leaving.

Seth, unfortunately, doesn't seem to share her cautious optimism. "I still fail to understand why you're putting yourself through this."

Sara puts the car in park, turns off the engine, and makes a show of putting things in her purse—just in case her father happens to be watching from the window. "I don't need you to understand," she hisses. "I need you to be *supportive*."

Arms crossed over his chest, he tosses her a dirty look. "I'm merely reminding you that your last visit ended with you barreling down that sad excuse for a highway at nearly double the speed limit. I am nothing *but* supportive."

"Things are going to go better this time."

"How could you possibly know that?" His expression is skeptical, but there's a thread of curiosity that makes the words sound more like an honest question than a hypothetical one.

She nods towards the front window, hand pulling the door handle. "He put up a tree."

"How on earth does that—"

She shuts the door in his face, biting back a smile at the glare it earns her.

Now that she's out of the car, she can hear Belle barking from inside; the high pitched whine that she always does when she gets overexcited. The moment Sara opens the front door, the spaniel is a flurry at her feet—tongue licking at her hands and so full of energy she practically *vibrates*. Sara reaches down to pet her, but she's distracted by the changes in the rest of the room. There are a dozen little differences—the tidiness, the warm smell of a ham in the oven in place of sharp liquor, but it's the pressed button-down shirt and the tentative smile her father wears that makes her wonder if she's hallucinating.

"Hey, how was the drive?"

It takes her a moment to find her bearings. In her hand, the door knob is cold—a sharp contrast to the hot tongue licking at her fingers. "Um, good. Missed the traffic." It's an overused joke—outside of Des Moine there is no traffic. Gently, she shuts the door behind her, readjusting the strap of her purse. "The, uh, place looks nice. I like the tree."

Belle whines, demanding her attention, and Sara crouches down to give her the enthusiastic hello the dog is obviously begging for. Her hands bury themselves under the soft fur behind her ears. "And you look just lovely, Miss Belle!"

The dog flops over, belly up, and Sara scratches her stomach dutifully. It's a good distraction—an excuse to avoid meeting her father's stare and the sudden presence she can feel at her back.

"Well," Seth says, surprise underlying his sarcasm. "Perhaps there's hope for a Christmas miracle, after all."

Dinner isn't what she expects.

The food isn't half as good as what Oma used to cook up—the ham is dry, the potatoes lumpy—but she can taste her father's effort in every bite. When he offers her a drink, the only thing in a glass bottle is apple cider.

She can't remember the last dinner they shared sober. If it weren't for the stash of whiskey she found hiding behind the salad bowl, she would almost have hope that it could last.

From the head of the table, her father clears his throat. "So, what's Jen doing these days?"

Sara's hands pause in cutting her slice of ham, remembering the conversation that triggered their last argument. From his spot, draped over the plaid couch in the living room, Seth scoffs. Her first instinct is to be wary, to prepare herself for another round of disappointment, but her father's expression is earnest—anxious even—and she suspects he wants this dinner to go well as much as she does.

"She's been pretty busy... she's taking a trip to China in a few months. She's really excited about it," she offers, careful not to disclose that the reason she's been busy is actually because of wedding planning and that the trip to her home country is doubling as her honeymoon.

Roy nods, taking a drink of cider before returning to his utensils. "Her wedding's coming up soon, yeah?"

Sara stiffens, warnings going off like sirens in her skull. Through the noise, she hears Seth curse. She swallows, looking down at her plate—her hand gripping her fork so tightly, her knuckles are nearly as white as the paper plates. "Yeah, February."

"Odd month for a wedding, isn't it?"

"She wanted it during Chinese New Year."

She waits for the blowup, but when she risks a glance, he seems more awkward than angry.

"I'm, uh, sure it will be pretty. Jen's always had an eye for that stuff."

Sara blinks. "Um, yeah. Yeah, she has."

Another nod, and he fidgets with his fork. "And the groom's a nice enough fellow?"

Seth appears at her father's elbow, staring down at him with a perplexed frown. Sara looks back down at her plate to avoid the temptation to read the meaning between his furrowed brow.

"His name is Miles," she says. "We've become good friends."

Again, her father nods. "Good. That's good."

Seth's head tilts. The questions in his eyes match her own.

***

"Princess, wake up."

She groans, opening her eyes. Seth hovers over her. "Wha—"

He hushes her, a finger to his lips. "There's something I believe you should see, but you must be quiet."

Sara frowns, trying to rub the sleep from her eyes. There's one muddled question at the forefront of her thoughts, but there's an edge in his gaze that tells her not to ask.

To *trust* him.

Her chest tightens, a thread of fear winding around her heart. Nodding, she pulls the covers back and stands. Seth's eyes flit over her Santa themed pajamas with a hint of a laugh hiding at the corner of his mouth, but makes no comment. It's his silence that makes Sara's heart race as she follows him, quietly, out of her room.

Her father's on the back porch, which isn't all that unusual, but the open expression on his face *is*. She takes another quiet step closer and is alarmed to see a wetness to his cheeks. Then she registers his voice, low and deep, filtering through the cracked kitchen window, and stills.

"—old bat, and I blamed you for a whole lot of shit you weren't really responsible for, but I bet you're laughing up there now. Aren't you? How many times did you tell me, Gertie?" He looks at the unopened beer in his hands, thumb picking at the label. "How many damn times, and I still didn't listen." He sighs, a large hand running over his face as he looks across the horizon.

Sara feels her heart seize at the mention of her grandmother's name; a still healing wound scraped raw.

"I'm losing her. Just like you said I would. Have been for a long time, now, if we're being honest. I used to blame you for it—for taking her all the time. Hard to compete against real food and cookies, you know? It was an easy excuse. I know that now. You've only been gone a short time and I'm already seeing it. No one but myself to blame, though. Ain't that right?" He laughs, the sound strangled and wet, and presses his temple against the glass bottle in his grip. "Oh, Gertie. I've gone and fucked it all up."

His face is hidden from her, but Sara can see the way his shoulders shake—hear the soft gasping between hiccuped breaths. She's only ever seen him cry one other time in her life; a week after her mother left them and it became clear she wasn't coming back. It was late—hours past the time she should have fallen asleep. He had thrown his empty beer bottle down the driveway, screaming curses until he became hoarse. Sara watched from the window, frozen and terrified, as he sank to his knees, buried his face in his hands, and sobbed.

This is different. There's no anger in him tonight, no broken bottles, only resignation. Sara quietly slips away, drifting down the hall with her heart in her throat and an unsteadiness in her feet.

When she curls back up in her childhood bed, quilt pulled up to her chin, she whispers into the darkness. "Does it even matter?" Is being sorry enough, is *loving* her enough, when all her father's given her the past sixteen years are bruised memories?

"Yes," Seth says, voice soft.

Sara swallows, eyes tracing the slanted shadow of the blinds on the wall. Her father left the front porch light on. "He's never going to stop drinking." Because she knows, at the end of the day, that's the biggest thing standing between them. His anger—all the hurt that stems from it—is the symptom and not the disease. There's no filter when there's alcohol in his system; no empathy to rein him in from selfishness. Perhaps, if he were to stop—

No.

She won't let herself go down that road of what-ifs and maybes. He'll never quit, not long term, because he'll never bother to really *try*. Because, at the end of the day, that's the kind of person her father is: someone who will complain about everything being wrong but never step up to help make it right.

Seth sits on the foot of the bed. It's perturbing to see him perched there, but not feel his weight dipping the mattress. "No. I rather suspect he won't." He meets her eyes, sympathy in his gaze. "I'm sorry. I thought—" he cuts off with a shadowed laugh. "No, I suppose I wasn't thinking at all. Perhaps you're right. Perhaps it doesn't matter."

Sara curls into her pillow, thinking of the way her father's tears shone under the porch light and feels her chest tighten. Her father loves her enough to recognize the rift he's sown over the years, but not enough to fix it. Sara can't decide if that makes it better or worse.

She swallows thickly, gravel in her throat. Eyes burning, she blinks away the threat of tears and rolls over to face the wall. Her old country music  poster, a remnant from her childhood, stares back at her with faded ink and curling edges. She used to listen to that album on repeat, wishing the happy songs resonated more than the sad ones.

"It matters," she whispers, voice cracking. "Just not enough."

"Fathers can be a right piece of work, I'm afraid. If it's any consolation, you're far from being the first person with daddy issues—certainly not the last."

There's a bitter edge to his tone that catches her attention. When she looks over her shoulder, he is staring through the slots in the blinds with a pensive frown. "Was yours?"

Seth turns to her, mouth twisting into a sneer. "A piece of work? Without question." He shrugs. "Though, I suppose it's unfair to complain, times being so different and all. I rather suspect you'd be hard pressed to find more legitimately happy families than miserable ones."

She sits up, back resting against the headboard and hugging her pillow to her chest. "You never talk about it." At his curious glance, she adds, "Your life before."

There's an almost imperceptible stiffening of his shoulders, but his expression remains neutral. "It's a long time gone. Hardly worth your time."

She doesn't believe that for a second, but the fact that he can say it means he *does*. Sara can't help but wonder if that's a reflection of his past or *her*. Either way, it coaxes a pang from her heart. Suddenly, it feels important that she know. "Will you tell me anyway?"

He hesitates. "Certainly, but... do you really wish me to? Truly?"

"Does that really surprise you?"

"Yes," he says, softly but without a hint of doubt. The tightness in Sara's chest grows, an aching pain. Seth must catch her flinch, because his expression changes into one of awkward embarrassment —hands sinking into his pockets. "It's only, well, no one has ever *asked*."

"Oh," she breathes, but the pressure in her chest doesn't lessen. If anything, it feels heavier. How could she be the only one, in all those hundreds of years, who cared enough to want to know? "Well, I *am*. And, you know, if you're ok with it, I'd like to hear about it."

He drags in a shaky breath, pulling his hands from the confines of his pockets and leaning against her dresser. "Very well then. Ask away."

She falters. "But if I ask, you'll *have* to answer."

Seth shrugs. "If you don't, I'll have no direction to begin."

Sara takes comfort in the relaxed line of his shoulders, the openly curious tilt of his chin. If their roles were reversed, she would be terrified, but Seth almost seems... eager. Still, she makes a point to keep her questions open enough for him to escape. "Did you have any siblings?"

"Unfortunately," he sneers. "Two older brothers. Both of them were utter pillocks." Glancing at her, seeing her awkward confusion, he rolls his eyes. "Idiots?"

"Oh." She shifts, picking at the seam of her pillowcase. "You didn't like having siblings?"

"Far from it," he glowers. "They were both over a decade my senior. By the time I came into the picture, our dear Father was already grooming them to be as heartless as he was. Carry on the family legacy and all that rot."

"Which was?"

Seth waves a flippant hand. "Managing the estate, overtaxing the tenants, making examples of the ones unable to pay. They were nothing but numbers on a page to him." His eyes harden, a sneer curling his mouth. "God forbid he see a person in the face of a peasant."

"So, regular grade-A asshole?"

"Precisely."

"And your brothers were the same way?"

"Worse," he says, the word spat with a level of contempt that surprises her. "Youth made them more ambitious."

Sara leans forward, chin resting on the end of her pillow as she processes what he's told her. She frowns. "But what about you?"

"What about me?"

"Your dad didn't want to teach you the family business?"

Seth laughs, the sound as bitter as it is harsh. "Goodness, no. I was the third son. Hardly worth the time when he already had two strapping young men ready to take over."

There's only one other family member she can think to ask about, but it takes her a moment to gather the courage. Sara thinks of her mother's red sedan, the dust and gravel it kicked up behind it. Sometimes she can almost taste it on her tongue, still choke on it. Her voice is little more than a hoarse murmur when she brings herself to ask, "What about your mother?"

His expression softens, his adoration so vivid it nearly makes her sick with envy. "Mother was… she was the only good thing in that family. My light. She was a poet, you know, and a fine one at that. Though no one ever cared to know it."

He goes quiet, soft smile dimming until it resembles more of a grimace. There's an old pain there, a regret, hiding in the furrow of his brow and the glassiness of his eyes. "I watched over her. From the day I became, well, *this*, to the day she died. I watched her suffer without me. Listened to her pray."

Sara's heart gives a sympathetic twinge. "Why didn't you answer?"

"I tried." His voice is level, but there's a reserved sort of agony tucked around the edges. A pain so deep, that even centuries worth of time were unsuccessful in completely smoothing the barbs. "Her only prayer was for my return. And, for however many times I tried, the magic refused to take."

Sara sucks in a breath, hands fisting in her pillow. Grief fills her, rising like floodwater the longer his words sit between them. Sorry is too soft a word, but she can't find any others, so she sits—lips parted around an apology she can't string together and her eyes burning with a sadness that isn't her own. "Seth…"

His hands are in his pockets again, fingers fiddling with the chain of his watch. "Don't fret over it, Princess. It was a long time ago."

That doesn't mean it ever stopped hurting, though, and in that moment—with the porch light casting slotted patterns across the room—Sara can almost see her pain reflected in his own.

Her mother abandoned her.

He abandoned his mother.

A mirrored image. Opposite, but somehow twisted into a pain so similar it *hurts*.

"What was her name?" Suddenly she needs to know. She'll never have a face for her, but she can have this. She can have a name.

For the first time in their entire conversation, there's a flash of hesitation before he laughs—breathy and full of secrets she doesn't understand. An inside joke she hasn't been privy to, not until he answers. "Sarah," he breathes. "Her name was Sarah."

His eyes catch hers, his smirk widening. "*With* an 'h'. Naturally."

# CHAPTER TWENTY-FIVE

I  FEELS LIKE WINTER BREAK ENDS FASTER THAN IT SHOULD (IT ALWAYS
does). The weeks go by in a blur of brightly colored paper and
peppermint until she looks at the date and realizes she only has four
days until classes start up again. Somehow, dread doesn't follow the
discovery.

There's an eagerness buzzing beneath her skin—excitement. It's
her last semester and she'll get to focus purely on her photography
classes. It's enough to make her palms itch in anticipation. Especially
after celebrating Jen's graduation a few days ago with board games
and alcohol. Not for the first time, Sara almost wishes she would
have followed in her friend's footsteps and just taken the extra
classes her previous semesters.

She's searching her fridge for something to eat when her phone
rings in her back pocket. Sara's relieved that it's Jen and not another
telemarketer. She perches the phone between her cheek and shoulder. "Hey, what's up?"

"Hey, bestie! What are you up to?"

"It's a trap," Seth says from his chair. He doesn't even bother to
look up from the television.

Sara shoots him a glare, fingers drumming on the fridge door as she holds it open. "Staring at the inside of my fridge and wondering if I'm going to eat cereal for dinner," Sara says, eyes flitting past the quart of milk and frowning at the suspiciously empty space beyond it. She wishes she was joking.

From his chair, Seth repeats, "It's a *trap*," a split second before Jen answers with, "We're going shopping."

Sara stifles a groan, closing the fridge door. Shopping with Jen was like running a marathon—she wouldn't be content until she searched every aisle, in every store, in the immediate area. "Why?"

"I have nothing to wear for my bachelorette party," Jen says, voice flirting on the edge of a whine. "Please, please, please come with me to find something?"

Sara knows, without a doubt, there's probably at least a dozen dresses stashed away in her best friend's closet that would be perfectly suited for a night out, but she bites her tongue. It's a special night, and while Sara doesn't feel the need to buy something new, she has no intention of disappointing Jen, either. "No more than five stores," she says.

"Six."

Sara recalls how many bridal shops they went to in search of a wedding dress and cringes. "Jen…"

"I have it all planned out this time, I swear! Six stores. All in the mall. That's *it*."

"When?"

On the line, Jen's voice turns sheepish. "… Now?"

She really doesn't want to go anywhere today, but a quick glance around her house gives her no viable reasons to say no. Sara sighs. "… Can we eat first?"

Jen laughs. Sara imagines her doing a victory dance. "Yeah, girl. We can eat first."

"Alright, but only because I love you."

"Yes! Ok, we'll be there to pick you up in about ten!"

Sara's heart drops. "We?"

"Yeah, Lisa and Mary are coming too!"

As pleasant as Mary's company is (especially with all the baby brother stories she loves to share about Miles) somehow it still can't make up for the absolute dread of having Lisa involved. Sara forces a smile, hoping it will make her sound more convincing when she says, "Sounds great."

From his chair, Seth chuckles—eyes dancing. "I did warn you."

THE MALL IS CROWDED, FULL OF PEOPLE DOING RETURNS AND EXCHANGES for their Christmas gifts. Sara thought Seth would follow her, but looking over the sea of bodies, she understands why he didn't bother to get out of his chair. She also understands his amusement when he told her to 'have fun.'

They've only made it through two stores, but Lisa's already ditching them for the high end retailers at the other end of the mall. Sara can't say she's angry about it (the less time she spends with Lisa, the better) but Mary makes no effort to hide her disapproval.

Shaking her head, braids tied back, she watches the blonde walk away until the crowd swallows her up. "That girl is something else."

Jen waves it off, the way she always does—an extra dose of chipper to help hide the disappointment. "It's fine. Really, I don't mind."

Sara and Mary share a look.

It's not fine at all.

Especially since Sara knows this is a long repeating pattern that's been going on since childhood. Lisa's always been selfish, and Jen has always been too forgiving to call her out on it. Sometimes Sara wonders if Jen would still bother trying if they weren't cousins.

Mary says nothing, but her lips purse as if she's tasted something sour. Sara has no doubt that she'll be sharing the details with Miles later. If anyone hates how Lisa walks all over Jen as much as Sara, it's him.

They make their way into the third store, their hands sliding the hangers and their eyes flitting over the dresses with a scrutinizing eye. A lot of it is more prom than club attire—full length adorned with incandescent beads and sequins—but they find some shorter ones, too.

"What about this one?" Jen asks, holding up a strapless dress.

Sara only needs one look at the neckline to dismiss it. "I don't have the boobs to hold that up."

"Like I do?" Jen presses it into her hands, putting on a mock serious face. "Tape is our friend."

Sara puts it back on the rack. "*No.*"

From another rack, Mary hums. "Word to the wise: don't trust tape at a bachelorette party. Alcohol and gravity are not friends."

Jen pauses, chin tilted as she considered. "Good point. Straps then."

They each pull a handful, the fabric draped over their arms as they take turns using the fitting room. The retailer is a small one, the two fitting rooms covered only by an emerald curtain in place of a door. One is already taken by a pair of teenagers prom dress shopping.

Mary tries on three, but none of them impress her. Sara suspects she's still thinking about the slinky gold one she tried on and liked at the first store. She's lost track of how many Jen has tried on (seven, maybe?) but Sara knows she won't be satisfied enough to choose any of them until they've scoured the racks of all six stores.

Sara takes in her one pick, despite knowing it probably won't be going home with her. She (and her bank account) will be far from heartbroken if she leaves empty handed, but it's still fun to try on.

It's nice—emerald green with a silhouette that gives the illusion of more curves than she actually has. Giving herself one last look in the mirror, Sara opens the stall door and is instantly greeted by both Jen and Mary's approval. However, before she can fully bask in their praises, she spots his familiar face behind them.

Seth gifts her with his usual crooked smirk, a finger to his lips.

"Uh, Sara?" Jen says, startling her out of her stupor. Both her and Mary look over their shoulders and back, trying to find what caught her attention. "What are you staring at?"

Sara fumbles for an excuse. "Oh. I, well—"

Seth taps on one of the hangers on the rack beside him, eyes dancing. "Try this one, Princess."

She latches onto the excuse, walking past her confused companions to pull the dress from the rack. An embarrassed flush is threatening to spill over her cheeks, but she tries her best to sound convincing. It's a struggle to keep her eyes on the black lace in her hands instead of Seth's infuriatingly amused expression. "Sorry, this dress just caught my eye, is all."

Mary frowns. "Honey, you passed that one up a good three times."

Brows furrowing, Jen tilts her head. "Because it's lace. You hate lace. You've *always* hated lace."

If she could manage it without making herself look even crazier, she would pin Seth with a withering glare. As it is, she holds the dress up so she has an excuse to meet his eyes just past the dress's neckline.

He raises a brow. "A little trust wouldn't be remiss. Besides, what have you to lose?"

It's bad enough that he's right, but the fact that he *knows it* is insufferable. "I don't know, maybe I just need to give lace another try?"

Jen looks at her like she's grown a second head. "First your hair, and now lace? Who are you and what have you done with my best friend?"

Sara rolls her eyes and takes the dress back into the dressing room to take a closer look without an audience. To be fair, it's not *all* lace—just the high neckline and the capped sleeves. The bottom half is a softer, stretchier material that feels like it could potentially be comfortable.

Still, Jen's not wrong about her usual distaste for lace.

With a silent groan, she slips it on—fingers fumbling with the button at the back of her neck before she turns to the skinny piece of mirror they've fit on the dressing room wall.

She stares.

From the front, the dress is modest. Completely covering her chest and capping her shoulders while still being form fitting. The extra fabric across her front seems to highlight the long expanse of her legs (though the effect is slightly ruined by her pink socks). She turns, admiring the way the low V accentuates the line of her spine, and gives a breathy laugh.

Leave it to Seth to find the one dress that would change her opinion on lace.

THE BASS HITS DEEP, AN ECHO OVER HER HEART; LYRICS SPRINGING FROM her lips half a beat late. Sweat makes her hair stick to the back of her neck, and in some distant part of her, she's thankful she cut it short. The alcohol is buzzing under her skin, making her lightheaded and warm. The dress hugs her, a second skin that stretches with every twist of her hips.

It's all flashing lights and music, sweat rolling between her shoulder blades and panting, humid breath. Jen and Mary dance beside her, looking way more balanced than she is and far less out of breath. Sara's legs ache, her feet begging her to strip out of her stilettos and go barefoot. It would be a lot more tempting if she couldn't feel her soles sticking to the concrete floor with every step. Still, with every song the pain in her calves and arches becomes more persistent, until it becomes enough for her to tap the bride-to-be on the shoulder and shout over the music, "I'm gonna go rest for a sec!"

Jen nods, shouting back, "Okay!" Then her arms are around Sara's neck, her lips pressing against her cheek in a clumsy kiss. "I love you!"

Sara laughs, because drunk Jen loves everyone. "Love you, too! I'll be back!" She has to push her way through the crowd to get to the outskirts, but the air already feels a little less thin. There are no available chairs, but there's an empty corner that calls to her like a siren.

She leans against the wall, the brick shockingly cool against her back in comparison to the humidity in the room, and catches her breath. Distantly, in the part of her brain that's still pretending sobriety, she realizes she's not the only one taking a break from the crowd. Her head lolls, eyes taking a moment to focus enough to recognize that the man looking back at her—brows raised—is a familiar one. "You're here," she blurts.

His lips quirk. "And you're intoxicated."

Sara doesn't bother denying it.

His hands busy themselves, straightening his sleeves. "The music is barbarically loud. I can't say I see the appeal."

Watching the way his fingers fiddle with his cuff, a muddled thought breaks through the fog. "Were you watching me?"

He stills, mouth twisting into a sardonic smile. "Yes," he hisses. "And even as addled as you are, I'm sure you can see how unfairly you phrased that."

Frowning, she tries to understand, but his words slip away faster than she can interpret them. "Ok."

Seth's brows arch, his foul mood disappearing nearly as quickly as it came. "My, no argument?" His eyes look over her, lips curling into a teasing smile. "Now I'm certain that last round of tequila has hit."

Sara blanches, the burn in her throat still as present as the warmth lingering behind her ribs. "God, I hate tequila."

"Yes, you looked right miserable choking it down," he says, chuckling. "I suspect it would be in your best interest to start drinking something *without* warnings on the label. The bride-to-be doesn't appear to be slowing down at all."

Nodding, Sara finds Jen still dancing her heart out in the crowd. "This was always more her scene."

"It shows. She's quite adept at—what is it you call it? Dropping it like it's hot?"

Sara snorts on a laugh, hand covering her smile. "Please, stop."

"What, precisely, am I stopping?"

"Trying to sound cool," she teases.

Hand splayed over his heart, he puts on a mask of offense. "Don't be salty because I'm out here high key slaying your ridiculous vernacular."

"Oh my *god*," she laughs, hiding her face in her hands.

He grins. "I believe you call that a *clap back*."

"Stop."

"Are you… *shook*?"

"Please, please stop. Millennial slang isn't for people over a hundred."

Seth shrugs, his smile refusing to dim. "You know, depending on how you choose to look at it, I'm only four years your elder."

Sara starts, her amusement fading into surprise as her buzzed brain finally catches up to the math. "You're twenty-six?!"

"I'm not sure if your response to that should invoke pride or if I should feel insulted."

"No, it's just, you seem older is all." Her words catch up to her, and she shakes her head. "I mean, obviously you *are* older. I just— ugh. You know what I mean."

"Despite your blabbering, somehow I do."

The alcohol is still making her head fuzzy; bolstering her courage and trampling her reservations. She stares at him—the smooth skin of his cheek, the absence of wrinkles and crow's feet lining his face— and feels foolish. Of course he isn't much older.

But then she meets his eyes, remembers the depth of them, and feels her pulse quicken. It's his eyes that give him away.

He tilts his head, eyes narrowing. "You *are* aware that you're staring?"

Mostly, but she's really too tipsy to care. "I've been getting a lot of compliments on my dress."

He huffs on a laugh—because of the sudden change in topic or the way some of her vowels slur, she can't be sure. "I have impeccable taste," he hums, hands disappearing into his pockets.

She frowns. "You know, there's something I can't figure out."

"Oh?"

"Well, you couldn't see it on the rack. And I know for a fact I never pulled it out to give it a better look." Her gaze slides to his, fingers playing with the lace at her collar. "I can't figure out how you knew to pick it."

In their corner, the lighting is dim at best, but she swears she sees the muscles in this throat work around a swallow. "Yes, quite the mystery."

She bites her lip, smiling. "Right? It was almost like you had scoped the place out before we got there." Her eyes find his. "But that would be ridiculous."

He shifts, looking away. "Ridiculous. Definitely ridiculous," he mutters, so low Sara barely catches the words.

She leans back, head tipping upward as she sighs. The brick is cool against her flushed skin, the club lights flashing behind her eyelids as she wills the world to slow down for just this one moment.

"It looks lovely on you, by the way."

She opens her eyes, head turning to look at him. He's staring out over the dance floor, expression neutral. For a moment, she wonders if he never said anything at all—if she imagined it. Then he meets her gaze in a fleeting glance, before darting away, and Sara knows she heard him correctly.

"Thank you," she says, voice softer than it should be considering their surroundings. It's only his subtle nod, the way his hands fidget in his pockets, that assures her that he heard. There's something between them—so thick she feels like she could almost reach out and touch it—but with the alcohol blurring the edges of her thoughts she can't figure out a name for it.

Sara's lips part, but before she can find the words, she hears Jen shouting her name and weaving her way through the crowd.

"Sara! Come on! It's our *jam*, girl!" Jen grabs her hand, pulling her back into the fray of people. Sara only has time to glance behind her once, but the sight of him—leaning casually against the brick with his eyes dark and his lips tipped into a soft smile—haunts her for the rest of the night.

# CHAPTER TWENTY-SIX

Sara loves her classes.

Of course, that might be the misery from the previous semester casting an extra glow to the current one. Still, she can find nothing but enthusiasm for the assignments (even though it's filling up her days faster than she ever imagined). She had always preferred land-scape photography over anything else—the scenery always seems a lot easier to deal with than people—but most of the projects this final semester are done within the studio.

Which, on one hand, at least means she isn't *having* to scout out settings. Unfortunately, it also means she has to deal with managing all the little things nature usually provides for her—lightings, back-drops, etc.

It takes up more time than she expected, keeping her busy when helping Jen with wedding preparations doesn't. She does manage to combine the two when she offers to take some studio portraits of Jen in her wedding dress (she can safely say that working with models is her least favorite thing about her classes, so when she can do her assignment with friends it's an instant win in Sara's book).

Jen's enthusiasm helps.

The pictures come out beautifully—the red of her wedding dress is a perfect match for the color assignment—but after they've packed everything up and headed to the campus coffee shop, Jen's mood shifts.

Her friend's fingers tap against her purse as they stand in line, fast and without rhythm. Sara assumes it's just wedding jitters—they're only a week away now—and doesn't push it. Jen is nothing if not open, and Sara knows she'll share if the weight is too heavy.

They sit at the corner table, up against the window so they can watch the snow as they sip from their styrofoam mugs. The warmth of their bodies, so close, fogs up the glass.

"Look," Jen says, twisting her fingers in her lap, looking about as nervous as the time she fessed up to accidentally cracking Sara's camera lens three semesters ago. "There's something I need to tell you. And, I don't know, you're probably going to be mad, or upset, or—"

Sara stops her with a look. "Jen, you're my best friend. Whatever it is, I'll deal."

Jen visibly swallows, nodding. "Um, well. You know how we sent the Mclintock's an invitation to the wedding?"

Her fingers twitch, but Sara manages to keep from flinching at the surname. It's nothing she wasn't aware of. Even if the invite wasn't sent before David had his accident, Jen's father was close friends with David's, so it's hardly a surprise. When she speaks, her voice is still steady. "Yeah, why? Are you having second thoughts? Because I told you, I'm totally fine with his parents coming to—"

"David's coming too," she blurts.

Sara pales, heart hammering in her chest and stomach flipping violently. She's suddenly very glad she skipped breakfast, because there's a very real chance it would be coming back up if she hadn't. "Oh," she breathes, the single syllable is all her anxious mind can manage.

Jen's hands grasp her own over the table, face eager. "I didn't know until last night, I swear. And if it's going to be too hard on you, I will *totally* ask him not to come."

Sara shakes her head. "No. It's... it's ok. I'm just, uh, surprised. That's all." The way Jen stares at her—a frightening mixture of pity and understanding—makes her feel stripped bare. She knows it's supposed to be supportive, knows the hands covering her own are trying to offer comfort, but right now all Sara feels is *trapped*.

There's no doubt in her mind that Jen would ask David to stay away for her sake, but she would hate every second of that phone call. Jen has always been the last person to risk hurting someone's feelings. Right now, her empathy feels like both a blessing and a curse, because Sara wants nothing to do with this decision.

If she asks Jen to disinvite him, it'll be at her friend's expense. David—God, as much as she wants to believe him to be the same, he just *isn't*. He's changed. The man that tore her down in the hospital room, that pounded on her door after midnight... how would he react if Jen told him not to come?

Sara licks her lips, gathers her courage, and offers the most convincing smile she can muster. "I'll be fine. It's not a big deal."

⌒⌒⌒

"OF COURSE IT'S A BIG DEAL," SETH SNAPS. "CALL HER, THIS INSTANT."

Sara doesn't look up, her voice muffled by the pillow she's burrowed her face in. She hasn't decided if she's done screaming. "She has enough on her plate."

"Yes, and she'll likely have more if she lets this happen. *Call her.*"

She pulls away from the pillow, glaring. "And say what?" she groans. "That the thought of my ex being in the same room for an evening makes me a little uncomfortable?" She runs a hand through her hair, wincing when her fingers snag on a tangle.

"A little uncomfortable," he echoes, disbelief making his voice dip low. "In what world would one describe 'fear for my safety' as 'a little uncomfortable'?"

Sara lowers her eyes, fingers fiddling with the hem of her pajama sleeve. She can feel the weight of his stare on her cheek, can pinpoint the exact moment he figures it out.

He stills; a looming shadow of disbelief. "You never told her."

She flinches, but hugs the pillow closer to her chest instead of denying it. "I didn't want her to worry."

"She *should* worry!" he seethes.

"It was only the one time—"

"It *wasn't*," he growls.

Sara stares, stomach dropping. "What are you talking about?"

Pacing, his steps are so violent she should hear the soles of his shoes slap against the floor, but each foot falls as painfully silent as the last. "I only have suspicions. I don't have any—"

"Seth." She stands, the pillow falling from her lap and onto the floor. "*What* are you talking about?"

He flinches, body stilling. "I saw him—just before Christmas. I believe he has been around far more than either of us realize. The odd calls, your car—"

"What about my car?"

He still won't look at her. "I suspect he may have poured water in your fuel tank."

Her stomach drops. Immediately, she thinks of the odd way he was acting weeks before—remembers his promise to tell her if something was worth worrying about—and feels her fear bow down to her fury. She stomps over to him, the sound of her feet making up for the silence of his. Sara doesn't stop until they're so close he *has* to look at her. "What is *wrong* with you?! How could you keep that from me?!"

"Because I don't have any proof!" he growls, eyes sharp—accusing. "How could I possibly come to you with my suspicions without it? You, who place your precious David on a pedestal of false hopes?"

"I never—"

"Don't," he bites, eyes closed and lips twisted. "Do *not* stand there and lie. Not when I'm denied the luxury of doing the same." He exhales sharply, his hands flexing sporadically at his sides. When he opens his eyes, they're alight with a bitterness that is more fire than frost. Sara wonders how long that flame has been burning.

She swallows down the urge to defend herself, tucks it behind the twinge of pain his accusations stir. "I would have listened," she says, words soft but gaze firm.

He breathes a laugh, but it's sharp at the edges. The heat in his gaze cools, the tension in his body softening into resignation. "You won't even allow yourself to admit he's *gone*, Sara."

It's a blow, as physical as words could ever hope to be, and made all the more painful because *he's not wrong*. Her lips part, but her voice is stuck somewhere between the lancing pain in her heart and the tightness in her throat.

Seth shakes his head. Somehow, the blank expression he wears still can't hide his disappointment. "I have no proof," he repeats, a soft murmur. "But I would not have you endangering yourself if my suspicions prove correct."

Sara sits, her hands threading through her hair and her palms pressed against her temples. "If Jen tells him not to come, he probably will anyway. She—I can't let this ruin their wedding. I can't."

"It is just a day—"

"No," she says, meeting his eyes and begging him to understand. "It's *their* day. One they're going to look back on forever and I want —" she sucks in a calming breath, wets her lips. "I *want* it to be happy. They deserve that."

"I don't disagree," he murmurs, kneeling down in front of her. His hands are flexing again, as if he's unsure of where to place them. They settle on his lap. "But you know as well as I do, what they would wish."

The smile she gives him is thin, weighed down by so much emotion she could almost choke on it. "I'll live."

# CHAPTER TWENTY-SEVEN

SETH WAS RIGHT.

It's a big deal.

She's jumpy, flinching every time someone enters the venue and simultaneously trying to look out the window and stand in front of the box fan so she doesn't walk down the aisle drenched in sweat. Jen keeps watching her, painted lips pursed with worry when they should be smiling *because it's her wedding day*.

Sara stays away from the window after that, but she can't help the nervous energy buzzing beneath her skin. When one of the bridesmaids—Miles' other sister, Kate—offers her a croissant, she takes it only because she knows it'll draw the bride's attention if she doesn't. She nibbles at the flaky crust, each tiny bite tastes like chalk, her throat is so dry. It feels heavy, leaden, when it hits her stomach, but she manages to force down half.

Jen keeps watching from the corner of her eye. Sara hides behind strained smiles, until it's finally time for the ceremony to begin.

When the music starts and she leads the rest of the bridal party down the aisle, she forces herself not to look at the sea of faces on either side. Instead, she keeps her chin high and a smile in place, and stares straight ahead and offers Miles as genuine a smile as she can manage. He returns it with a nod, his hands clasped tightly in front of him. There's no nervous edge in his gaze, only a giddy excitement that Sara would find absolutely adorable if her own heart wasn't on the verge of beating out of her chest.

When she finds her marker and turns toward the crowd, she finds safety in the arched doorway where Jen is still waiting for the song to change. She looks absolutely beautiful in her red gown, the satin material hugging her body before flaring at the hip. Sara tries to concentrate on Jen's happiness, lets her best friend's beaming smile act as a balm for her frayed nerves.

By the time Jen makes it to the altar, Sara's trembling, near faint from the strain, when Seth appears at her elbow. Sara has more than half a year's worth of practice by now, but it still takes everything she has not to look away from the bride and groom. He must know, because he moves into her line of sight with purpose—putting himself between her and the ceremony so she can see his face. His expression is gentle, sympathetic.

"He's not here, Princess," he says, eyes soft. "You're safe."

A small, hiccuped breath escapes her, but it gets swallowed up by the cheering of the crowd. Seth steps aside, and Sara catches the tail end of her best friends' first kiss as husband and wife. The relief she feels is so great, she can't even be angry about missing it.

SARA'S NOT SURE IF IT'S THE LINGERING ANXIETY OR THE MOTHER-OF-the-bride that drives her to the bar immediately after the bridal party finishes with the photographer (both, it's definitely both). Regardless, she's quickly making good on the fully stocked bar Miles and Jen paid for.

She's really liking the red cocktail Jen picked out—she's pretty sure it's pomegranate she's tasting underneath the bite of vodka. Giving the bartender a beaming smile, she takes her (fourth?) glass from him before navigating through the sea of bodies surrounding the bar. Miles and Jen are still busy doing their photos, and everyone else already seems too tied up in conversations she's probably too drunk to follow anyways. She makes her way to the back door—propped open to let some of the heat out from the hundreds of bodies crammed into the room—and slips outside.

The air is freezing, snow reflecting the moon's glow with a gentleness that borders on peaceful. Sara wraps her arm around her waist while the other hand lifts her drink to her lips. She forgot her shawl inside... somewhere. The cold bites at the exposed skin of her arms and neck, but she's glad Jen at least chose bridesmaid dresses with a halter so her chest could escape the worst of it.

Sara sees him before he speaks, which is unusual actually. Perhaps he's decided she's had enough surprises for today. "Lovely ceremony," he says, leaning against the railing across from her. The leather of his shoes almost touches the pink satin hem of her dress. "Care to place a bet on how long the ceremonial love tree survives?"

Sara stares at him, trying to repeat his words in her head and failing. "What?"

He looks at her—a dawning realization lighting his eyes. "You're *pissed*."

Sara frowns, raising her cocktail and correcting him. "Excuse you, I'm a *happy* drunk."

"Bloody American vernacular." He stands in front of her, bending until he's closer to her eye level and makes a tally on his fingers. "Sloshed. Smashed. Wasted. Pick your favorite, but you are undeniably *drunk*."

"It's a party! You're s'pose to drink at parties."

"It's a *wedding*," he hisses back, looking over both shoulders as if checking to see if they were still alone. "And you're the maid of honor!"

A giggle escapes her. "You're funny."

"And you're bloody well screwed. Did you forget you have a speech to deliver?"

Sara pales. Seth curses.

"WE COME ON THIS DAY," SETH DRONES, A STEP BEHIND HER, "TO celebrate the joining of two wonderful people."

Sara raises her glass of champagne, all too aware of the crowd of eyes watching and forces a smile through her nausea. "We come on this day, to celebrate the joining of two wonderful people."

She repeats his every word faithfully, copying his every intone. It's not until she's about halfway through, that she realizes the speech she's giving is the very same one she has written on fancy stationery in the bridal suite. She wonders, drunkenly, how he managed to memorize it.

When she finishes, raising her glass and calling for a toast, the crowd follows suit and cheers. Sara takes the smallest sip out of respect (and perhaps a little superstition) for the couple. She never was a fan of champagne.

WHEN SHE FINALLY GETS HOME, SHE BARELY GETS HER HEELS OFF AND her dress replaced with an oversized t-shirt before collapsing into bed.

"Thanks. You know, for helping," she murmurs into her pillow. She can feel her mascara catching on the cotton. She should probably wash her face, but she can't summon the motivation. Her body—her eyelids—feel so heavy, she can't bring herself to look at him. "Was sorta nice of you."

He scoffs, but the sound is soft—more affectionate than anything. "Oh dear, is my devilish reputation suffering? Shall I tell you, my reasons were purely selfish and I merely couldn't stand the thought of suffering such second-hand embarrassment?"

"Seth," she groans, "Shut up now."

A soft chuckle. "Very well, Princess."

A few moments, a hair's breadth away from her subconscious wading into sleep, and a thought distracts her. A nagging little thing she can't bring herself to leave alone. "What did you do?" she mumbles, forcing her eyes open.

It's too dark for her to see much more than the shadowy outline of her dresser, but (somehow) she knows he's still there. She can feel him, hovering just outside of her vision.

He takes too long to answer, and when he does, it's too vague to be completely honest. "Nothing you need to concern yourself over. Now go to sleep, Sara. God knows you'll need it to face the hangover you'll be feeling tomorrow."

She forces herself to sit up with a groan. Even with the pounding headache at her temples, and the fuzzy feeling on her tongue, she's sober enough now to know this is important. Knows it with the same certainty that his answer is complete bullshit. He's a shadow at the foot of her bed, but there's just enough light for her to make out his expression—blank.

The same neutral mask he always wears when he wants something hidden.

She glares at him. "What did you *do*?"

"There... might have been an unfortunate incident in regards to the family dog."

Sara thinks of the floppy-eared basset hound David used to fuss over. The one that was so old he could barely hear. "Freddie?" The implication dawns, and the fatigue evaporates under her horror. "Oh my—*what did you do*?!"

Seth raises his hands in... surrender? Mercy? Sara's past caring she's so livid. "He's unharmed! He just got... conveniently lost."

"You lost their dog?!"

"Only temporarily."

She falls back into her bed with a groan, face in her hands. "I can't believe you."

"Well, I'm terribly sorry if you don't approve of my methods, but it *worked*."

Sara peeks at him between her fingers, not entirely surprised to find him looking completely unrepentant. "Why?" she murmurs.

"Well, it's not like I could distract them myself, could I?"

She shakes her head. "No, I mean, why'd you do it. I could have handled it."

"Maybe," he says, voice soft in the dark. She wishes she could see his face; read his expression. "But you shouldn't have to."

Curling onto her side, a pillow hugged to her chest, Sara murmurs, "You're right." Her eyes are so heavy, it feels like lashes are covered in lead instead of mascara. "But neither should you."

If he replies, the words are lost between them—buried in the darkness behind her eyelids and the unconscious pull of sleep.

THERE'S A TEXT WAITING FOR HER WHEN SHE WAKES—THE NUMBER unknown, the message vague enough to feel threatening.

*Hope you had fun.*

Sara deletes the message, blocks the number, and tries to calm the racing of her heart.

She doesn't tell Seth.

# CHAPTER TWENTY-EIGHT

SHE CONTINUES TO GET PHONE CALLS FROM STRANGE NUMBERS, BUT SHE doesn't receive any more texts. Sara tells herself it's fine. If—*if*—it's David on the other line, he hasn't made any move to escalate things. The calls are no more frequent than what they were before, and the days and times are just as random. Months go by, but David doesn't come knocking on her door again.

Sara's done worrying about it, but she knows Seth isn't (even if he won't admit it).

The rest of the semester sweeps by in a blur of camera flashes and shutter clicks. Her first love is, and always will be, landscape photography, but she finds little ways to make the portraiture assignments her own. She takes the lines of the model's bodies and makes valleys out of waists and mountains from their shoulder blades. She dresses one model in white tulle, soft and nearly transparent, and adjusts the settings until the image captured is as much fog rolling over the fields as a beautiful woman.

Seth always stays out of her way as she works, but his presence is always there—a quiet shadow at the edges of her vision. Sometimes she catches a strange smile on his lips. It's soft, gentle in ways that look out of place when he's hiding in the dark corners of the room.

It's only when he comments on her finished portfolio, that same smile dancing at the corners of his mouth, as he tells her she's done well, that she realizes it's *pride*.

Her answering grin is warm and a little teary, but it's honest. She hopes he can read the 'thank you' tucked at the edges.

When she finally walks across the stage with a rolled up piece of parchment symbolizing her diploma in her hand, she looks across the auditorium and finds his face in the crowd first.

"WHERE DO YOU GO?" SHE ASKS WHILE HER HANDS ARE BUSY FIDDLING with the height of the tripod.

It's been almost two weeks since she graduated, full of lazy mornings and marathoning Seth's newest tv obsession (a historical fantasy she actually finds herself liking as much as he does), but it feels good to be outside again. It feels even better to bring her camera and take some photos just for the love of it and not because there's an assignment due.

Her question is as out of the blue as the sky, but it's been on her mind for a while now, so when she feels his gaze at her back, it's the first thing to come to mind.

"Pardon?"

She looks up from her viewfinder, tracing his frown with her eyes. The abandoned stretch of railroad tracks, all stubborn weeds and rust, behind him is a sharp contrast to the clean lines of his suit. "When you disappear. Where do you go?"

"Oh." His frown softens into curiosity—as if he's surprised she even thought to ask. "Wherever else I'd like to be, I suppose. There's no specific place."

"So you can just… snap your fingers and be in Paris?"

A smile teases his lips. "It's a touch more complicated than that, but yes. In theory," he hums. "I'm rather more limited at the moment."

"Why?"

He hesitates, long enough to feed her curiosity. "I'm... tied to you. I can only go so far."

"Wait. Really?" Suddenly, she thinks of all those times she yelled at him for sitting in on her classes. Did he really have nowhere else to go? "How far?"

"I can reach most of the city provided you're home."

She can't deny she's relieved. The thought of him having to shadow her every footstep, blinking behind corners and closed doors, is a sad one. "So when you're not, uh, *tied* to someone. You can go anywhere?"

"Technically, though not in a single jump. And it's bloody exhausting to be honest. I much prefer to fly. Do you know how comfortable the seats are in first class on international flights? That they don't make them all that way is criminal."

"Really?" she asks, a smile in her voice. "You have magic powers that can take you anywhere in a couple of snaps and you're hitching rides on planes?"

"I told you, the seats are comfortable. Besides," he looks up at the sky, a wistful smile curling his mouth. "The view is much more pleasant."

"I've only flown a couple times," she admits. "When I was little, we went to visit Dad's parents in Georgia once or twice before they passed away."

"It's invigorating. The fact that you can fly at all... people take the miracle of it for granted." He turns to her, eyes soft. "The world is a big place, Sara. It would be a shame to live your life and only see a tiny corner of it."

Dropping her gaze, she picks at the leftover pink nail polish from graduation. Jen had insisted they get manicures together to celebrate. "It's not like I don't want to," she murmurs. "I wanted to go to the West Coast for college, but the prices..." She shakes her head, folding her knees up to her chest. "I could barely afford the in-state tuition *here*."

Seth studies her for a long, quiet moment before turning his attention back to the sky. "You'll have the opportunity and I'll be here to ensure you take it. You are meant for bigger things."

Her laugh is breathy, a knot she wasn't even aware of loosening in her chest. She remembers how Oma's friend, Janice, had assured her of the same thing. "You don't think I'll end up a penniless want-to-be photographer?"

"I don't," he says, softly. It sounds like a promise, and with the way he looks at her—like he truly believes it—coaxes her into believing it. Then his smile turns teasing. "Not penniless anyway. There's always the casinos."

Groaning, she tosses a pebble at him. It passes through his middle without resistance. "You're terrible."

"Perhaps a little," he admits, but his grin is wide and unrepentant. Then a frown knits his brow. "You have a ladybird in your hair."

"A what?"

"A lady—blasted American butchering of the English language." He sighs, resigned. "I believe you call them lady*bugs.*"

Sara grunts, blindly inspecting her hair with careful fingers. "You call insects birds, but we're the ones that screwed up the language? If you ask me, I'd say we fixed it."

"Not bloody likely," he gripes. "And you're doing an abysmal job, honestly. At the rate you're going, you're going to crush the poor thing."

She drops her hands with a huff. "Well, would *you* like to do it then?"

"I would, in fact. Unfortunately, I have this rather pertinent handicap." He holds up his hands. "Ghost. Remember?"

"That doesn't stop you from petting Ansel," she grumbles.

"We have an agreement. He asks, I provide," he says, waving a hand flippantly before pointing at her head. "I strongly suspect that your ladybird won't share the sentiment. Besides, I doubt it can even see me."

"Ugh. Fine. Can you just—I don't know, show me where it is at least? I can't feel it, and I don't really like the idea of bug guts in my hair."

He stills, eyeing her strangely. "You... want me to touch your hair?"

That was not at all what she had in mind, but (actually) that would be a hell of a lot more helpful. "Yeah?"

She can visibly see him swallow and there is a jerkiness to his limbs that betrays his awkwardness. "Very well. Move your bumbling digits aside, then."

Folding her hands in her lap, she holds still as he moves to her side—just out of her peripheral vision. His fingers are gentle, coaxing, as he separates a lock of hair from the others. Sara fights the hitch in her breath.

"Your hand."

"What?"

She can hear his sigh. "Give me your hand."

Tentatively, she raises her right hand. The feel of his long, tapered fingers against her pulse (so terribly soft and yet incredibly intimate) nearly has her snatching it back, but his grip is gentle and guiding. Cool against her flushed, sun drenched skin.

He guides her fingers toward her crown, holding her still until Sara feels the tiny tickle of feet crawling over her fingertip.

"There we are," he murmurs, slowly lowering her hand until it hovers in front of her nose. "One ladybird."

Turning her head up to look up at him, she feels her hair slip through his fingers and struggles to withhold a shiver. There must be something in her wide-eyed expression, though, because his eyes are dark and hooded—lips soft and parted with an emotion Sara doesn't dare interpret.

It is nothing short of terrifying.

She licks her lips; tries to ignore the fluttering in her chest and *get ahold of herself already*. "Thank you."

"Of course," he breathes, gaze lowering to her mouth. "Happy to be of service."

Her heartbeat drums in her ears, a flush rising up her neckline. He can't possibly know what he's doing to her, can he? There is a glassiness, a *drunkenness*, to his gaze that makes her suspect he mustn't. She clears her throat, praying her voice won't break. "You can let go now."

He blinks, eyes darting to their connected hands, and has the decency to look mildly uncomfortable. "Ah. Yes, of course." His grasp loosens, fingers unfurling from her skin. She doesn't miss the way his hand flexes once it's returned to his side.

She lowers her gaze, studying the number of spots along the ladybugs shell. Five. "Oma used to say if you found a ladybug with less than seven spots, it meant there would be a good harvest."

"That's preposterous. The number is clearly indicative of how many happy months await you."

Sara laughs under her breath, turning her hand so the ladybug can crawl across her palm. "Oh yeah?"

He nods, mockingly solemn. "Oh yes. That and how many children are in your future."

Snorting, she sends him a disbelieving look. "You're making that up."

His smirk is wide enough to dimple. "Not fond of that one, I take?"

"Not even a little bit," she admits.

"It's mere superstition. An excuse to look forward to something that might not come." His eyes follow the ladybug's path from her finger to her elbow, before she collects it with her other hand. "Still, I will confess I always find myself a touch more cheerful for seeing them."

Sara hums, unable to disagree as she coaxes the red bug from her thumb to her forefinger. Its wings open, a split second warning, before flying off her knuckle. It passes right through Seth's shoulder.

He chuckles, turning to watch the ladybug disappear into the horizon. "Suppose that confirms it."

Sara frowns in the direction it disappeared. "Why, though? What's the difference?"

"Hm? Oh. Well, I suspect it's intelligence. Cats and dogs—certain birds—seem to have no trouble."

It should make sense—at least to the degree that anything ever does when it comes to him—but it doesn't fit. Not quite. "But then people—*other* people—would see you, too."

"No," he murmurs, smile dimming. "We're too selfish a species to see what's in front of us. Not until it affects us, anyway."

"Well, don't sugarcoat it."

"Sugar is overrated."

"Maybe because it's been too long since you had any."

He smirks, crooked and dimpled. "Touché."

Sara chews her bottom lip, fingers playing with the hem of her sleeve. "We should make a cake," she says, trying to slow her heart long enough to sound casual. "You know, when you're human again."

Seth is silent for so long, his gaze a weight. She can't help but glance up. His expression is unreadable—a mix of so much she can't name.

She shrugs, offering a nervous smile—anything to break the stillness. "Don't you think?"

"I think it's too much to hope for," he admits, so softly it's little more than a chime on the breeze. "But it's a lovely thought, isn't it?"

Sara leans back, grass tickling her ears. The clouds are pretty today—full and scattered. "What kind?"

He tilts his head, brow furrowing in thought. "The kind with those ridiculous rainbow colored chocolate chips."

She fights a smile. "You want your first dessert to be something you can mock."

"Absolutely. Someone ought to encourage you to have better taste."

Her birthday is in eleven days. She almost wants to get that kind of cake just to tease him, but the thought quickly sours. Jen and Miles have already planned something for her, a small get together at their place, to celebrate. She knows Seth will be there too, but suddenly the difference between being *there* and being *part* of it, is painfully clear.

SHE DECIDES ON CHOCOLATE.

Jen makes it from scratch (because of course she does) and Miles lights the candles. Sara has a ridiculous plastic crown on her head. The tines keep getting caught in her hair, but Jen whines every time she tries to take it off. Leaning against the wall, Seth's grin is equal parts infectious and irritating. She knows what he's thinking before he even says it, but it hardly stops him. "I must say, that crown is rather fetching on you, Princess."

She can't tell him to shut up, but she's sure her glower gets her point across.

"Alright," Jen says, smiling wide as she dims the lights. "Let's get this party started!"

They sing "Happy Birthday" (Jen is off key, but Miles is annoyingly good) as they set the cake in front of her. Jen has decorated the top with her loopy handwriting and clusters of strawberries. When they finish, Jen claps her hands and reminds her to make a wish. As if Sara doesn't know, as if she hasn't had one in mind for a little over a week now.

Sara takes a deep breath, meets Seth's eyes, and holds the wish against her heart long enough for her lungs to burn. Then she blows out the candles. Miles and Jen cheer, but Seth is still—his eyes knowing and a little sad.

She can see the admonishment there, brimming around his irises. *Birthday wishes don't break curses, Princess.*

And in that moment, between one breath and the next, Sara feels her hopes break. There's shards of it, splintered and sharp like glass, stuck in her throat, but she swallows it down. Tempers it with heat and determination until it melts and cools into something new. Something stronger.

Wishes won't save him, but she *will*.

# CHAPTER TWENTY-NINE

S<small>UMMER IS HER FAVORITE TIME OF YEAR.</small>

Iowa comes alive in the warmer months. Corn grows, reaching tall and swaying, along the highways in rows just begging to get lost in. The fields turn dry and golden, as warm as the sun kissing her freckled shoulders. She sighs, content, as she lays back onto the quilt she's laid out.

They're miles from the city, tucked away from the trails and any wayward hikers. Her camera sits beside her, just in case, as she stares up at the clouds. "When's your birthday?"

It's been bothering her for a bit now—ever since she celebrated her own over a month ago—but she could never really bring herself to ask until this moment. He's been part of her life for a year now, give or take. Knowing that his own birthday must have come and gone, unrecognized and uncelebrated, makes her heart ache.

Seth gives an aggravated sigh. It takes her a moment to realize it's because her question forces an answer. "The sixth of October."

Sara frowns, sitting up on her elbows. "Why didn't you say anything?"

His eyebrows rise, a picture of skepticism and amusement. "As I recall, you were still rather preoccupied with *hating* me at the time."

Sara flounders. "Oh." It feels so long since she's hated him. She tries to pinpoint when things began to change… when she started to see him as a man instead of a monster. A blessing instead of a curse. It's all so impossibly tangled up, but she knows one thing for certain. "I didn't hate you."

The look he gives is full of skepticism. Sara rolls her eyes. "Not by then, anyway."

He hardly looks convinced. "Is that so?"

"It is," she says, trying (and failing) to match his fancy accent.

His grin is wide enough to make his cheeks dimple and eyes crinkle in the corners. Sara wishes he would smile like that more often. "Your impression is atrocious. How do you manage that so terribly when there's only two words?"

"I don't think you get to judge after that butchering of my generation's slang."

Seth waves a hand dismissively. "That was in fun. I wasn't actually *trying*." He tilts his head, eyes gleaming. "Is this American enough?" he teases, all traces of his accent gone.

"You can ditch your accent?"

"Don't be ridiculous, I didn't lose it. I adopted yours."

"I don't have an accent!"

"*Everyone* has an accent, Princess." He taps a finger against his ear. "Just because your ear is deaf to it, doesn't mean it's not there."

She huffs, shaking her head and laying on her side with her arm folded under her head. "Can you do any others?" Part of her actually wants to know. A bigger part just wants to see that dimpled grin of his again.

He doesn't disappoint her. "What would you care to hear?"

She names a few from the top of her head, delighted (and a little amazed) when he's able to pull off every single one convincingly. Hearing his voice in a southern drawl is almost as surreal as hearing him use 'clap back' in a sentence, and she chokes on a laugh.

She's ready to ask for another, but his smile has been replaced with a baffled frown—his gaze fixed across the field, over by the river. "What is that?"

Sara sits up, looking over the grass and searching until she spots movement along the tree line to their left. It takes her a full second to recognize what the mass of brown is. She crouches deeper into the grass, shoving her camera in the bag as quietly as possible despite the shaking in her hands. She debates on how and if she should even try to grab the blanket.

Seth pales. "Sara, what is *that*?"

"Shut up," she hisses—a plea and a prayer all rolled into one.

The creature's head turns, the antlers crowning its head in a nightmare of bloodied, shredded velvet. Its eyes, deep and dark, meet hers, and Sara knows they've been spotted.

Seth's voice goes shrill, edged with the same panic she can feel rattling her bones. "What the *bloody hell* is that?!"

"It's a moose, now will you *please shut up*."

"It's a monstrosity is what it is, good God. I've never seen anything more horrifying in my life."

"*Seth*." Maybe it's the use of his name, or the fear in her voice, but he finally looks at her—finally sees the numbing fear saturating her brow in sweat. Finally, *finally*, realizes what she had known from the start.

It can see him. Can *hear* him.

He stills—a monument of flesh and bone in a sea of swaying grass. Slowly, he sinks down beside her, but it's too late. The moose shakes his massive head, fleshy velvet ribbons swaying like corpses, and takes the first lumbering steps towards them.

"Run!" The word is hissed through clenched teeth, the only warning he gives her before blinking away. For a terrifying moment, Sara thinks he's abandoned her, but then she hears him—yelling from the other side of the valley. "Come on, you stupid beast!"

Sara doesn't look to see if the distraction works. She's running, camera bag slapping painfully against her hip. Seth's taunts, the bull's bellows, echo in the valley—somehow managing to sound both too close and too far—and she urges her legs to go faster despite the burning in her lungs and the cramping stitch in her side.

The car is in her sights now, a football field away, when her foot finds the gopher hole. Her ankle twists, sending her sprawling. Dirt and rock bite into her hand, her chin bashing painfully against the ground. For a dizzying moment, she struggles to find her breath, but she forces herself to stand. To hobble. The car is so close, and she can still hear Seth's voice casting echoes across the valley—goading snarls that tell her she's not yet safe. She's never been so appreciative of his talent to annoy.

Her hand finds the door handle, jerking it open with enough force that it nearly bounces back closed. She slides into the driver's seat, slamming the car door behind her. With shaking hands, she fumbles for the key ring around her neck, releasing a loud curse when the lanyard gets momentarily snagged in her hair. Clumsily, she inserts the key into the ignition. The moment the engine sputters to life, Seth appears in her passenger seat. He's more disheveled than she's ever seen him, hair wild, pale skin flushed. "Go, go, for the love of God, *go!*"

She peels out, gravel and dirt kicking up from the tires and leaving a cloud of dust in its wake.

The radio plays, but it's too soft. Between their panting breaths, Sara can't make out the genre, let alone the song. When the gravel gives way to asphalt, their eyes meet; a second of shared relief, and then a giggle escapes her. A laugh. Sara has to pull over, because it's leaving her like a flood—uncontrolled and too late to pull it back. Seth stares, baffled concern playing across his face, but it only makes her laugh harder.

Then his lips twitch, a chuckle, and suddenly he's joining her. Head back, throat exposed—his chest rising and falling with the force of each breathless burst of laughter.

Sara quiets, mesmerized by the dimples in his cheeks and depth of his voice. It dawns on her that this is the first time she's ever heard him truly laugh. The realization is sobering; a glass of ice water breaking through a haze of wine.

He looks at her, smile dimming when he sees her expression. Then his gaze lowers... her mouth? Is he looking at her mouth? He frowns, body turning towards her more fully.

"Your chin."

Sara blinks, hand instinctively raising to touch the bruised, scraped flesh and flinching. "Oh, yeah. I, um, tripped."

On his knee, his hand flexes—once, twice—before hovering in the space between them. "May I?"

She nods, sand in her throat and drums in her ears. Hooked fingers under the line of her jaw, he coaxes her to tilt her chin with a pressure so light she could almost believe she imagined it. His frown deepens, lips pursed. Sara wonders if he's aware of how close his thumb is to the corner of her mouth. "Are you hurt anywhere else?"

"Um, my ankle. I twisted it a bit." She doesn't mention the burning sting in her palms, but apparently she doesn't need to. He's already cradling her hands, turning them over until he can see the damage. The car is becoming increasingly warm...the AC never worked well while idling. Sara decides to blame that for the flush heating her skin instead of the simple, whispered touch of his fingers tracing her palm.

"I put you in danger. I'm sorry."

He can't lie to her, but even if he could, Sara knows he means it. There is regret there, darkening the rims of his eyes.

She wants it gone.

She isn't thinking, *obviously* she isn't. He's just so close and her heart is still high on adrenaline—his touch so reverent. She leans towards him, her lips a gentle press against the hollow of his cheek. His sharp intake of breath—nearly inaudible—rings, echoes, in her ear. Somehow, Sara knows the sound will haunt her later, when things are quiet and the room is dark.

Pulling away is harder than it should be, but meeting his eyes is harder. There are questions there, as plain as the flecks of amber in his irises and the surprise parting his mouth. She doesn't make him ask. "Thank you."

She can feel his exhale, a brush of warmth against her lips, before he leans away—shaking his head. A muscle in his jaw jumps, brow drawn and lips pulling in a sneer. "Don't," he says, the word a hiss between his teeth. "There is literally nothing for you to be appreciative over."

He settles into his seat, staring at the road ahead of them instead of meeting her eyes. "Take your shoe and sock off that foot before the swelling gets worse. I hear St. Mary's has a passable Urgent Care clinic."

She glances down at her left foot, cringing. It's definitely swollen, her sock visibly indenting her skin, but as bad as it looks, there isn't nearly as much pain as she expected. In fact, it's strangely numb. Maybe Seth was right about taking the shoe off now instead of later. Carefully, she reaches down to undo the laces, wincing. "I'll be fine," she tells him, working out the last of the lacing before gingerly removing her heel from the sneaker. "It really doesn't hurt that much."

"Because you bloody well broke it," he snaps, before looking away. "Sprained at best."

"How—"

He sends her a pointed look. "I've spent a lot of time in Emergency. Shadowing the residents was far more preferable than boredom."

Sara winces as she removes her sock, eyeing the shadow of bruising. "It really doesn't—"

"Sara." Her name is a command on his lips; no room for arguments. She wonders how he gets away with sounding like he has any say in the matter. He must notice her skepticism, because his eyes narrow in warning. "I will pester you every waking moment and, might I remind you, I don't *sleep*."

She grumbles complaints under her breath, lips pressed into a thin line as she puts the car back into drive. The air coming from the vents starts to feel a little bit cooler.

It's late when they finally get home—half past ten—and Sara is so bone weary she could fall into bed without even bothering to take her shoe off. Ansel weaves between her feet, meowing so obnoxiously loud that she feels like she's being scolded. "I know, I know," she grumbles, fumbling with locking the door behind her. The crutch under her left arm digs uncomfortably into her armpit. "I'm not happy about it either."

Seth appears in the living room behind her and, not for the first time (but perhaps the most fervently) Sara wishes she could move from one place to another in the span of a blink. Particularly now that she's stuck with this stupid, clunky walking boot for the next few weeks. With a grumbled curse, she readjusts the crutch.

The glare she sends him must give her away, because his answering smile would be appeasing if not for the guilt behind it. "Be grateful it's merely a sprain." Ansel abandons her to rub, mewling, against his ankles in a demand for attention. Seth concedes with a scratch behind the ears and a fond, "Yes, yes, I see you. No need to have a fit."

Suddenly, it dawns on her with enough force to make her stagger —her crutch falling to the ground with a metallic clang. "Oh."

Seth steps toward her, hands hovering at her elbows as if preparing to catch her if she falls. "What's wrong? You didn't use—"

"You could have been hurt," she breathes, the realization a weight on her chest. "That moose. It—it *saw* you. Like Ansel sees you. It wanted to hurt you."

The breath he releases is small. Relieved. It only makes her heart twist more. "Yes."

"But you taunted it, anyway."

"Also yes." He says it like it's obvious; like it's as inevitable and mundane as gravity. Like it's something that just *is*.

"It could have *hurt* you."

His hands twitch towards her before he catches himself. She wonders, if he knew he could, where he would have reached—her hands, her face? He ducks his head, meeting her eyes. "It didn't."

"But—"

"Sara," he says, a soft demand. "The only injury of any consequence here is your ridiculous ankle. Come sit."

She doesn't want to sit. There's too much unsaid dancing in the space between them. He risked himself for her. Even if he can't die, she knows he feels pain. He has to know. She *needs* him to know—

She kisses him.

Soft. Sweet and chaste—the innocent pressing of lips worthy of childhood fantasies. Her fingers grip the lapels of his coat as she leans into him for balance—stretching up to meet him as best she can. When she pulls away, he follows—lips hovering so close she can feel his every breath.

"Sara..." Her name is a prayer; wine and chocolate off his tongue. Goosebumps dot her flesh. His lips graze the corner of her mouth and his hands—trembling—slide along her jaw with a reverence that makes her weak. When she dares to look, his eyes are dark. Hooded and drunk. "Please, I beg you, don't tease. Not with this."

He towers over her, his body curling around her, and yet—somehow—he feels small beneath her palms. Vulnerable. The way he watches her... as if every shift in her expression holds the power to either save or condemn him. In some ways, Sara knows she *could*.

She swallows thickly, a battle of nerves and wishes clashing in her chest. "I'm not," she whispers. "I wouldn't." She wants to tell him she's not that cruel, but the words are stuck in her throat.

His breath is a laugh, soft and pained with truth. "You do," he murmurs, thumb tracing her bottom lip. "You don't mean to, but you do."

Sara could argue—list all the reasons why he's wrong, highlight why she's right—but she's tired of the back and forth. Tired of the fragile line they've been dancing around. Tired of wanting more, but being too afraid to grasp it.

She leans up, her good ankle straining despite her full weight leaning against him, and lets her lips linger at the corner of his mouth—basking in his sharp intake of breath. "I'm not teasing," she murmurs against his lips. Beneath her hands, he trembles around heaving breaths. His fingers slide into the hair at the base of her skull, his full bottom lip sliding against her mouth with a diligence that makes her pulse thrum.

Then he's kissing her—deliciously, tortuously, slow—and *oh god*, no one has ever kissed her like this. Like every taste is treasured, every hitch in her breath coveted. He moans, low and deep, and it's enough to make her toes curl and her heart ache.

Her hands push past the lapels of his coat, sliding up his chest in search of skin—

Seth hisses, recoiling from her touch so abruptly she nearly stumbles. For a moment, she thinks maybe she went too far, but there's something in his expression—his parted, panting mouth and the furrow of his brow.

"Seth?"

He shakes his head, his hands bracing her shoulders as he steps away from her—refusing to release her until he seems satisfied that she's balanced. His eyes drop to his chest, pushing his coat aside to reveal a stain over his heart—red and blooming across the white cotton peeking beneath his vest. "Oh."

There's static in her ears. Shaking, her fingers touch the stain and come back wet. "You're bleeding." She stares, dumbly, at the red coating her fingers before the implication lands like a bomb. She's thinking of doves—of blood and feathers; brittle bones and broken hearts.

Her hands can't move fast enough; they're pushing the coat off his shoulders, fumbling with the buttons of his vest and pulling at his shirt. "You're bleeding!"

"Yes," he snaps, shrugging out of his coat and vest. "I can *see* that."

He swats her hand away, pulling his collar down and inspecting the damage himself. On the left side of his chest is a spattering of small, weeping punctures. Seth stares, mouth working silently before a breathy, sardonic laugh leaves his lips. "Well, that's just not bloody fair."

He reaches back, pulling his shirt up over his head with a pained growl, and deposits the blood stained fabric on the floor. Sara is horrified to find the rest of his lean chest is a battery of angry, molted bruises. He glowers, words hissing between his teeth. "Not fair *at all.*"

She raises a trembling hand, fingers brushing against a purple bruise blooming at his collar. Her eyes flit between the rapidly appearing injuries in growing horror. "What is this? Why—"

"They're old," he says distractedly, prodding against his bloodied flesh and hissing. "Pillock had to use the blasted shotgun."

Sara freezes. "This is from a *gunshot*?!"

"Rather relieved he never decided to give the rifle a try," he mutters, flinching as he presses against a tender spot.

Sara watches a bruise bloom across his jawline, molted purple and in the shape of her knuckles, and pales—bile rising in her throat. "These...these are injuries people *gave you*!?"

He looks up at her, the edge in his gaze softening. There's a calmness, an apathy, in him that has no right to be there—not when she can feel her blood boiling and freezing all at once. "Nothing to fret over."

"That's *not* what I asked!" she snaps. Her nerves are rope, fraying with every new bruise and blemish marring his pale skin. "Who did this to you?!"

Seth's mouth holds the barest hint of a smile, his hands reaching between them to caress her cheeks. He ducks his head until their noses touch and all she can see are the flecks of amber in his dark eyes. "It will heal, Sara."

The urge to stomp her foot, the same way she did as a child, is nearly overwhelming. "That doesn't answer my question!" A beat of silence passes between them, and a whole new realization dawns. "You... you didn't answer my question."

His thumbs trace the freckles over her cheeks, lips pressing a soft kiss to her forehead. "No."

Under his stare, she wavers. The air feels thin. "I—I don't understand."

Seth chuckles, brushing a stray piece of hair away from her eyes; fingertips gliding across her skin like a whisper. "Don't you?" His head tilts, regarding her with a smile so warm—so *adoring*—it's a small miracle she doesn't melt. "I'm Laura, the foolish mortal that fell to temptation and ate the cursed fruit." He rests his forehead against her own, his lips so achingly close she can feel every breathy word. "And you, my dear, beautiful Sara, are my Lizzie."

His fingers trail down, thumb brushing her bottom lip—eyes hooded. "'Eat me. Drink me. Love me.' Wasn't that the line?" A laugh, small enough to fit in the space of a breath, leaves him—hot and wanting on her skin. "Always a kiss that breaks the spell."

Sara swallows, willing herself to ignore the heat stirring in her lower stomach. Damn him. Damn him for making this hard. "We need to stop the bleeding."

He hums, still transfixed by her mouth—her skin. His fingers sweep across her jaw with a diligence that scares her. The bruise on his face stares back, a taunting reminder. She reaches for his wrists, stopping their progress. "Seth..."

A grimace, as if her words cause him more pain than the lead in his chest. "I've waited so, so long." With her hands still grasping his, his palms burn—warm and real—against her cheeks. The eyes she had once thought to be so cruel, beg her for mercy. "The wound—it's nothing. Truly. I just..." he trails off, words hitching in his throat. Sara can hear him swallow, feel the slight tremble of his hands across her flushed skin. "Let me feel you. Just a little longer. I—"

After David, she didn't believe the crack in her heart could widen any further, but she can feel it—deep and splintering—in her chest like a physical wound. She thinks of that moment in the rain when he told her he was hers; the break in his voice when he spoke of trading one Hell for another.

*How can it be anything else?*

Her eyes burn, jaw aching from holding in the sob that wants to tear itself from her chest. Her grip loosens, fingertips trailing down his arms—his skin shivering beneath her gentle touch—until she finds the crook of his elbow and delivers a coaxing pressure.

He doesn't want to release her; it's as clear as the flash of pain in his gaze, but he surrenders—lets his hands lower away from her face. "Sara..."

Her name has never been so heartbreaking; each syllable a blow. It's too much.

She steps into the empty space of his arms and hugs him—holds him. Quietly, the tears (one, then two) slips free.

He sucks in a breath, the uninjured side of his chest rising beneath her cheek, before his arms—trembling—wrap around her with near bruising force. One hand tangles in her hair, his face dropping to the crook of her neck with a sound that is half sigh, half sob.

Sara doesn't let him go.

# CHAPTER THIRTY

Mostly minor bruising, but the splattering of dime sized wounds across his chest and shoulder looks gruesome and there's a cut along his ribs that makes her worry the more she looks at it. One of her good friends is an emergency doctor—she should know what to do —but she's frozen in disbelief as new marks appear across his skin faster than she can process the one before. It's not until Seth wads up his shirt and presses it over the wound at his side that she remembers the basic first aid lesson Miles gave her when she sliced her finger on a paring knife.

Stop the bleeding. Keep it clean.

"Sit down," she ushers, relieved when he obeys without argument. With some difficulty (damn that boot), she kneels between his legs and ignores the way his eyes widen.

"What on earth are—" he yelps as her hands cover his, pressing the cloth more firmly against his side.

With his thigh pressing intimately against her ribs, she doesn't dare meet his eyes. "Pressure, right?"

His breath hisses between his teeth as he leans his head back onto the cushion. Beneath her palms, his hand trembles. The pained grunt would be hard to interpret if not for the sharp nod. "Pressure."

They fall silent, the only sound Seth's rasping breaths and the hammering pulse in her ears. "How long?" Her murmur sounds louder than it is, plucking at her nerves like a guitar string.

His thumb strokes the back of her pale knuckles, crimson smearing over her skin, and Sara realizes that she's trembling too. "A while yet, I'm afraid. Perhaps another ten minutes."

Jerkily, she nods—tries to swallow down the panic she can still feel clawing at her throat. She can't stop staring at the blood streaking their hands.

"I must confess, when I dared to imagine it, I envisioned us partaking in much more enjoyable activities," he jokes, words breathy. His eyes are dark, rimmed with pain, but his lips are turned up into a smile that borders on flirtatious.

Sara knows it's an act; an attempt to distract her from the anxiety clawing at her chest. She loves and hates that, in some small part, it works. "You're bleeding all over the couch. Maybe now isn't the best time to clue me in on your sexual fantasies."

His grin is wicked. "I was talking about the cake you promised. But, please, do tell."

Sara's laugh is breathy, but at the tail end it sours into a sob. She hears her name, a sigh on his lips, and the tears come faster than she can stop them.

"Shh, breathe, Sara. Breathe."

"You're hurt. There's—the blood and the bruises, how can you even—"

"Look at me." There's a gentle command in his voice, one that begs for no arguments. When she obeys, his face softens. "I promise you, I'm in no danger. It looks far worse than it is." Gently, he lifts their hands away from his wound, exposing the cut along his ribs. The bleeding has stopped. "There now, see? Right as rain."

"There's nothing right about this," she snaps, voice hoarse.

He hums. "There are a few aspects I wouldn't mind repeating, but faced with the overall situation and your temper, I will concede defeat. Also, I'm afraid I need to borrow your shower."

Shower. Right.

Stop the bleeding. Keep it clean.

She helps him up, leads him down the hall with a hobbled gait. The bathroom is too small for the both of them—it's a struggle to keep a respectable distance when the very walls seem to push them together. "The towels are in that cabinet there and, um, you can just use my shampoo if you want."

She turns to look at him, but his eyes are trained on the mirror.

On his reflection.

"Oh," she breathes, chest tight. "This is the first time since…?"

Seth nods before clearing his throat. "Yes."

He continues to stare, his hand raising to his cheek as if he's lost in the shape of his face. It strikes her as an intensely private moment —one she probably shouldn't be witnessing—but he's blocking the doorway and, well, despite the intimacy of the moment, he doesn't seem uncomfortable with her being there.

She steps closer to him; their reflections standing side by side. "Well, it looks like you."

It's a weak joke, but he huffs on a laugh, his hand dropping from his face and eyes meeting hers. "That is a relief," he murmurs, before turning back to his reflection. "It's strange. I thought…" his words trail off, a frown furrowing the smooth skin between his brows. He seems entranced by the change. "Tell me, is it terrible that I don't recognize myself?"

Sara's hand folds around his own and he starts as if he had, in that moment, forgotten that he's as human as she is. "No," she says, bypassing the mirror to look at him directly. "But it is kind of sad."

Seth swallows thickly, before he clears his throat and tears his eyes away from his reflection. "It is, isn't it?"

The smile she offers is weak. "Do you need any help?"

"Undressing? No, I'm fairly certain I remember that much."

Her face flames. "With the *shower*. Do you know how the knobs work?"

"I like to think myself capable of figuring it out."

"And you won't pass out, right? You're not—"

"I promise you, I am fully capable of washing myself without further injury."

"Right. Ok, yeah, but if you need anything—"

"You'll come wash my back?"

She returns his teasing grin with a glare. "Please don't die in the shower."

"I shall try my very best."

Sara nods, throat tight, before closing the bathroom door behind her. She sits with her arms wrapped around her bent knees and her back against the door, and listens to his grumbled curses as he fiddles with the water temperature. Then she catches his pained gasp, and she flinches. She's a second away from asking if he's ok, when he gives a long exaggerated moan. Sara flushes, burying her face in her hands and muttering under her breath, "Oh my *god.*" She can still feel the imprint of his lips, the branding touch of his fingers. She *really* doesn't need to add on to the list of ways he will haunt her.

He yells, voice picture clear over the sound of running water. "This is *bloody brilliant.* Why does anyone ever get out?!"

Sara takes a deep, calming breath—tries to cool the heat in her cheeks—and clears her throat. "There's this thing called utility bills," she yells back, grateful there's no hitch in her voice to give her away. "And you only have about ten minutes before the hot water runs out."

"That's criminal!"

"Welcome to the real world, Casper."

HE COMES OUT OF THE BATHROOM WEARING THE SAME BLOOD STAINED trousers and holding the bottle of antiseptic wash she had stashed under the sink. Sara knows, even before she presses the cloth to his skin, that it's going to hurt, but his reaction still makes her jump.

He hisses, body arching off the couch. "Bloody *buggering*—"

"Sorry!" she squeaks, hastily removing the rag. "Should I stop?"

His words pass through clenched teeth, his hands clenching and unclenching at his sides as he eyes the bottle in her hand venomously. "No. Pain is temporary, infection isn't." Seth lays his head back, eyes staring at the ceiling. "Be kind and get it done quickly."

Sara licks her lips, eyeing the wound with growing trepidation. "I —shouldn't you have X-rays? Or something? What if the BBs are still in there?"

He laughs. "Oh, they're most definitely there. It'll be a terribly fun time getting through TSA in the future."

She stills. "You want to *leave* them?"

Shifting his weight on the couch, he grimaces. "As opposed to you digging around my chest with a pair of tweezers? Most certainly." He looks at her, sees the horror painted across her face, and sighs. "It will be fine."

Everything is so, *so* far away from 'fine', she wants to scream. "There's a hospital right down the street."

"And they will ask for identification I don't have." He takes her hand, thumb stroking her knuckles. "I don't exist here, Sara. There will be questions that I'm unprepared to answer."

"But the BBs..."

"There's no need to remove them." He gives her hand a gentle squeeze. "As I've said, it will be fine."

She stares at him, eyes tracing the shape of his smile. "You're hiding something," she murmurs, frowning.

His fingers twitch against her skin, a grimace painting his face. "It's not worth you fretting over."

"Tell me."

Seth hesitates, eyes flitting over her determined expression before releasing a resigned sigh. "I'm not worried about the shot. I'm worried about the infection that could follow." He nods toward the rag in her hand. "This... may not be enough."

"You need medication," Sara breathes, bile rising in her throat.

"*Possibly.*"

"They would still treat you. They have to, right? They do that, that Hippomatic Oath thing."

The corner of his mouth twitches. "Hippocratic, Princess."

"Whatever! Point is, we're going. Let's go."

"No."

"But—"

"Do you have any idea, precisely how broken the American healthcare system is?"

"That is *not* the point."

"I have *nothing*, Sara. No identification, no money." He gestures to the wound on his chest, eyes dark. "This isn't an emergency. My life is far from endangered. There's a fair chance it will heal well enough on its own, no antibiotics needed."

"But what if it doesn't!?" she snaps, frustration rising. "You can't just leave something like this up to chance! You can't break the curse only to—" The word sticks in her throat.

*Die.*

*Leave.*

She swallows, chest tight and eyes burning. "You just can't."

Seth reaches for her, fingertips brushing her own in a coaxing whisper. "Sara." Tenderness softens the edges, but her name leaves his lips like an apology. "I swear to you, the moment it becomes a danger I will go, but not a moment before then." His fingers curl around her own, squeezing gently. "Believe me, I have no wish to be anywhere you aren't."

"I really think it should be looked at." She bites her lip, eyes trailing over the gash spanning over his ribs. There is no doubt in her mind that it would at least *benefit* from some stitches.

He stares at her, lips thin. "Fine. What about your friend, then?"

"Miles?"

"Well, I certainly wasn't referring to his other half."

"He's a resident."

"Yes, I'm well aware," he says. "Good thing he won't be able to order a slew of unnecessary tests."

Standing, Sara paces the living room, one hand carrying the rag in a white-knuckled grip while the other tangles in her hair. "This is insane. I can't—how does that conversation even go, Seth? There's no way."

He rolls his eyes, pushing himself off the couch. "Right, I suppose

I'll do it myself then. I apologize in advance for the mess. Do you have a needle and fishing line?"

"What?! No! Ugh! Sit back down. I'll call."

"Will you make up your bloody mind?"

Sara doesn't respond—she's already pulling her phone from her back pocket and hitting the call button before she can talk herself out of it. Even though she dials Miles' number, it's Jen that answers. "Hey, it's like, almost midnight. You ok?"

Sara cringes. She hadn't even thought about the time. "Yeah, um, well sort of? I'm not in, you know, danger or anything but—"

Seth takes the phone from her. "Yes, hello Jen. Terribly sorry to intrude, but would your husband, perchance, be available?"

Sara grabs the phone, hand slapping over the receiver and hissing at him, "What is *wrong* with you?! *Perchance?*"

He shrugs. "Good manners get you anywhere."

If he wasn't injured she'd smack him, as it is she lets out a frustrated growl before bringing the phone back to her ear. She sends him a glare before hobbling into her bedroom and shutting the door. "God, I'm sorry. I really—"

"There's a guy in your apartment."

Sara winces, heat pricking her cheeks. "Yes."

"A guy, with an accent like *that*, is in your apartment. *Right now.*"

Sara doesn't have time to respond before there's a scuffling sound of the phone changing hands. In the background, Sara can overhear Jen squealing that, "there's a guy in Sara's apartment" just before Miles speaks.

"Am I happy or worried for you?" he asks. "Because considering the time, I'm leaning toward the second. Do you need me to call the police? Just say yes."

"No, no, it's nothing like that. I'm not in any danger, Seth is a..." Oh god, what were they now? "Friend."

There's a moment of silence on the other line. "You hesitated."

Sara bites her lip, releasing a long, internal scream. "I haven't exactly had time to figure out our relationship status, ok?" she hisses into the phone, trying not to think of the shirtless sort-of-something-more sprawled across her couch.

"Whoa, wait, relation—"

"Miles, I need your help," her voice cracks, threatening to break.

"Sara, you're seriously starting to scare me, girl. You sure you're ok?"

She sniffs, rolling her eyes in frustration. "Yes, I'm fine. It's just— it's been a really *crazy* day, there was this moose and now Seth's hurt and he's being a stubborn jerk and refusing to go have someone look at it, even though I really think he could use some stitches, and—"

"Ok, ok. Take some deep breaths for me, alright? I'm putting some clothes on now. I'll grab my bag and be over in about fifteen minutes. Sooner if I can manage it. Ok?"

Sara breathes a sigh of relief. "Thank you."

"He hurt anywhere else?"

Sara thinks of the lead in his chest, the myriad of bruises decorating his skin, and swallows. On the other end of the line, she can hear the sound of their front door closing. "Yeah, but he says none of it's an emergency."

"Everyone's a doctor," Miles grumbles, car beeping in the background. A moment later, she hears the start of the engine. "Put him on." He must sense her hesitation, because his voice softens. "I'm just making sure there isn't actually an emergency." A beat of silence, then, "You did mention a moose, right? Or was I hearing things?"

Sara swallows, opening her bedroom door. "It's a long story." From the couch, Seth tilts his head questioningly. She's relieved to see no new injuries, but there's fatigue in his gaze that wasn't there before. "Miles wants to talk to you."

He blinks, drowsily, but holds out his hand expectantly. "Very well, then. Hand it over."

Sara places it in his palm, sitting in the empty seat beside him and wringing her hands in her lap. She can hear the murmur of Miles' voice, the questions in his tone, but can't make out the words.

Seth releases a long sigh. "I assure you, there's no cause for concern. No head injuries to fret over, no breaks to throw out any clots. The only thing that could use some attention is a laceration along the upper left quadrant. I would suture them myself, but I'm afraid I'm left-handed."

Another garbled question from the other line, and Seth frowns—eyes meeting hers across the room. The weight in his gaze makes her breath still. "No." Miles says something, and Sara can almost feel Seth's irritation. "Because it isn't." He pauses, listening. "Well, because she won't stop *fussing*."

Overhearing Miles' laughter, Sara takes the phone back. "I'm *not* fussing."

"Yeah, ok," he says, sounding entirely unconvinced. "Where'd you find this guy?"

Somehow, admitting that she met him in front of her hometown's emergency room seems like the gateway to a longer conversation than she can deal with right now. "Uh, you know, around."

"*That* doesn't sound suspicious at all. How long have you two been—"

No way she's letting him finish that question.

"I'm going to get him a glass of water. I'll see you soon, bye." She hangs up, collapsing on the unoccupied section of the couch. There's five missed messages displayed on her screen. Apparently, Jen has been texting her during the call.

*How long have you been seeing this guy?*

*Is he cute?*

*Because he sounds hot as —*

Sara drops it onto the couch without bothering to read the rest, hiding her face in her hands with an embarrassed groan. When she looks up, Seth looks as if he's fighting a grin.

"You're truly terrible at this. A child lies more convincingly."

"I was trying to avoid lying, actually."

His expression softens, smile warm. "I know. It was a commendable effort." He sits up with a growling hiss, a hand resting over a large bruise spanning across his side. They look deeper than before, more angry. She wonders if she should be worried about broken ribs, too.

"What are you doing?" she scolds. "Lie down!"

"You're too far away," he grumbles, sitting up until they're shoulder to shoulder. "It feels strange."

His bare arm brushes hers, and she tries to suppress a shiver.

Strange is definitely a word for it, though it isn't the distance so much as the *feeling* that's alien. "What do you mean?"

Head tilted back, the long expanse of his pale throat exposed, he closes his eyes. "The pull is gone."

Sara shakes her head. "I have no idea what that means."

He yawns, jaw cracking. The hand cradling ribs lifts to tap at the center of his chest clumsily, his voice a tired murmur. "Here. It's all empty. Feels strange to have to look for you without it."

It hardly answers her question, but Sara can't bring herself to ask anything else. There's an unguarded softness to his expression—lips parted, dark eyelashes trembling with an effort to remain open. He's exhausted; beaten and bruised. How long has it been since he's been able to rest? Her heart pangs, her hand reaching for his. She knows it's been far, far too long. "I'm right here," she assures him softly.

She catches the smallest of smiles before he drifts off to sleep.

IT TAKES EXACTLY TWELVE MINUTES FOR MILES TO ARRIVE; HIS KNUCKLES a soft rap against the door. Too soft to wake the man beside her.

Slowly, Sara untangles their fingers—relieved when his breathing remains steady. Rising from the couch is a struggle, but she manages to grab her crutch and limp her way down the hallway before the knock can sound again. She's barely opened the door, when Miles pins her with a knowing look.

"Don't think I don't know when you're trying to avoid a question."

Sara's face heats. "This really isn't the time."

Miles hums skeptically, shouldering his duffle bag and closing the door behind him. "Mmm...that long, huh?"

"Keep it down," she shushes, "he's sleeping."

He steps through the threshold, his smile falling as he notices her foot. "What the hell happened?"

"It's just a sprain."

"And you didn't think to mention it to your friend, who's a *doctor*?"

"I told you, it's been a *really* long day."

He only looks more concerned. "Right... you going to explain that whole moose bit?"

Sara closes the door, locking the deadbolt. "I was taking pictures. There was a moose."

"Please," Miles deadpans, eyes lingering on the scrape on her chin. Sara wonders how bad the bruising is now. She hadn't checked since leaving the clinic. "Don't bore me with the details."

Sara can't even summon the energy to retort, the day weighs on her almost as heavily as the anxiety. Instead, she leads him into the living room—thankful for the wall that blocks Seth from sight until the moment they've turned the corner.

Miles freezes. "That's a shotgun wound." Then, his eyes flit over the rest of the injuries—cataloging every bruise, every scrape—before grabbing her arm and pulling her back around the corner. "Sara, what the hell is going on?"

"I—"

"No." He cuts her off, finger in her face. "No lies. You suck at them. Why the *hell* does your boyfriend look like he just came out of a leading role in BBC *Fight Club*?!" His eyes search hers, more serious than she's ever seen him. "What have you gotten yourself into?!"

She swats his hand away. "It's not like that, ok?" she hisses. "And keep your voice down or you'll wake him!"

Seth's voice materializes from the living room, tinged with sleep. "Too late for that, I'm afraid." He stumbles around the corner, leaning against the wall. Sara notes that his short nap doesn't seem to have done him any favors... if anything he looks paler. The bruises under his eyes deeper. "Hello, lovely to meet you. Now, will you please tell her I'm not going to die in my sleep so we can all tuck in and call it a night?"

The muscle in Miles' jaw jumps. "When we talked on the phone, you didn't think to mention you've been *shot*?"

Seth gives a slow blink. "No, not particularly." When the other man's expression darkens, Seth sighs, hand gesturing lazily to the wound. "It's merely tissue damage. You're more than welcome to verify it for yourself."

Miles' seems less than impressed—shoulders tense and hands fisted—but he nods stiffly. "Fine. You want to lay on the bed?"

"And risk getting blood on the sheets? Don't be absurd. There is a lovely couch around the corner."

"There's a *hospital* around the corner, where you wouldn't have to worry about getting blood *anywhere*."

"Why does everyone keep saying that as if it isn't already common knowledge?" Seth grumbles, already making his way back to the living room.

Miles pins her with a look, his voice a harsh whisper. "Don't even think we're done talking about this."

Sara glares back, unmoved. "It's not what you think."

How could it be?

His jaw works silently, but he doesn't push the conversation further. He stomps into the living room, instead. Sara follows, flinching when his medical bag—his old army duffle he keeps jam packed with supplies—hits the ground.

From the couch, Seth raises an eyebrow. "Very dramatic, bravo doctor."

Mile's doesn't look up as he unzips the bag, pulling out some supplies and lining them up on the floor—antiseptic, a bag of gauze, and a box of gloves. Ansel sniffs at the last before Sara picks him up, holding him against her chest where he'll stay out of the way. "You going to tell me how this happened?"

"There was a gun and I was *shot*," Seth quips, tone dry. "I thought that to be fairly obvious."

Miles' mouth tightens, snapping on his gloves. "Was there a reason *why*?"

"If memory serves, it was because he believed me to be the devil." Seth frowns, hissing as latex hands prod the wound. "I'm not. For the record."

Sara sends him a pointed glare that she can only hope screams *shut up*. Seth's attention seems more focused on her lips—or maybe Ansel? He keeps rubbing his face against her chin, purring loudly against her cheek.

Miles pauses. "And the rest of it?"

Seth glances down his body. "More or less the same, actually."

"…Uh huh."

Seth rolls his eyes. "Give it a few more years, *doctor*—I'm sure you'll find much stranger cases."

Miles looks at her, eyebrows raised in what Sara can only interpret as 'where the hell did you find this guy'?

Sara doesn't dare even try to answer. Glancing at the deep purple bruising along Seth's side, she asks, "What about his ribs? You don't think they're broken, do you?"

Miles huffs on a laugh. "You know? That's a great question, Sara. If only there was a place your boyfriend could *go to find out.*"

Sara doesn't even have the energy to correct him. In her arms, Ansel squirms—nails biting into her shoulder—until she sets him down. He scampers down the hall, no doubt beelining for the spot he's made for himself under her bed.

Miles pulls out sutures, opening the package with careful, aggravated hands. "You look like shit."

"I haven't slept in—well, ages really."

Miles' eyes narrow. "Are you on something?"

"No, unfortunately. Though I wouldn't say no to a spot of gin."

"There a reason you're not sleeping?"

Seth's expression hardens. "None I care to share at the moment, no." He grunts as the hooked needle slides in, glaring. "Feel free to drop this irrelevant line of questioning. If you absolutely must know, I have no plans of hurting or involving her in something that could."

"Yeah? That why her foot's in a boot and her chin's all banged up?"

Sara doesn't miss the way Seth recoils, face paling. Scowling, she resists the urge to slap Miles' shoulder, but only because his steady hands are preoccupied knitting Seth's flesh back together. "Will you stop? That wasn't his fault."

Miles scoffs. "Right. It was the *moose.*"

Seth doesn't answer. He's too exhausted.

Sara can see it in his face—the way his eyes struggle to remain open, the hitch in his breath the moment he catches himself drifting too deep. She suspects it's only the pain and sheer stubbornness that keeps him awake. The silence is tense, suffocating, as Miles finishes his work. It's only when the last stitches are tied and the open wounds nearly dressed, that Seth speaks.

"Antibiotics," he murmurs, eyes lifting drowsily. "Do you have any?"

"No, because carrying a pharmacy around is illegal," Miles grumbles, tying off the last bandage with a little more force than Sara believes to be strictly necessary.

Seth winces.

Sara glares.

She's tempted to accuse Miles of being petty, but the truth is both of them have done nothing but push at each other's buttons the entire time, and she really doesn't have the energy to play peacemaker. Not tonight. "Should we be worried about infection?"

Seth makes a small sound in the back of his throat—probably irked that she's even asking—but Miles seems more concerned with her phrasing. "Oh, so it's *we* now?"

"Miles…" She says his name like a warning.

He rolls his eyes. "I can write a prescription," he grumbles, rifling through his bag. "Make sure his pasty ass finishes it."

Pulling out his prescription pad, he clicks a pen and begins to fill out the blanks. "Last name?"

Sara pales. "He doesn't—"

"Hastings," Seth says, eyes closing. "However, being that I have no identification it hardly matters."

Miles' hand pauses, a muscle in his jaw jumping as the words hiss between his clenched teeth. "Of *course* you don't."

Sara sets a hand on his wrist, eyes pleading. "Could you prescribe it under mine?"

"You *do* know that's illegal, right?" The hand holding the pen shakes. Sara's never seen Miles so furious. "It's *fraud*."

From the couch, Seth sighs—his eyes closed and head tilted back. "It'd be easier to just tell him at this point, Princess."

Miles' eyes narrow, flitting between them. "Tell me *what*?"

Seth holds her gaze patiently, waiting for her approval. Sara's chest is so tight she can barely find the space to breathe let alone answer.

"Sara, what the *hell* is he talking about?"

She closes her eyes, sends a small prayer to whatever power that will listen, as she forces herself to speak the words. "He doesn't have any ID," she says, voice thready and weak, "because, until a few hours ago, he was a ghost."

When she dares to open her eyes, Miles is staring back at her like she's spoken a different language entirely. Considering what she just admitted, she may as well have.

"Do you honestly expect me to believe that?" She wonders what kind of diagnoses are going through his head, what kind of tests he's on the verge of calling up and ordering. There's a worried edge to his voice, an unsung plea for her to tell him she's joking. "*Honestly?*"

From his spot on the couch, Seth grunts. "How else would she have cleaned the table on your poker night? She can't lie to save her life."

Sara offers a weak smile. "I did tell you I had an invisible friend."

# CHAPTER THIRTY-ONE

It takes more convincing—a *lot* more—before Miles' complexion goes ashen.

Sara knows it's Seth's recounting of how Miles tucked himself away in one of the patient rooms to deal with his leg pain in privacy, that does it. The way he's able to give details he should have no way of knowing. Sara jumps in before Seth can make a mess of the situation by divulging too much. She has no doubts that, in all the times he's "checked in", he was bound to have stumbled in on something more personal than he should have.

Struggling to keep her voice steady, she tells Miles how they met —of the curse that bound them together and the miracle that wasn't one. She tells him how she broke it. By the end, he has sunk into the wingback chair. It's weird seeing someone who isn't Seth sitting there.

Sara lays a hand on his shoulder. "Miles—"

He holds up a hand. "I am not ok." The words are muffled by the fist in front of his mouth, elbows planted on the floral armrest and his glasses dangling from his finger while he massages his temples. "Please, *please* do not ask me. This is so far from fine."

Sara bites her lip, wringing her hands in front of her. She glances to Seth, looking for support or guidance, only to frown. He's fallen back asleep. Sara tries to quell the concern that inspires. Their discussion hasn't been quiet.

Miles follows her gaze, sighs, and puts his glasses back on. "This... all this is crazy. It's unbelievable."

"I know," Sara murmurs, fingers lacing. She stares at the skinned flesh of her palms. They still sting whenever she lets herself think about it. "But you believe me anyway, right?"

"Kinda have to, at this point," he grumbles, giving her a considering look. "So what really happened, then? With his injuries. Last I checked, a moose can't pick up a shotgun."

She swallows down the bile that rises in her throat. "He was telling the truth." Cringing, she looks at the floor. There's a fur ball with Ansel's signature color halfway hidden under the coach. "It's— they're injuries people have given him over the centuries."

"Centuries," Miles echoes, horror and awe straining his voice. He runs a hand over his scalp, eyes darting to the sleeping man on the couch. "Fucking *hell*."

Honestly, she couldn't have said it better.

"But how—" Miles' phone rings, cutting him off. They both know it's Jen. Besides the fact that no one else would call this late, the sing-song *'it's your wife calling'* ringtone gives it away.

He silences it without answering, finger tapping against the case as he stares at the screen. When he speaks, his words are careful. "I'm going to go home, but we aren't done talking about this—I have so many questions, I—" he shakes his head, in his hand the phone rings a second time. Jen again. "Dinner," he says, meeting her eyes. "Tomorrow. All of us."

Sara nods. "Tomorrow."

Miles stands, sending Seth one last lingering look, before picking up his prescription pad and his abandoned pen. He scratches an order onto the paper, his eyes serious as he tears it from the pad and hands it to her. "For your ear infection."

The laugh she gives is shaky and short, fitting in the span of a breath, as she takes the prescription from him. She hugs him. Maybe it's the stress of the day, but Sara feels the breath leave her lungs in a stuttering sigh against his chest and holds him just a little bit tighter. "Thank you. For everything."

He pulls away, ruffles her hair the way he knows she hates (but really kind of loves). "Stay out of trouble, yeah? And call me if you need anything."

It's an easy thing to agree to.

After she locks the door behind him, she returns to Seth's side. Gently, she nudges his shoulder—murmurs his name.

His eyes blink open, staring at her for several long seconds with a sleepy frown pulling at his lips. "Sara?"

"Hey, Miles went home. Are you ready for bed?"

The furrow in his brow deepens, an adorably confused look stealing across his face. "There's this odd... empty feeling in my stomach. I think, perhaps, I may be starving."

She raises her eyebrows. "May be?"

"I'm quite out of practice."

"Let me see what we have," she says, studying him. "Do you think you can stay awake long enough to eat?"

He hums, eyes slipping shut before drowsily reopening. "I make no such promises."

Right. Something quick, then. She grabs a few protein bars from the kitchen, hoping he can stay awake long enough to eat at least one.

"I believe some of that ghastly excuse for cake was promised."

"Yeah, I don't exactly keep that on hand."

He huffs, a shadow of a smile teasing his lips. "Pity. An obscene amount of sugar would be welcome about now."

Sara hands him one of the bars, ignoring the skeptical look he gives it. She cuts him off before he can complain. "Gift horse. Mouth. Don't complain."

Scowling, he grumbles an obscenity under his breath as he tears the wrapper. Taking a bite, he pauses, making a face before forcibly swallowing. "This is vile."

"Beggars can't be choosers."

"But surely they're still allowed to gripe." He glares at the half-wrapped bar, a frown on his lips. "A piss poor substitute for cake."

He sounds so much like a petulant toddler, that it's *almost* funny. "Will you please just eat it so we can sleep?"

He takes another bite, not bothering to hide his displeasure as he chews. Forcing himself to swallow, he gestures to her room. "Help yourself. Don't let me keep you."

"If I trusted you not to fall asleep and choke on your food, I might. Besides, you can barely sit up straight. Even if you don't pass out, I doubt you're getting off the couch by yourself."

He blinks at her, slow and lazy. "Off? Why would I do that?" He holds up the remaining third of the protein bar. "Are you aware of how dry these are? How on earth do you stomach it? I rather suspect I'd find more moisture in a handful of sand."

Sara rubs her eye, fighting back a yawn even as she heads to the kitchen to get him something to drink. He's not the only one who finds the bars unappetizing (which is why she still has them, despite being overdue for a grocery run). "Can't get to the bed if you can't get up."

Seth freezes. "I'm not taking your bed."

Sara rolls her eyes, pulling a glass down from the cabinet. "You're injured." She glances at his wound—still angry and raw. "And it's not like you fit on my couch."

"Perhaps I stuttered," he deadpans, completely unfazed. "I am *not* taking your bed."

"Seth, when was the last time you slept? Before tonight?" His silence—his *stillness*—is answer enough. She sighs, running a hand through her hair. "Look, I really don't mind. Ok? I'd rather you have it."

"It's not—" he cuts himself off, looking more uncomfortable than she's ever seen him.

"Not *what?*" She watches, in amused fascination, as a flush darkens his cheeks.

"It's not... *proper.*"

She blinks. "Proper. *You* are worried about what's proper?" When he remains stubbornly silent, she chokes on a laugh. "Really? *This* is the line you won't cross?"

"I resent that. I've been nothing but a gentleman."

She shakes her head, filling the glass under the tap. "You've been stalking me the past year and living in my apartment *rent free*." Three quarters full, she turns the water off. "We're practically—" *Dating,* she thinks. Thankfully, her mind catches it before her mouth can say it. "Roommates."

He catches her almost-slip, though—gaze lowering to her lips. "Oh," he breathes, more distracted than boastful. "I think we may be a touch more than that." He meets her eyes, eyebrows raised. "Wouldn't you say?"

The heat crawls up her neck, but she refuses to look away. She does shove the glass of water into his hands, though. "Then you won't have a problem using the bed."

Seth scoffs, a frown turning his mouth. "I will not have you sleeping on the couch or, heaven forbid, the floor." He brings the glass of water up to his lips.

"Well," she says, watching the way the muscles in his throat work as he drinks, "we could share."

He chokes.

Sara pats his back firmly, trying to ignore the heat and feel of his skin against her open palm.

"Cruel," he wheezes. "You're bloody *cruel*."

She shrugs, averting her eyes. "Well, those are your options."

"You're... you're not *serious*?"

Heat pricks her cheeks. "Stop looking at me like that. It's sharing a mattress not, you know."

"It's even more improper than your previous suggestion. What on earth makes you think—"

"You're greedy," she challenges, arms crossed under her chest. "You said so yourself."

His eyes drop to her mouth distractedly. "Yes, you cruel thing. There are things I want desperately, but that doesn't mean I deserve them."

"Ok... couch it is, then. Let me just grab a pillow—"

He grasps her wrist, stopping her before she can leave. His hold is gentle, but she can see the force in which he's grinding his teeth in the straining line of his jaw.

"Change your mind?" she asks, eyebrows raised.

"Yes." The look he pins her with is more exasperated than heated. "I've decided to take it back. You're not Lizzie. You're the bloody goblin."

Her mouth purses, a small effort to hide her smile. Considering the glare he's giving her, she's failing. Miserably. Her hand slides into his, fingers curling against his palm. "Come on. Goblin's tired."

He grumbles under his breath, but accepts her help.

ON HIS BACK, HE LIES AT THE VERY EDGE OF THE MATTRESS; HIS BODY SO stiff, Sara can practically feel it from the other side of the bed.

She sighs, turning towards him. "You know, this really isn't as big a deal as you're making it out to be."

He glances at her, a brief moment of connection, before he goes back to staring at the ceiling. "For you, perhaps. The last time I shared a bed—" He cuts himself off, eyes darkening. "Well, it was a very, very long time ago."

Blinking, Sara shifts her weight onto her elbow so she can better see his face. "Wait. Is that why you're being so weird? You're worried about being out of practice? Because that's *not* what's happening here."

"How is it you manage to misinterpret nearly everything I say?" he mutters, as much disbelief as irritation pulling at his lips. "Truthfully?"

"How else was I supposed to interpret it?" she asks, settling into her pillow—her body facing his. "Isn't 'share a bed' old time talk for sex?"

A muscle in his jaw jumps, his hand reaching up to cover his eyes. "Yes, but I was quite hoping you would know better than to think I would mean it that way."

"So you *don't* want to have sex with me?"

He makes a sound in the back of his throat, head snapping to face her. "You... you're teasing me."

The corner of her lips twitch. "Maybe."

"Why?"

She hums, "Payback. Definitely payback." Her fingers pull the sheet closer to her chest. "It's nice that you're the flustered one for a change."

"I believe I preferred it when you hated me."

She smiles. "Liar."

"Perhaps," he murmurs. After a few beats of silence, he sends her a dimpled, suggestive smirk and adds, "I suppose the kissing was rather nice."

Flushing brightly, her eyes flit to his lips. "I suppose it wasn't too terrible."

He coughs on a sharp laugh, cringing when it pulls on his wound. "Below the belt there, love." His hand reaches up, cradling his injury. "Bloody hell, that hurts."

Sara sits up—tries to ignore the way her pulse thrums at his slip, but it keeps echoing in her ears (*love, love, love*). She swallows thickly, distracts herself with his pain. "Let me see," she mutters. The words sound loud in the dark as she nudges his hand aside.

He lets her, his hand draping over his bare stomach instead. She can feel his stare, tender in ways that make her heart skip, as she gently peels the bandage back. It looks worse—bruising darkening the skin around the wound in molted purples and greens—but nothing has reopened and there's little to no blood staining the gauze. "I still can't believe someone would do this to you," she says, carefully resealing the bandage.

Her eyes lift to the bruising along his jaw, her heart giving a painful squeeze. She traces the edge, feels him shudder beneath the gentle touch. "I can't believe *I* did."

Seth takes her hand, bringing her palm to his lips. "It was an accident."

No... it wasn't. She had wanted, so desperately, for him to hurt that it manifested into something tangible—something real. It doesn't matter that she didn't know her hit would actually land, doesn't matter that she was hurt and angry. "I'm sorry."

"You've mentioned." His lips linger over the fragile skin of her wrist, a whispered kiss against her pulse. "It's forgiven. Has been for a long time. Just because you see proof of it now is hardly reason to feel guilty for something that's long passed."

"But—"

"Sara, it's *fine*."

"It's not," she snaps, eyes screwed shut. "You didn't deserve it. You didn't deserve any of this."

His hand skims up her arm, her shoulder, her neck, until his palm warms her cheek. In the dim lighting, his eyes gleam. "I'll live."

In her chest, her heart gives a painful lurch. He can't possibly understand what those words mean to her, the pain and resignation embedded in each letter. He *can't*. Because the way the syllables curl on his tongue is reverent, the hush in his voice as soft and honest as his smile.

His thumb traces a path over the ridge of her cheek, eyes half-lidded with a fatigue so heavy she's surprised he's able to keep them open. His lips curve, giddy at the corners. "And isn't that a thought?" he breathes, wonder in his voice. "To *live*."

Sara doesn't answer. Even if she knew how to respond, she suspects he doesn't really expect her to. His eyes drop to her lips, words escaping his own in a murmured prayer. "What a thought..."

Throat dry, Sara swallows down the temptation to lean down and kiss him. She lays her head on the pillow, facing him. "You need to sleep."

Seth hums, eyes closing. "That does sound like an accurate assessment." He meets her gaze, brow furrowing thoughtfully. "May I—" He swallows, jaw tense as he scowls up at the ceiling. His hand, the one laying between them, flexes once, twice, before fisting in the sheets. "Never mind. It's ridiculous."

It's not, she thinks, but she knows better than to try to pry an answer from him. There's no time for his riddles and deflections when his eyes carry the bruises of centuries' worth of lost sleep. She stares at his hand, eyes lingering over his pale knuckles. She has a pretty good idea of what his request was, anyway.

She coaxes his fingers loose, unwilling to meet his surprised stare. When she clumsily laces their fingers, their palms pressed together, a stuttered sigh leaves his lips. The tension he was holding onto leaves with it. "Thank you," he breathes.

Sara squeezes his hand, frowning when he doesn't return it. A quick glance and she understands why. In the same way he used to come and go, disappearing between one blink and the next, he has fallen asleep.

Smiling softly, she whispers, "You're welcome."

She doesn't release his hand.

# CHAPTER THIRTY-TWO

SHE WAKES UP WITH A WEIGHT DRAPED OVER HER WAIST AND THE muffled sound of her phone humming. Groggily, she looks over her shoulder. Seth still sleeps, his face relaxed and his lips parted around shallow breaths. Stripped of the years of torment and guilt, he looks younger.

From the floor, her phone goes silent for only a second before the vibrating starts up again. Another glance proves that Seth is having no trouble sleeping through it, but she's glad she left it in the soft fabric of her sweatshirt pocket instead of the usual spot on the night-stand. She settles back onto the pillow with a soft sigh. The arm draped over her middle twitches when she shifts, his fingers brushing against her clothed stomach.

Her eyes slip shut; content. She imagines he'll be mortified when he wakes up. Sara's lips quirk into a smile at the thought.

Then her phone goes off again—this time short bursts that indi-cate rapid fire text messages—and she sighs. She really should get up and check it, but when she shifts away, Seth pulls her closer.

"Don't go," he mumbles, gravel in his voice. The sound stirs something in both her lower stomach and her heart.

"I thought you'd be embarrassed," she confesses, settling back in. "I was kinda looking forward to teasing you."

"Too tired." His jaw cracks around a yawn. "Stay. It's Sunday."

Another violent burst from her phone has her frowning. "It's Monday." Not that it matters. The only schedule she has to keep is her own.

Seth is quiet for a moment, but Sara can practically hear him struggling to put the days together. "Damn it all. You're right."

He sounds so dejected at being wrong, it pulls a small laugh from her. "I think we deserve to sleep in," she says softly, shifting onto her back so she can see him more easily. It's probably just Jen trying to fish some answers out of her, anyway.

The look of relief and the "thank god" he murmurs under his breath are equally endearing. The way he falls, almost immediately, back into sleep is even more so.

Feather soft, she brushes the hair away from his eyes. If she didn't know she loved him before, she knows it now—can feel it simmering in her chest, a tangle of emotions she's too tired to sort through. She holds his hand and drifts back to sleep.

THERE'S A POUNDING ON HER DOOR.

Sara's eyes fly open, a gasp pulling into her lungs. Beside her, Seth mumbles something incomprehensible and shifts further under the covers. A quick glance to the window shows that it's late morning and she groans.

Jen.

Or Miles?

No, he'd be patient enough to wait till dinner. It's gotta be Jen.

Swinging her legs out of bed, she rushes to get up as the beginnings of guilt seep into her stomach. Sara runs a hand through her hair hastily, cringing when the knocking continues. She should have at least sent a quick text assuring her friend she was ok.

Biting her lip, she closes the bedroom door softly behind her— hoping Jen won't be so loud as to wake the man sleeping in her bed.

The way he nodded off last night... he needs rest. Not just to heal, either. She has some strong suspicions that it goes deeper than that; the same way she's almost certain he will wake with a voracious appetite. Hundreds of years with no food, no sleep... if his injuries caught up with him, she has to believe everything else will too.

God, her grocery bill is going to be horrendous.

Sara grabs her crutch from the spot on the wall, careful to keep her weight off her injured foot. She'd taken the boot off to sleep and doesn't want to deal with velcro straps, but she knows there'll be hell to pay if Seth catches her walking on it unprotected. Hobbling to the entry, she unlocks the deadbolt and opens the door, her lips parting around an apology only for it to wither before she can even speak the first syllable.

It isn't Jen.

Sara stares at him, the breath knocked from her lungs and her mouth parting around words she can't find. David stares back at her —blonde hair sleep-mussed and blue eyes panicked but clear. The freckles on his face hide behind a flush; skin dewy with sweat as if he ran the entire flight of stairs. She knows, in that very second of looking at him, that he's back.

*Her* David is back.

Somewhere beneath the numbness, she recognizes that she should feel happy.

"Sara?" Her name is a hope and a prayer all rolled into one. She feels it sink into her skin with a familiarity that used to be comfortable. Now it just feels stale.

"David," she says, body numb. His name tastes foreign—an echo of a bad memory. "What—"

"I remember," he blurts, letting himself through the door of what was once supposed to be *their* apartment. "I remember everything and I—God, Sara. It's all just this jumble, but I remember and—"

"We should sit down," she says, cutting him off. The room feels off-kilter, her knee wobbling threateningly despite the crutch under arm. Her lungs don't seem to be working right—struggling to pull in a full, even breath. "Please."

He must see how pale she is, see the shock edging the rims of her irises, because the words stop falling out of his mouth (even though she can see the way he has to bite his lip to keep them in). He closes the door and follows her into her living room. Sara makes a point of sitting in Seth's chair.

Nervously, David glances around the room before sitting stiffly on the couch across from her. He licks his lips, swallows, before speaking again. They're still jumbled, but significantly less rushed. "What happened to your foot?"

Sara shrugs awkwardly, keeping her answer short in hopes that he'll drop it. "I tripped."

He fidgets, seeming to get the hint. "Sara, I'm so sorry. I—I have no idea what came over me. Those things I said—and your car—I wouldn't even believe it if I didn't remember doing it. That—that's not who I am. It's not—that wasn't *me*. I would never—"

So Seth was right. He did mess with her car.

Sara runs a hand through her hair, not missing the way his eyes caught the motion or the slight frown creasing the smooth skin between his brows. He used to love her long hair, would twirl in around his fingers and watch it coil like a spring. "All the phone calls? That text message? Was that you, too?"

His expression confirms her suspicions before his voice can. "I'm so—"

"David, it's ok. I know."

And she does. She's known for a while now that the words he said—the ones that cut her—weren't from the same man she'd fallen in love with. What she's struggling to understand is why it *changed*. "When," she swallows, tries to recapture her voice. "When did you remember?"

"This morning," he says, leaning over the coffee table between them and grasping her hands. Sara lets him, frozen despite how unfamiliar they feel. "Right when I woke up. I tried to call, but you weren't answering and I—well, I couldn't wait. I figured you had to be here."

This morning... Her eyes flit to her bedroom door, realization dawning with the subtlety of a knife.

Seth.

Kissing him didn't just break his curse, but David's too.

"I—" she trails off, unsure of what she wants to say—what she feels. There's a tangle of emotion in her chest, squeezing on her heart, but she's too busy drowning in the shock of it all to begin untangling it. Then she hears her bedroom door creak open, and it feels like the world stops.

"Sara?" Seeing them, Seth freezes in the hallway. Sara can tell the exact moment when he figures it out. His head tilts, his brows furrowed and his mouth parted in a perplexed frown as he stares at the man across from her. "You're *back*."

David looks between the injured, half-naked man in her home to her, and back. "Uh, who are *you*?"

Seth's gaze finds hers; a brief meeting. Too brief. "No one of consequence, I assure you. I'll be in, well, the only other room. Pardon my interruption."

The silence that falls between them is punctuated only by the click of the door latch.

David can't seem to take his eyes off her door, eyebrows furrowed in what she recognizes as concern. "… Who was that?"

If *that* wasn't the question of the week. Sara settles for the closest thing to the truth. "A friend."

"He came from your bedroom." He blinks, shaking his head. "He went *back* to your bedroom."

Sara's eyes close. Of course, he remembers the layout of the apartment. "A *good* friend." When she opens her eyes, David is still staring at her as if she owes him more of an answer, so she adds, "His name is Seth."

"Ok… should I be worried?" He gives a nervous laugh. "I mean, there's a half-naked guy hanging out in my girlfriend's bedroom."

Sara's heart drops. Rises. There's an ocean in her ears; a flood of static white noise threatening to drown her.

Oh.

Oh *no*.

"David…" she breathes, struggling to find the right words. She hates that she can't find any—hates that there *aren't* any. "I'm not— our relationship ended a *year* ago."

He pales, grasping her hands. A look of panic pinches his features. "No. No, no. I know—I really messed up, but I swear I didn't remember anything until this morning. I *swear*. I—I still *love you*."

Once, months ago, she would have begged to hear those words from him. But now... her gaze lingers on her bedroom door. The David sitting in her living room is the same person she fell in love with, but she *isn't*. The trauma of being abandoned by him, of losing Oma, has changed her. Being with Seth—seeing the regret he carries, the way he forces a smile through his suffering... The way his mask slipped, little by little, until she saw the man shielding himself behind it.

The way David looks at her now—on the precipice of self-righteous anger—she understands why Seth embraced the role of a villain for so long. There's nothing she can say that won't make her seem cruel. Maybe, in some ways, she is. But she won't force herself to try when she knows it's destined to fail. She won't sacrifice the happiness she's found, the *love* she's found, trying to salvage a relationship she's already given up on. Not when she can't even look at him without remembering the way he tore her life apart—without hearing the echo of his fists pounding on her door.

Sara swallows thickly, regret heavy on her heart. "I'm sorry, David." She stares at him, urging him to believe it. "I really am. But... I've moved on."

He stares back at her, mouth parted, before shaking his head. "So, what? You're not even going to try?"

"I *did* try," she reminds him. "I tried for *weeks*."

"That wasn't—I didn't remember!"

"I know," she says, voice soft. "But, David... it still happened. Whether you remembered or not, that doesn't just erase everything *I* went through." She stares at him. "Did you really expect me to just sit here and wait for you?"

He doesn't get it though, she can tell by the slap of his expensive shoes against the floor as he paces her living room, by the way his hands fist at his sides. "I can't believe this," he growls, face twisted. "I didn't think you'd be so *selfish*."

Sara thinks of what Miles has always insisted—that David has never wanted for anything—and sees what he was trying to warn her of. David was everything she could have wanted in a boyfriend, but only because she was everything he wanted from *her*. The moment she didn't live up to his expectation, the second he didn't get what he felt he was owed, this is the type of response she'd get.

A tantrum.

She shakes her head, disappointment making her heart ache. "I think you should leave now."

He stills, has the nerve to be surprised. Maybe he thought his accusations would encourage a change of heart. A year ago, maybe they would have. "Sara—"

"Now, please."

He stares at her, as if he's turning the words over and over in his head. His expression softens, a scowl transforming into a wince. "I'm sorry."

There's regret lacing his voice, quiet as it is. Sara doesn't have any problem believing them. "I know." The words, *but I still need you to leave* go unsaid, but he must read them in her expression.

He doesn't slam the door on his way out, but Sara locks the dead-bolt behind him, anyway. Just in case.

SETH IS LAYING ON HER BED, HIS FINGERS IDLY STROKING THE CAT CURLED up against his neck. Ansel is purring so loudly, Sara can hear it from the doorway. Seth can probably feel the vibrations. She smiles at the sight, but when Seth doesn't acknowledge her, Sara's heart plummets at the thought of him being upset with her too. Then she notices the shape of her earbuds perched in his ears, her phone in his hand. She's too relieved to wonder when he figured out the password.

"Seth?"

He starts, blindly reaching for the earbuds and flinching when the movement pulls at his chest. Ansel mewls pathetically at being jostled, but only puts his head between his paws and goes back to his nap. The apologetic scratch Seth gives him behind his ear probably helps. "Sorry. I thought—" He grimaces, making a wide gesture with his free hand. "Well, the walls are rather thin."

"Oh." She shifts, chewing her bottom lip anxiously. "Um, thanks. You didn't have to do that."

His expression darkens, gaze falling to the earbuds in his palm. "Yes, I'm afraid I did." Clearing his throat, he holds the pieces out to her. "Apologies, but I was mostly certain you wouldn't mind."

"I don't," she assures him, taking them gingerly. "What were you listening to?"

"Music, but honestly I'm not always convinced your generation understands the meaning of the word."

She rolls her eyes, taking her phone from his other hand to see what's currently playing. When she sees the artists, she blinks—legitimately surprised. "Dolly Parton?"

"The world is undeserving of her talents."

Sara bites back a smile. "I never would have pinned you as a fan of bluegrass."

"It's not the genre," he says, eyes lingering on her phone. "It's her voice."

She can't argue there.

Fingering the neckline of her pajamas, she shifts her weight. "Anyway, I'm going to get dressed and get going. I shouldn't be gone too long, though."

"Ah," he says. Sara can't help but notice the weight hiding behind his thinly disguised indifference and the way his gaze seems to drop away from her. "Going to lunch with some friends, are you?"

Somehow, she knows it isn't quite what he's asking. Eyebrows raised, she says, "I'm picking up your antibiotics. Also, we need food. And *you* need clothes."

He blinks, glances down at himself as if just realizing he has literally nothing else to wear. "Oh."

"Yeah..." She clears her throat. There's something horribly (wonderfully) intimate about going to pick out clothes for him, but she doesn't dare unleash him on the world in his bloodied clothing two centuries out of date. "I don't suppose you know what size you are?"

Seth frowns. "I don't have any money."

"I know, so don't expect me to be bringing home Prada." No matter how good he would look in a suit. "I'm guessing that's a no on the size?"

Her answer only serves to make him more disgruntled. "No," he grumbles.

She kind of suspected as much. Even if they *did* have a sizing system back then, it would no doubt have changed since. "I'll just grab a few things then, until we figure it out." She eyes the shadow lining his face and adds, "And maybe a razor."

Frowning, he runs a hand over his jaw, wincing at the stubble. "Ah, didn't miss that bit."

Sara ducks her head, hiding a smile as she rifles through her drawers to pull out a fresh set of clothes. She can feel Seth's eyes on her, but reminds herself that there is literally nothing embarrassing about him being able to see into her underwear drawer as she pulls out a clean pair. "Alright, don't do anything stupid while I'm gone. There's some cereal left in the cabinet if you get hungry, but do *not* try to use the stove."

His nose wrinkles. "I am perfectly capable of turning on an appliance."

She levels him with a warning look, but she suspects the pile of clothes in her arms might be sabotaging her efforts. "No stove."

"So little trust," he grumbles. When she doesn't budge, he sighs. "Fine."

"Thank you." There's only a little bit of sarcasm lacing her voice. "I'm gonna get dressed and go. I'll be back in a few hours, ok?"

He nods, face solemn, but when she turns to leave, he stops her. "Wait."

She pauses in the doorway, patiently waiting for him to continue. He licks his lips, hands fisting in the material of her comforter. She can see the tension in his shoulders, the corded muscle stark against his lean frame. "The pocket watch," he murmurs, eyes lifting to meet hers. "The gold one. It's in the pocket of my vest."

Sara's brow creases, confused. "You want me to get it for you?"

He doesn't meet her eyes when he answers, "I want you to have it. Sell it."

"What?" she breathes, not quite believing she heard him right. "But it's—"

"I know what it is," he snaps.

She frowns. Sure, she tries to be frugal in her spending, but since Oma's inheritance went through, she's far from poor. Certainly not to the point where he needs to sell anything to cover the costs of a few outfits. There's a stubbornness in his gaze that leaves no room for arguments, though, and she's too physically and emotionally exhausted to fight over it.

However, when she finds it in the vest wadded up on the living room floor, she takes her time studying it. She turns the watch in her hand, admiring the warmth of the metal and the delicate curves of the filigree. Seth doesn't pull it out often, and only ever when he seems to think she isn't paying attention, but she's caught him fingering the chain when he's deep in thought. That alone is enough to tell her there's more value to the timepiece in her hand than just the gold.

She finds the latch, momentarily impressed that it's still ticking when her eyes snag on the engraving opposite of it.

'For my favorite son'

Sara swallows, closing it softly. She feels like she's intruded on something private, but she can't bring herself to regret it. If she had any hesitations about its fate before, it's gone now.

The watch in her hand is the last thing Seth has of his life from before; the only tangible connection to his mother—the other woman in his life with the same name but a different spelling. The one, she knows, who loved him too. There's no price in the world worth parting him from it.

# CHAPTER THIRTY-THREE

AFTER FILLING HIS PRESCRIPTION AT A LOCAL PHARMACY, SHE ENDS UP AT a thrift shop. Mostly because she doesn't know his size and she hates dealing with returns, but also because she suspects he's less likely to fight her on the watch if she can keep the costs down. Plus, she still has to grab groceries and toiletries, so she'll save where she can.

She hobbles straight to the men's section. The crutch is uncomfortable under her armpit, but she's too busy scanning the racks with mounting glee to notice much.

They're full of plaid.

BY THE TIME SHE COMES HOME, HE'S TORN THROUGH A BOX AND A HALF of cereal. One of them lies empty beside him as he shovels another spoonful of chocolate-flavored cereal into his mouth. When he sees her, he quickly swallows his bite, gesturing to the bowl enthusiastically with his spoon. "This is... I've always found the look of it quite unappealing, but it's *delicious*."

His excitement over cereal is nothing short of endearing. "Wait till you try ice cream." Then she spies what he's wearing below the table and blinks. "Those are my sweatpants."

It's stating the obvious, but seeing him in her pink sweats—so short on him they look more like capris—has her brain short circuiting.

He looks down at himself, shrugging. "My trousers were dirty. Besides," says, nose wrinkling in distaste, "after two centuries, I'd be just as happy to burn them." He puts his hands in the pockets, smiling giddily. "I must say, while I wouldn't dream of wearing them in front of company, they are quite cozy."

"They're also very, very pink."

He waves her off. "Color is nothing more than a social construct."

"A lot of guys would disagree."

"A lot of *guys* would be cowards," he says primly. "Though I dare say I'll let you keep the other pair. I still find the labeling of one's buttocks to be peculiar at best."

Setting the bags on the table, Sara fights a smile. The thought of him wearing the pair with 'juicy' stamped across the backside is both hilarious and somehow... arousing? Probably something to do with him still walking around shirtless.

She pulls his antibiotics out of her purse, setting it in front of him. "One every twelve hours."

"Thank you," he murmurs, already screwing off the cap. A pill lands in his palm and he pops it into his mouth before swallowing it down with a gulp of milk leftover from his bowl of cereal.

Then he stands, reaching for the bags of clothing. The waistline of her sweats stretches with him, pulling the fabric low on his hips, and Sara flushes ten shades of red as she realizes her crucial mistake. "I forgot underwear."

He jerks, eyes wide and voice a notch higher. "What?"

"I forgot to buy you underwear."

"Oh. Well, that's fine."

She bites her lip to stifle her smile as she starts unpacking the grocery bags. "Pervert."

His mouth tightens. Suddenly, he's much more interested in

investigating the clothes she brought home. He looks through the first bag, his hand pausing when he sees that one is full of plaid. The glare he shoots her is venomous.

She shrugs, trying for innocent. "That's all they had."

"Somehow, I'm not inclined to believe you."

"Would you forgive me if I told you I got cake mix, too?"

"… Possibly." The smile teasing his lips says otherwise. "Is it the one with the—"

"The ridiculous rainbow chips?" Sara finishes, grinning. "So little faith."

His laugh is nothing more than a huff of breath, but it's so genuinely pleased it makes her heart ache. She busies her hands, folding her reusable bag and wondering how to address their evening plans. "By the way… do you feel up to dinner tonight?"

He's still picking through the clothing—disgust warring with gratitude. "As opposed to going hungry? Certainly."

She shakes her head. "No, I meant—last night. Miles asked if we could do dinner. Tonight. At their place."

He stills, eyes finding hers. "Is it an invitation or an execution?"

Sara rolls her eyes. "He didn't exactly get the whole story last night, Seth. And Jen—"

"You don't need to justify it," he grouses. "I'm merely curious. He doesn't seem to be my biggest fan."

"Yeah, well, in his defense, you weren't exactly looking like prime boyfriend material, last night." She's teasing when she says it, but the way his lips thin and his brows draw together—the way he seems happy to look at anything but her—makes her smile fall flat. She can't tell if he's upset with the assumption or the poor first impression.

"So, yeah, anyway," she mumbles, fingers picking at the folded corner of the bag. "Do you think you're up for it?"

"Do you want me there?"

It's such a ridiculous question, it inspires a breathy laugh. "Don't be stupid. Of course I *want* you there. But if you're too tired, I totally understand."

He wets his lips. "Very well, then." He runs a hand over his jaw, wincing at the stubble. "I don't suppose you remembered a razor? If I'm to be forced to wear that ghastly print, I would like to do so with a clean face."

Sara sifts through the bag, finding the razor at the bottom, and hands it to him. "Do you remember how to use it?"

"Your faith in me is nothing short of astounding."

Sara does her best to hide her smile. She's not nearly as successful when, half an hour later, he emerges from the bathroom with pieces of tissue paper decorating his jaw.

Before she can comment, he shoots her a warning glare. "Say *nothing*."

He's been fidgeting with his shirt the entire drive over—the cuffs, the buttons. Sara finds his petulant frown hilarious, but she does feel a little bad about the hint of unease she sees straining his eyes. She wonders if first impressions are more or less stressful when you know the person, but they know nothing about you.

"Will you stop messing with it?" she says, giving him a gentle nudge with her shoulder as they wait on the front step. In the grocery bag looped over his wrist is the cake she promised him. The frosting is a little melted—she should have let it cool longer—but she hopes he'll be pleasantly surprised by the taste. "It looks fine."

"That's impossible," he grumbles, but his fingers stop plucking at his cuff. "But with your skewed sense of fashion, I have no doubt you believe it."

Sara lets the snarky comment slide, linking her arm through his and giving a gentle squeeze. The effect is immediate. The tension slides off his body like oil on water, the harsh line of his scowl softening into a subtle smile that hints at gratitude. "It's going to be fine," she tells him.

"Your optimism is adorable."

The door opens before she can answer, Jen's tiny frame filling the doorway. "Hi! Oh my gosh, I'm so happy to meet you! I'm Jen, Sara's best friend since forever." She's so excited, she's practically vibrating.

Sara knows it's coming, but the smaller girl's arms wrap around Seth in a friendly (and awkward with the cake between them) hug before she can put a word in to stop it.

Seth grunts, flinching.

Jen pulls back, horrified. "Oh! Oh god, I'm so sorry! I totally forgot—are you ok?"

"Quite," Seth wheezes, smile strained. The hand holding the cake sports white knuckles. "Lovely to meet you. Officially."

Jen's nose wrinkles. "Officially?"

A dagger would be duller than the glare Sara sends her best friend's husband. "You didn't tell her?!"

Miles holds up his hands. "If you thought, for one minute, I was going to even try to explain that level of crazy, you're tripping."

Jen looks between them, smile faltering. "What—"

"Let's continue this conversation inside," Seth says, cutting her off before she can finish asking. "Shall we?"

Nodding hesitantly, Jen gives Miles a questioning look as she steps aside for them to come in.

Miles meets her stare. "Don't look at me like that. Baby, *trust me.* You're gonna need to hear this shit straight from the source."

Sara swats him on the arm as she hobbles past.

JEN FROWNS, HER FOOD BARELY TOUCHED AND HER FORK BALANCING IDLY between her fingers. Sara's not sure if it's made it to her lips even once. "So you were dead."

Seth doesn't seem to be having the same problem (he's already helped himself to three more pieces of garlic bread). He twirls the spaghetti around his fork, frowning when the pasta doesn't cooperate. He sighs. "No, no. I was *cursed.* Quite different."

Jen still seems to be struggling to process everything, but she's handling it better than her husband had. "But you were invisible."

"To anyone outside of Sara, yes."

"But then she broke the curse."

"She did."

"How?"

Seth grins. "I'm afraid that's classified."

Beside her, Miles rolls his eyes and takes another long drink of wine. Sara's not exactly sure what glass he's on. "She kissed him."

Sara's cheeks grow hot (Jen's excited squeal doesn't help). She catches Seth's surprised stare before she hides her face in her hands.

"It's like a fairytale!" Jen sighs, hand clasped to her chest.

"Maybe minus the bullet and stab wounds," Miles grumbles.

Sara sneaks a glance at Seth's expression, but he seems more uncomfortable by Jen's enthusiasm than embarrassed. She wishes she could say the same. "Cake," Sara blurts, skin hot. "I'm gonna grab the cake."

"Sit down," Miles scolds, already pulling out his chair. "You gotta stop walking on that boot."

"I was going to use my crutch," she grumbles, even though it's a total lie. She's eighty percent sure he's more concerned with taking her escape route for himself than her actual foot.

Miles responds with, "Yeah, right" the same moment Seth says, "Doubtful." There's a grudging respect in the fleeting glance they share, but Sara knows better than to point it out.

Jen's lips purse, a sad attempt at smothering her smile. She saw it, too. "Guys, I have a *great* feeling about all this."

"Your optimism is charming," Seth says, shifting in his seat. "However, I still suspect the 'fun' in the name is more advertising than truth."

Jen looks ready to correct him, but Sara sees his words for what they are—an effort to change the subject. "It's rainbow chips," Sara says. "Big difference."

Catching on, Jen looks between them curiously, but goes with it. "She's right. Chocolate is *way* better than sprinkles."

"I don't know why you always gotta hate on my sprinkles like that," Miles says, setting the cake on the table with one hand and a stack of old paper plates with the other. Sara recognizes the plates as being leftover from her birthday dinner.

"It's not about the sprinkles, it's the *frosting*," Jen stresses, already cutting into the cake. She hands the first slice to Seth, her smile wide. "We'll make the other one next time. Maybe you can convince Miles that it's just his childhood nostalgia lying to him."

Seth's returning smile is small, but genuine as he takes the slice of cake from her. "I'll make no such promises." Taking a bite, he chews thoughtfully—his gaze meeting Sara's playfully. "It's… disgustingly sweet," he answers before his fork dives in for another bite. "But I suppose it's not terrible."

THE RIDE HOME IS QUIET, BUT NOT REALLY *UNCOMFORTABLE*.

Sara knows he's tired. It's not that late by the time they get in the car, the clock just creeping past nine, but Seth wears his fatigue like a weight. Sara can see it pushing down on his shoulders and making his feet clumsy. Catching him nearly passing out at the dining table was what prompted her to head home in the first place. So when he falls asleep in the passenger seat on the ride home, the leftover cake clutched protectively on his lap, she's hardly surprised.

What *does* surprise her, is the awkwardness that comes after. When she wakes him gently, her hand on his shoulder, he leans away from her touch once he blinks the sleep from his eyes. Then they're walking, side by side, and there's something uncomfortable hiding behind in his silence that she just can't put her finger on. Something deeper than the hobbled echo of her single boot or the way he keeps adjusting his gait so she can keep up.

"I'm sorry," she blurts, her steps pausing. It's only when he stops too—when he *looks* at her with that baffled crease between his brows —that she continues. "If I made you uncomfortable. You looked… well, embarrassed, maybe? That Miles knew I kissed you."

Seth huffs, head canting to the side. She gets the sense that he's studying her expression as diligently as she is his and, somehow, that inspires more relief than discomfort. "Don't be ridiculous. You're the one who went red."

Sara shrugs her good shoulder, fighting the urge to chew her bottom lip. If she lets her gaze drop now, she's worried he'll drop his too. "I guess I wasn't really prepared for Jen to know. Her enthusiasm can be…"

"Overwhelming?"

The laugh she gives is breathy and short. "That's one way to put it."

He nods, the corners of his mouth curling into a subtle smile. "I was…surprised," he admits, his hand rising in an invitation to continue walking. "I didn't expect you to tell them."

Sara shrugs, limping forward . "After dropping the curse bomb, it seemed silly not to."

"And now?"

Sara frowns, looking at him. His face is carefully (infuriatingly) blank. "And now, what?"

He doesn't meet her eyes. "Do you wish it remained a secret?"

Sara's heart drops, her fingers grasping his sleeve urgently. "Do *you*?"

Seth has the decency to pause, sighing through his nose before giving her a disgruntled look over his shoulder. "It's bad manners to answer a question with a question."

"Yeah, because I'm really worried about that."

"It certainly wouldn't kill you to try on occasion."

"Ugh, you're ridiculous," she huffs, hobbling forward and linking their arms. She's relieved when he doesn't pull away.

The crutch makes it ten times more awkward than she'd like, but he moves with her as best he can. "I believe that's my line."

Before she can respond, her door comes into view and whatever words she might have said are lost. There's a huddled figure sitting, back pressed against the door and head resting on his folded arms. Sara knows who it is before his head lifts—she remembers buying the Carhartt jacket for him two Christmases ago. Beside her, she feels Seth's body go rigid.

David eyes their linked arms, cringing as he stands. "Hey."

"Hey," Sara murmurs. She doesn't know why he's there, but she has her suspicions.

He never was one to let things go.

"Can we talk?"

Sara chances a glance at Seth, but his expression is blank. She hates how good he is at hiding behind that mask. "Sure," she says, because the sooner she does, the sooner it will be over. She pulls her keys out of her purse and presses them into Seth's palm. When he finally meets her stare, she gives him her most encouraging smile. "Could you just set the leftover cake in the kitchen?"

There's a tension in his jaw that gives him away, but his voice remains even. "Of course."

"It'll just be a bit," she promises. She hopes he can hear all the things she leaves unsaid, but he's shielded his expression well enough that she can't be sure.

David waits until Seth has closed the door behind him, his blue eyes glaring daggers at his back, before he offers her his hand. "Do you need—"

"I'm fine," she says, adjusting her crutch. She doesn't want to offer him any reason, intended or not, to hope. "I got it."

His hands disappear into his jacket pockets, leaning back on his heels. Sara can't help but think that the motion is much more refined when Seth does it. "Can—I mean. Could we, I don't know, go for a walk or something?"

She stares at him. "My foot's in a *boot*."

"Oh. Right. Well, what about dinner? There's—"

"David," Sara sighs, shaking her head. "Just say what you came to say. Please."

"I'm sorry," he says, the words rushed. "For this morning. You were right. I don't—I shouldn't have expected—" His breathing is deep, his chest heaving with the force of it. "I just really want to make this work."

"David," she murmurs, voice soft. She sounds older, even to her own ears. Wiser. Maybe she is, because the past year has been a tangled mess of curses and miracles—of heartbreak and healing— and in it all, she found the one thing she hadn't been looking for. "I love him," she says, with so much feeling it would be impossible for David to deny the truth of it. "I love him and I'm *happy*."

She loves the way he only tells her good morning when she

wakes up in a decent mood and isn't afraid to suggest she get herself a cup of coffee when she doesn't. She loves the way he explains things to her in a way that's simple enough for her to understand, but complex enough that she doesn't feel like he's talking down to her. She loves the way he tries.

The way he inspires her to be better; to be *happy*.

David runs a hand through his hair. The smile he gives her is strained. "That's really it then, isn't it?"

"Yeah," she murmurs. "It is."

"We can at least be friends, right?"

She knows the answer just as well as he does, but some truths hurt less when they hide behind white lies. Seth taught her that. "Sure."

Scuffing the toe of his boot against the rug, he looks down at his feet. "I'm going to miss you," he says, eyes raising. "Hell, I already do. Is that weird?"

"No," she answers, and this time it's honest. "But it'll get easier." One day, he'll hear her name and think of her as just an important person in that single stage of his life. A memory worth keeping, but not a relationship worth saving.

"I guess it has to, right?" he jokes, but the humor in his voice sounds as false as it is. He leans in, giving her an awkward half-hug. His breath tickles her hair. "Goodbye, Sara."

Sara returns it, lets herself take a moment to reflect how his arms somehow feel familiar and foreign all at once. "Live a good life, ok?"

"Ok," he promises, pulling away. "You too, yeah?"

Her smile is bright, free from the doubts that stain his. "I will. Goodbye, David."

He nods, shoving his hands in his pockets as he walks past her. Sara watches him leave and is glad when he never once looks back. A sigh, tired but relieved, leaves her. Suddenly, it feels so much later than it is. She's looking forward to finding out if Seth's arms will find themselves around her in the night, or if he'll give up on pretenses altogether. But when she finds him, he's fast asleep on the couch—so still that if it weren't for the deep rise and fall of his chest, she'd worry.

He looks so peaceful with Oma's crocheted blanket tucked up to his chin, Sara doesn't have the heart to wake him.

# CHAPTER THIRTY-FOUR

'PATIENCE' BECOMES A MANTRA.

A not-so-subtle reminder that her wishes don't outweigh his comfort. Even if she thinks it's insane for him to continue sleeping on the couch night after night when they've technically already shared her bed. The urge to tell him *exactly* how backwards and outdated the whole thing sounds is enough to make her jaw ache from forcing herself to stay quiet. To stay *patient*.

He's still healing, she reminds herself. Still adjusting to living as someone who is part of the world instead of just a bodiless bystander. Jen and Miles have been more than welcoming—they've gone to see them more than a handful of times in the last few weeks—but she can tell that the whole idea of being known by more than just her still feels alien to him. She makes an effort to invite him wherever she goes, but he declines more than he accepts. It must be overwhelming, trying to navigate the changes when he's spent centuries being invisible. The times she can see him biting back the urge to say something he would have so freely said before, when only she could hear him, are as frequent as his showers.

God, the man takes *so* many showers.

She was willing to overlook it before with his wounds, but

they're practically healed now and his bathing habits are still excessive. She's giving him another week before she starts rationing his hot water.

Patience.

She stirs creamer into her coffee, watching it go from a bitter dark to soft caramel. Seth still hasn't found a taste for it, but he's been drinking an ungodly amount of tea. Sara's not sure if it's because he actually missed it or because everything he does seems to be in excess lately. Either way, she's made a point to mix some decaf in the tea box before he turns himself into an addict.

Taking a sip, she closes her eyes and sighs. Her bare feet are tucked beneath her, and she relishes finally being able to curl up on the couch without a bulky walking boot.

Seth is sitting in his chair, an ankle crossed at his knee and looking so at home it would almost feel like old times if it weren't for the flannel of his shirt and the book in his hand. He has the sleeves rolled up to his elbows today, the pale lines of his forearm flashing with every turning of the page. With the morning sun streaming through the window, casting soft shadows across his face, Sara struggles to tear her eyes away from him.

Of course, that's nothing new. She finds herself watching him way more than she should, tracing the lines of his face and the shape of his mouth. She's not the only one. When her back is turned, and he thinks she's too busy to notice, she can feel the weight of his stare as clearly as her reaction to it—skin flushing and pulse quickening. The air between them feels thick; ripe with a temptation she's too hesitant to take.

Besides his looks, he's given her no indication that he wants to move forward. Hasn't brought up their kiss or the sheets they shared. She doesn't think he regrets it, but she does think he might need more time.

Because *patience*.

"You're staring," he says, turning the page without bothering to look up. "I don't suppose you're reconsidering your choices in my wardrobe?"

She doesn't even bother entertaining his question (she's mostly sure it was a joke anyway). "Can I photograph you?"

His eyes lift, the corner of his mouth lifting into that teasing half-smile he wears so well. "I suppose it would last longer."

It's permission, obviously, but instead of getting her camera she finds herself rooted; captivated by the curve of his lips and the heat it inspires. In her chest, her heart thrums—the sound echoing in her ears like the shrill screaming of cicadas in the summer.

His head tilts, smile dimming into something concerned. "Sara?"

*Patience,* she reminds herself, but it's so weak it may as well be a whisper in a storm. *Patience.*

"Why haven't you kissed me?" She blurts, setting her mug on the coffee table before standing. "Or did I misread something?"

Seth blinks up at her, the hand holding his book going lax. "I beg your pardon?"

"It's been, like, a month," she blurts. There's a heat crawling up her neck, but she stands her ground despite the outrageously blank look he's giving her. "So. Yeah. I—if you aren't interested, you could at least—or if you're needing more time to adjust—"

"Sara," he interjects, her name rolling off his lips like champagne —soft and dizzying. "Do you mean to tell me, that you *want* me to kiss you?"

She hates that she can't make sense of his expression—can't tell if he's eager or irritated—and it only fuels her own frustration. "Are you for real right now? Because I've been pretty obvious about it."

His lips part briefly, then shut, twisting into a frown. Closing his book, his knuckles white as he grips the edges, he tries again. "I... rather thought you to be the monogamous sort?"

"I... am?" she says carefully. Then a thought strikes, and she blushes a whole new shade of red. "Wait. Are you *not*?!"

Brow furrowing, he only looks more confused. "I don't understand."

"Well, that makes two of us."

"You want me to kiss you," he says, each word carefully formed, "despite your relationship?"

"*What* relation—" she stops, eyes widening as realization dawns. "Oh my *god*. You think I'm still with *David*?!"

Seth stares at her, the book sliding from his lap and onto the chair as he slowly rises. His breathing is deep, chest straining against the flannel of his shirt, as he steps towards her. "Do you mean to say you *aren't*?"

The edge in his voice, the *heat*, makes her shiver even though the whole situation makes her want to scream. "Of course I'm not! How could you even think—"

He kisses her.

It's everything their first kiss wasn't. Hungry and frenzied; weeks worth of pent up passion bursting at the seams matched only by her own. His hands slide over her jaw, fingertips burying in her hair as his lips slant over hers around a gasp. "You infuriating woman," he pants between kisses, "Why didn't you say anything?"

The words slip out between a gasp, breathy and weak. His lips graze her jaw, and the friction is electric. "I didn't think I had to?"

"I just assumed. For so long, you wanted—I thought—" Her fingers drag over his shoulders and he groans, low and deep against her neck—his breath hot and panting against her collar. "Bloody hell, you're magnificent."

She guides him back to her mouth, her fingers fumbling with the buttons of his shirt. "Less talking."

He smirks into the kiss. "Think you rather like it when I talk."

"I don't."

He nips her bottom lip. "Liar."

Her fingers run over the puckered, scarred skin over his heart—feels the hitch in his breath against her mouth. "Sorry," she whispers. "Does it hurt?"

"Does it hurt?" he echoes, laughter coloring his voice, lips brushing against her jaw. "As if everything you do doesn't tear me apart." The hand at her hip slips under her shirt, palms gliding over her waist until his long fingers fan over her ribs. "As if you wouldn't have me begging you to continue."

A small sigh leaves her lips as he peppers kisses along the line of her neck. His hand is dangerously (deliciously) close to her breast, his thumb tracing maddeningly along the edge of her bra. She swallows thickly, eyes closing. "That's a no, right?"

He smiles against her skin. "Yes, Princess. That's a no." Leaning back, he brushes a stray hair from her forehead. "How did I manage to find you?"

"You must be lucky."

"Was it luck?" he asks, a question she doesn't have an answer to. "To find you. Here of all places? In the very last place I would have chosen to look?" he murmurs, the words tickling her ear. "Must be, mustn't it?"

"Seth," she breathes. "You're still talking."

"Sincerest apologies," he murmurs. Sara doesn't believe him for a second. Especially since she can feel his smirk against her cheek. His nimble fingers are making steady work out of the buttons of her shirt.

Hers aren't doing too shabby either.

By the time they make it to the bedroom, both of them have lost their flannel to the floor. By the time they get to the bed, his pants are hanging precariously low on his hips thanks to her, but he seems to be having greater trouble.

"I miss skirts," he grumbles, struggling with the button of her jeans.

Sara bites her lip, smothering a laugh as her hands reach down to help him before shimmying them down her legs. She's a second away from teasing him, but the surprised parting of his lips, the way he stares at her hip, stalls her.

Her tattoo.

It's so small, no bigger than a nickel. He shouldn't have even noticed it right away. But he's always been too perceptive; has always had a knack for zeroing in on her weaknesses. Seth is so familiar with her—knows her in ways she doesn't even fully know herself—that she never realized the ink embedded in her skin would be news to him.

His thumb brushes over the spotted flesh, a smile in his voice and a question in his eyes. "What's this, now?"

Sara licks her lips, her mouth painfully dry. She knows he's thinking of their afternoon in the field, laughing about spots and old wive's tales. It would be easy to let him believe that, to lie by omission, but she can't. Of all the people in the world, Seth is the only one she wants to share her pain with. The only one she trusts to be unburdened by it.

Her face must reflect her feelings, because his expression softens. "You don't—"

"It's for Oma," she blurts. Quick. The ripping of a bandaid that's been pressed against her heart for far too long. "After she... it's for Oma."

"Ah," he breathes, a sigh in the dark. His fingers trace the lines, his eyes following their path. "I... never knew your grandmother, but I know you. I've seen your love for her—your suffering. I have no doubts she was an amazing woman." His gaze finds hers, soft with sympathy but firm with conviction. "I'm sorry she's gone."

Sara swallows thickly. "Thank you," she murmurs, chest tight. A watery laugh escapes her, teeth sinking into her bottom lip to keep it from escalating into something more—something deep and guttural. "She would have really, *really* liked you."

Humming, he places a gentle kiss on her hip, just above her tattoo, and Sara's breath hitches. "I believe you," he says, words whispering over her skin. "I am, after all, *incredibly* likable."

She rolls her eyes, but the smile he inspires is wide. "Incredibly arrogant, maybe."

Another kiss, just as soft but not even half as innocent, to her lower abdomen. "Less than seven spots," he croons. Sara can feel his smirk, breath fanning dangerously close to the hem of her underwear. His eyes, dark and heady, are entirely focused on her. "Suppose that means a lifetime of happiness, yes?"

"Harvest," she says, correcting him with a smile. "Oma said it was harvests."

He shakes his head. "No, no. Not when you have no fields," he murmurs, thumb tracing over her hip. "I have it from a very reliable source that it is happiness."

"That being?"

"Myself. I'm old and very reliable."

"Except you can lie now."

"True," he hums. In the dark, his eyes gleam. "I suppose you'll simply have to trust me, then."

The thing is, she *does*. Oh, she does. Despite the way he teases, touch feather-light and tauntingly slow, as they remove the rest of their clothing.

His lips are everywhere—tasting the inside of her knee, the dip of her waist, the curve of her ribs—while his fingers dip languidly between her thighs. Keening, her body arches off the sheets, moving against his hand in a frenzied search for more.

She gasps his name, and it's a command and a plea all rolled into one. His scalp must be stinging with how tightly her hand has wound in his hair, but he only places another kiss, sweet and soft, at her breastbone.

"Patience," he murmurs, breath hot. Another kiss, this one at the hollow of her throat.

The sound that escapes her is a cross between a whimper and a moan. It trails off into a gasp as his teeth drag against her pulse, the hand between her legs shifting just *so*.

How he's able to hold back, take his time in exploring her, when he's had no one to touch for centuries, mystifies her. Her body is a tangle of humming, nerve endings coaxed tight as guitar strings until she feels like she's straddling the line between singing and *snapping*.

She growls, throwing her leg over him until he's under her. "I've been patient," she reminds him, hands fanning over his ribs and hips grinding down. The groan she pulls from his lips is poetry, the way his head tosses back and exposes his pale throat is art. She could fill a portfolio with the lines of his body.

Seth's eyes are dark. Endless. He sits up, one hand caressing her jaw—fingers threading into the hair at the nape of her neck—and the other a delicious, bruising pressure at her hip. The curl of his lips against her mouth, hovering just shy of a kiss, steals her breath as effectively as his words. "As my Princess demands."

Sara wants to scold him—at least send him a glare—but she likes the sound of *my* too much to argue. She kisses him instead, hand reaching between their bodies, and basking in the way his breath hitches as she grasps him.

He groans, head dropping to her shoulder. The hand in her hair travels down, fingers tracing the curve of her breast. "Permission to go through your nightstand?"

"My nightstand?"

His mouth follows the path his fingertips have mapped over her skin, breath fanning over her heart. "Isn't that the quintessential storage spot for condoms? Or has media failed me?"

She adjusts her grip. His body trembles. Sara's free hand runs through his hair, her answer a sigh against the shell of his ear. "IUD. You don't come with any mysterious 18th century diseases I should worry about, right?"

His laugh is hot against her collar. "None that showed up on my labs, anyway."

She stills, ignoring his soft whine. "Labs?"

"Miles was particularly insistent on the matter," he hums, lips tracing patterns along her neck. "If memory serves, I believe his exact words were, 'If you give her the clap, I'll kill you.'"

Sara's torn on whether to thank Miles or smack him.

She'll decide later.

Preferably when Seth's arms aren't pulling her against him— palms open and warm against her back as he presses in, chasing the emptiness away with himself.

When she doesn't have his every panted breath whispering encouragements and endearments against her skin; when her lips aren't busy shaping words like "please" and "more" while her nails decorate his shoulders in crescent moons.

When Time and Space isn't condensing, revolving around the way their sweat-slicked bodies push and pull, pressure building. Ecstasy disguised as a spring. With every turn of his hips and every brush of his fingers, her body coils tighter, tighter. It's too much and not enough and her name is a tattoo on her heart for how many times he murmurs it against her parted, gasping mouth.

He shifts, or maybe the world does—she can't be sure—but the pressure snaps and she is spinning. Suspended in the moment, his name on her tongue and his eyes—deep and dark in ways she knows will haunt her in the best of ways—holding her own as his grip tightens and he shudders against her.

HIS FINGERS TRAIL OVER HER SKIN, TRACING THE CURVE OF HER HIP, THE line of her spine. Languid and so gentle the touches are borderline ticklish, but it's the look on his face—the adoration she sees there—that makes her melt.

"I don't think it was the kiss," she murmurs, voice quiet between them.

"Oh?" His fingers push a piece of hair away from her face, his eyes dark and sated in ways that make her heart thrum. Beneath the covers, their ankles tangle together, knees knocking.

"Well, maybe not *just* the kiss," she amends, gaze dropping. She traces the line of his collarbone before laying her palm flat over his heart. The scars are like braille under her palm. She wonders what it would say, if she could read it. "I think, maybe, it's been breaking a little bit at a time." Sara's brow furrows, chewing her bottom lip. "I hated you. I thought—I *really* thought—you were evil. The villain in my own screwed up story. But then you weren't. And I…"

She takes a breath, lets the words sit on her tongue until she's certain they're the right ones. "I realized, the miracle you gave me was a curse, but *you* weren't. You weren't the monster you pretended to be." Her eyes lift, pulse quickening at the absolute reverence in his expression. She swallows, wets her lips as she searches his eyes—struggling to put it in a way he can understand. "I *forgave* you."

His exhale is a sigh against her lips, shaky and brimming with emotion. His mouth parts, throat working around the words he can't find. He kisses her, instead. Softly. Lovingly. The hand tangled in her hair trembles. "You should have turned me down," he breathes, lips whispering over hers with every syllable. "I'll be impossible to be rid of now."

Sara smiles. "Good, because you kind of already threatened me with forever." She can feel his mouth curling, his eyes bright with the force of his smile.

"Forever then," he whispers, a promise sealed with a kiss to her forehead.

Sara curls into him, rests her cheek over his chest and listens to his heartbeat. It feels like the future is rolled out in front of them, inviting and warm with promises.

One of these days, sometime soon, she'll set her alarm and drive out to her favorite hilltop and wait—camera in hand—until the light spills into the valley. It's time for her to capture a sunrise.

# EPILOGUE

<small>Twelve years later, and he's still the most physical person she's</small> ever met.

It feels natural to her now—the hand resting at the small of her back while they're maneuvering through a crowd, his fingertips tracing invisible patterns on her calves while watching TV on the couch. When her days at work are particularly long, she feels the absence keenly—an itch under her skin—and knows he's at home feeling it three times worse.

On those days, she usually comes home to more food than either of them can eat and a mess in the kitchen. Or, if he's feeling particularly anxious, the house will be spotless, but his stomach empty—the whole day gone by in a flurry of detergents and sprays. It's easier, he tells her, when there's something for his hands to do. To touch. The pen dragging over paper and the clicking of his keyboard isn't enough, no matter how many words are dancing in his head or how many writing deadlines he has to meet.

There are laugh lines around his eyes now. When she points them out, a strange expression softens his face. Sara has never known anyone to be happy about wrinkles, but he admires them in the mirror with a giddiness that leaves her baffled. "It will be wonderful," he says, gaze warm, "Growing old with you."

He still manages to steal her breath with just a handful of words. Of course, words have always been his to mold—a weapon and a shield, a lure and a deterrent. After centuries of having nothing but his voice, Sara can't say she's surprised at how well he's honed this skill. That she's still so affected by it, over a decade later, is another story.

She shivers in response to his whispers, burns when his voice dips low. He knows her weaknesses, her strengths, more than anyone; plays her body like an instrument with nothing but gentle, teasing touches and sing-song promises. Never does he leave her wanting.

It's not the perfect arrangement—nothing ever is—but they've made it work. Her photography career keeps them both busy traveling from place to place, but Seth hardly seems to mind. If anything, he's thrilled to show her the parts of the world he's familiar with, and eager to experience the new ones by her side. Sometimes they spend weeks living out of their suitcases. Home is wherever they're together; where they can lay their heads and whisper to each other in the dark.

Though, that's all about to change now.

Washing the dishes, she feels his arms slide around her waist from behind—his lips smiling into the bare skin of her shoulder in a way that makes her body hum. "Damn the dishes," he murmurs. "They'll still be there in the morning."

"Yeah, except even grosser."

He sighs, his hands sliding over the swell of her stomach. She gives him credit for not correcting her grammar even though she can tell the temptation's there. "This *is* an unfortunate truth." His palms rest over the taut skin, a patient pressure. "How are my favorite girls this evening?"

Sara shakes her head, an exasperated smile pulling at her lips. "What if you're wrong?"

He places a kiss along her jaw, his words a soft but firm murmur in her ear. "I'm not."

"But if you *are*?"

"Then I suspect you will never fail to remind me."

"Well, you got that part right, at least," she says with a laugh. "What makes you so sure, anyway?"

"When do you ever fail to remind me of the times I was wrong?" At her exasperated glare, he grins—kissing her nose. "Just a feeling, Love. Just a feeling."

"You're sure it's not just because you *want* a girl?"

He pulls her closer. She still has another two months to go before her due date, but her stomach is still big enough to get trapped between them. Seth seems to find it as amusing as she does annoying. "I assure you, I want nothing but the two of you safe and happy." He reaches up, fingertips brushing over her skin as he pushes a stray hair from her face. "The rest of it, who they are, doesn't matter. Because they are *ours*."

Sara smiles. She feels the same way. "Jen's still disappointed we aren't finding out."

"Jen has her own child to mind. She should have no problem waiting with the rest of us." He kisses her temple before releasing her, picking up a towel to dry the dishes as she finishes them. "Tell me, is Shaun still struggling with his reading?"

Sara shakes her head, handing him a plate. "Jen said he's been doing a lot better since you gave her the name of that series. Apparently he's going through them so quick, she thinks he'll probably finish them before we get the chance to visit for Christmas."

Seth hums. "I told her. He was simply bored with the reading material that asinine—"

She silences him with a look, and he grumbles the rest of his complaints about the American education system under his breath. *That* particular discussion has been beaten to death, especially since they've moved back to the states to be closer to Jen and Miles.

A tiny foot presses against the inside of her ribs, prompting her to shift. Her pregnancy was... not a mistake—she could never bring herself to call it that—but far from planned. A gift neither of them thought they wanted until two pink lines proved it had been given, anyway.

It had encouraged them to put down roots; to pick a place and stay there. It took a few months of back and forth before they settled on a home in Chicago. With three bedrooms and two bathrooms, it felt huge despite being small in comparison to the size of homes being sold in the suburbs outside the city. Now, with many of Oma's belongings (lovingly stored for all these years) filling the space, it feels just right.

While he finishes drying, Sara begins to turn off the lights in the other rooms, but when she gets to the hallway, she pauses. Her hand hovers over the switch, her eyes staring past the open door into the second bedroom. There's still no fresh paint on the walls, and it's lined with boxes that still need unpacking, but in the corner is a doll-house. The same one her grandfather made and her grandmother kept. The same one she almost said goodbye to.

She's no wordsmith—her art is visual, not written—but she thinks there's something poetic about those miniature rooms and tiny shingles. A physical symbol of the hopes family has the power to pass down; the dreams they can inspire when nurtured with kindness...

A reminder of the legacy Oma gave her, of how her patience and love helped Sara bloom despite the lack of light at home. It's fitting that it find a home in the nursery.

Seth's hand touches her lower back, his lips a caress against her temple. "You look so serious, my dear."

She leans into him, head resting on his chest. "We're going to be good parents, right?"

His chest falls with the depth of his sigh. "Ah, now that *is* a worrying thought, isn't it?" He reaches for her hand, lacing their fingers. "I believe we'll try our very best. And, I think, that alone will make the difference," he murmurs, raising their hands and placing a kiss on her knuckles. He waits until she meets his eyes before adding, "We are not our fathers."

No, they're not. Sara will die before she chooses the bottle over her child, and Seth would turn the world over before he let them feel unwanted. Both of their fathers are gone now, his to Time and hers to liver disease, but somehow the shadows of their mistakes remain. Sara's determined that they learn from them—be *better* than them.

Seth gives her a peck on the cheek before flipping the light switch. "Now, let's save the parenthood panic for tomorrow, shall we? I'm knackered."

He's not—no doubt he'll spend another two hours reading before even trying to go to bed. It's just that he knows her well enough to understand that the fastest way for *her* to sleep is to convince her to get under the covers. He uses the same tactic whenever she's tired, but being stubborn about it.

Tonight, it's enough to convince her to follow him to their bedroom, but her mind is still buzzing and—for once—he's the one that falls asleep first. His arm drapes over her waist, his even breaths fanning across the nape of her neck. It's the slow rhythm of his chest at her back, the warmth of him, that soothes her anxious thoughts until they're silent.

Her eyes close. Sleep beckons. Sara dreams.

She is surrounded by the gentle rolling hills of her childhood, a sunrise spilling across the cornfields and painting the green leafy stalks in golden hues. Flashes of jeweled red dance around her, light glinting off their iridescent wings.

Ladybirds—thousands of them. Sara catches one on her fingertip, counts the spots, and smiles.

It's going to be another good year.

THE END

# ACKNOWLEDGMENTS

Much love and thanks to Krys for being this story's number one fan when it was nothing more than a few thousand words and a vague idea of a snarky ghost boy. Your enthusiasm was, without a doubt, the reason this book was completed on time.

So much love and appreciation to Sarah, who has not only given such spectacular feedback but has also been beside me on this author journey longer than anyone. I cannot describe what your continued support means to me.

Thank you to Renee for your praise and love for these characters, and to John for your suggestions and ever amazing typo spotting talent!

Lastly (but perhaps most importantly) thank *you*, Dear Reader. Thank you for reading my words and letting me share my story with you. I adore hearing from my readers and live for your feedback! If you take a moment out of your day to submit a review, it will make this author's day!

# ALSO BY R. RAETA

**She sits at the same bench, in the same park, every night.**

Lily doesn't remember her death, or even her reawakening, but she knows this: the sun is to be feared, words are her salvation, and—above all—the bench facing the playground is hers. She is the pin holding the hands of the clock, watching the world move and change around her while she remains fixed, lonely, and unchanged... until a boy takes a seat beside her.

A story about love, loss, and what it means to live forever.

# ABOUT THE AUTHOR

R. Raeta is a two-time IAN Book of the Year finalist for her debut novel, *Everlong*. *Ladybirds* is her second novel of what (she hopes) will be many more to come. She lives in Northern California with her husband and young son. When she isn't agonizing over word choices, she enjoys telling the dog how handsome he is and sitting in on the nightly therapy sessions the cat so generously provides for her. She is a Trigiminal Neuralgia survivor, and believes in living your best life day by day.

If you would like to follow R. Raeta's future works, you can visit her website at www.rraeta.com or find her on the following social media platforms.

Printed in Great Britain
by Amazon